APPOINTED TIME

SANDS OF TIME TRILOGY

C.J. PETERSON

ISBN 978-1-952041-40-2 (paperback)

ISBN 978-1-952041-41-9 (ebook)

Published by Texas Sisters Press, LLC.
Lufkin, TX U.S.A.

The story, all names, characters and incidents portrayed, and the names herein are fictitious. No identification with actual persons (living or deceased), places, buildings, and products are intended or should be inferred.

Texas Sisters Press, LLC

2021

CONTENTS

DEDICATION

This book is dedicated to my loving husband and dear family who love and support me. You all mean more to me than you will ever know. Thank you! I love you!

This trilogy is also dedicated to my mom, **Sue Mann**. We lost her in January 2021. She never hesitated to take other kids under her wing to guide, direct, and pray for them. She was a prayer warrior and an encourager until the end! Her legacy of praying the family through all our good times and bad will never be forgotten. I only hope to continue to grow in my prayer life to be as strong as she was! Mom, you are loved and missed, but we all know you're up in Heaven making sure to keep an eye on all of us!

A portion of the proceeds from this series go to:
www.daretodream-dallas.org
Their mission: To pick up the broken pieces of the lives of wounded youngsters in group homes, shelters, detention centers, and orphanages by providing life-skills education and ministry through role model speakers, cultural experiences (art, music,

and dance), and one-on-one mentoring. **Who they serve:** Youth between the ages of ten and eighteen, living in shelters, foster homes, group homes, detention centers and orphanages. Many have been abused and neglected and do not have a father present in their lives. Partnerships have been developed with Juvenile Departments, State Youth Commissions, youth shelters, group homes and orphanages.

To learn more about C.J. Peterson, you can find her online at:
http://cjpetersonwrites.com/
'While the stories are fiction, the journey is real!'

SUMMARY

All we have in this life is the time we are granted. Like sands on the sea shore, our lives depend on where we land. Some grains of sand land in an oyster, and are turned into beautiful pearls. Some land in the bottom of the sea floor, and become beds for bottom feeders.

Blake and Holly Hunt, and Adam and Deanna Roth all were created for a purpose by Professor Noah Roth. There were many years the genetic manipulation did not allow the babies to be viable…until the four. He had big plans for the children. Two nurses, Ben and Grace, had a different idea.

This is a tale of two sets of gifted children. One pair raised in a caring environment, and taught to strengthen their gift with love and respect. Meanwhile, the others were raised under the strict and abusive conditions set by Professor Roth. When Deanna and Blake, who were raised by Professor Roth, are set free to retrieve the other two by whatever means necessary, chaos ensues. The first explosion will take place in a quiet little East Texas town called Willow Bend.

Proverbs 27:1 – "Do not boast about tomorrow, for you do not know what a day may bring."

"Time slips through our hands like grains of sand never to return again. Those who use time wisely are rewarded with rich, productive and satisfying lives." Robin Sharma

CHARACTERS IN THE SANDS OF TIME TRILOGY & SERIES

Ben   Hope   Wyatt

Professor Roth   Alex

Holly   Blake   Deanna   Adam

Charlie   Eddie   Freya   Gemma   Isabelle

The Gifted Maine Teens

Willow Springs Teens

SANDS OF TIME

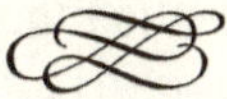

"The two most important days in your life are the day you are born and the day you find out why." Earnest T. Campbell

"*H*elena! Helena, it's time!" Hope Hunt shouted for her sister. "Call the number! Let them know it's time!"

Running downstairs into the living room, Helena asked, "Are you sure?"

A contraction spiked just as Helena asked the question. It was intense. Hope could not form a thought or speak a word. The piercing pain started from her mid-back, and then screamed around to the front. The sheer velocity in which the contraction hit shocked and stunned her.

Helena grabbed her phone, quickly dialing the number for the clinic. She had her doubts, but those at the clinic always seemed to come through. With all the testing and experimental treatments Hope went through to become pregnant, she knew it would be worth it to hold the next generation in her arms.

"Ahhhhhhh-eeeeee!" Hope screeched as she dropped to the ground on her hands and knees. She looked down and cried out for help as blood seeped through her sweatpants. "Helena!" Hope breathed heavily. She rolled over, grabbing her stomach. "Helena, help me!" Tears poured down her cheeks. Her body shook uncontrollably.

"They're on the way," replied the operator at the clinic after Helena explained the situation. "They should be there momentarily. Just keep her comfortable."

"Yes, ma'am," Helena said into the phone that was tucked between her neck and shoulder, while she finagled her way behind Hope to hold her. "Hold on, Hope! They're coming!" she said to her younger sister. "Just hold on."

"I'm bleeding," she said, panting in agony. "My-my chest hurts. Oh! My head!"

"They're on the way," Helena said calmly, trying not to let her sister know how much panic churned through every muscle in her body. Listening to the instructions the operator gave her, and briefly answering those questions asked, Helena functioned on automatic.

"Holly. Name the baby Holly," Hope said, and then let out a yell as the pain spiked again. "Promise me..." she said through gritted teeth, "promise me...you'll name her Holly!"

"What if it's a boy?" Helena asked, waiting for Hope's pain to release.

"No." Hope panted. The pain finally subsided enough for her to speak. "No. It's a girl. Helena, the room's spinning. I don't feel right. Something's wrong. Too much pain."

"Just breathe like we learned in class," Helena coaxed, stroking Hope's strawberry-blond, wavy hair. "Come on. You can do this."

"My arm hurts," Hope said, grabbing her left arm.

"What did you say?" Helena asked. She was momentarily distracted by the instructions being given to her by the operator.

"Arm hurts." She grabbed her head and screamed in pain and agony. "Head!" she screeched. Blood oozed from her eyes, nose, ears, and mouth.

"Hope, talk to me!" Helena begged.

Hope did not say another word. Her arms collapsed as she closed her eyes, shallow breathing.

"Hope!" Helena yelled. "Hope!"

"What's going on, ma'am?" the operator asked.

"Hope!" Helena's heart raced. "Hope, please!" Helena dropped the phone and eased Hope to the ground. Tapping Hope's cheek, Helena yelled, "Hope! Oh! Please hurry! She's not waking up!" Hearing the sirens, Helena screamed so the operator could hear her, "They're coming! I can hear them."

"Just hold on, ma'am. They're almost there." The operator's voice came through the dropped phone calmly. "Is she awake yet?"

"No." Helena's tears crawled down her cheeks. "She's not moving. There's so much blood." Putting her head to Hope's chest, she gasped. "She's not breathing! Please hurry!"

"Ma'am, they should be pulling in," the operator said as the red and white lights flooded the living room, piercing through the darkness of the night. When security for the compound arrived, their red and blue lights joined the ambulance lights, lighting up the neighborhood. "You have to let them in."

Everything seemed to move in slow motion around her. The paramedics knocked on the door, but there was no answer. Helena was not letting her sister go. Her arms wrapped around Hope, Helena slowly rocked, singing *All Through The Night*. It was an old Welsh lullaby their mother sung to them when they were little.

"Sleep my child and peace attend thee, all through the night." Her tears flowed unrestrained down her cheeks. "Guardian angels God will send thee, all through the night."

The paramedics and security pounded on the door. "Open the door! Ma'am! You need to open the door!" they shouted.

"Soft the drowsy hours are creeping, hill and dale in slumber sleeping." Helena brushed Hope's hair with her fingers, barely able to make out the details of her sister's face through the tears. "I, my loving vigil keeping, all through the night."

Security kicked the door in.

"While the moon her watch is keeping, all through the night." Helena used her sleeve to clean the blood off Hope's face. "While the weary world is sleeping, all through the night."

The security officers ripped Helena away from Hope so the paramedics could get to her.

"No! Hope! Give her back to me! Hope!" Helena screamed, reaching for her sister.

The paramedics ignored her, as they focused on Hope's lifeless body to get the baby released.

"Stop! Stop it! Give her back to me!" Helena shouted, arms flailing, trying to get to Hope. Seeing them cut Hope's stomach open, she yelled, "You're hurting her! Stop it!"

"Get her out of here!" one of the paramedics yelled over Helena's objections. "We need to save the baby!"

While security drug her out of the room kicking and screaming, Helena barely saw into the other room. She had to get to Hope! "I need to see her! Let me go! I mean it! Let me get to my sister! Hope!

Then she heard it! There was a distinct cry of a newborn…at least she thought she heard it.

Shouting and sobbing, Helena fought the security officers even harder to get to her sister and the baby. Any amount of force was met with equal force as it took two security officers to hold her.

"Hold her down," the paramedic said. He injected something into Helena's arm.

"What is that?" she demanded. She felt the warm wave wash

over her. "Let me go!" she shouted. She fought it for only a moment. "I will sue this place for everything it's worth! That man will pay! I want my sister and her baby."

"I'm sorry, ma'am. They didn't make it," the paramedic said as he stood. "Keep ahold of her. She's going."

"Thank you," a security officer said.

"Let me go!" Helena shouted, getting a second burst. "I heard the baby! You're lying! I hear her!"

"There is no baby," the paramedic insisted.

"There!" she said, hearing a baby cry. "What's that?"

"I don't hear anything." The paramedic shook his head. As Helena's eyes closed, and her head dropped to the side, he said, "She's done. C'mon, Sam, let's load everyone up and get them to the clinic."

Helena swore she heard a baby cry. The world spun around her in a blur. *Was it real? Which portions were real? Would she wake to find this nightmare not real? Did Hope's baby live...or did she die with Hope?*

⬥⬥⬥⬥

EVERYTHING SOUNDED like an echo as Helena moved in a daze after waking up in the hospital. She slowly made her way down to the ER waiting room. Barely functioning, she saw a doctor walk in wearing blood-covered green scrubs, with a green operating cap over his head and booties over his shoes.

"I'm sorry, ma'am. We did everything we could. We couldn't save either of them," he explained.

She looked up at him, her eyes glazed.

"Is there someone we can call for you?" he asked.

"No. I'm fine. I'll be fine."

"As you know, the home provided was only for those in the program. You will have fourteen days to find a new location to live."

"Yes. I know how the program works. I understand." Helena nodded. "I was there when Hope signed the papers." Looking up at the doctor, she asked, "When will I be able to see their bodies?"

The doctor shook his head. "Ma'am."

She narrowed her eyes as she growled, "That was my sister and her baby! I demand to see them."

"Ma'am, I don't –"

"My name is Helena Hunt. Not ma'am. Not even Miss. Hope Hunt was my sister. She was the only family I had left. That child was to continue our bloodline. Do you understand?"

"Yes."

"Then you walk your little self down to doctor what's-his-name, and tell him –"

"Professor Roth," the doctor corrected her.

"I don't care what his name is!" Helena stood, putting her hands on her hips. "You tell him not only do I want to see both of them, but I also want to know when I can have their bodies to bury in our family's plot. If he doesn't have the decency to understand that, then I will see him in court!"

"Ma'am…I mean, Helena," the doctor said, resting his hands on her arms.

She jerked away. "Don't touch me!"

"I'm sorry." He lifted his hands. "If you were there when she signed the papers, then you know Hope signed a paper stating in the event something went wrong during the program, her body would be donated so we can determine what happened. Her baby is part of that."

"You can't be serious!"

Crossing his arms, standing his ground, the doctor simply responded, "I am serious."

Helena took a step back. "You mean I can't even bury her?"

"She chose to be cremated. I can show you the paperwork,"

the doctor offered. "You can have the ashes of the mother and the baby when they're ready."

"They have names," Helena snapped.

"I meant you can have the ashes of your sister, Hope, along with those of her baby."

"This clinic is a joke!" Helena shouted. "That creepy sleazeball of a boss you have insisted she signed the papers before he started. I have more humanity in my pinky than that man has in his entire body! Science!" She huffed. "What about simple human decency?"

"Helena, if you don't calm down –"

"Calm down?" Helena cut him off. "Calm down? This is me calmed down. I'm reigning it in for your sake. You didn't do this. He did."

"I will call security and have you forcibly removed from the premises if you do not garner some self-control. If you leave now, you can have the time you need to pack your and your sister's belongings."

Helena stared at him, speechless.

"I don't mean to be callous. I have a lot of work to do. There are multiple patients here I'm responsible for who I really need to get back to. I'm sorry for your loss, but you and your sister knew the risks before she signed up for the program."

Bottom lip trembling, her body shook. She felt like a volcano about to explode. Helena narrowed her eyes at him. Through gritted teeth, she said, "I lose everything, and your only response is to tell me she signed the paperwork? What is wrong with you?"

Opening the folder cradled in his arms when he walked in, the doctor pulled the photo from the chart and handed it to her. "I know it isn't what you want, but it's better to remember her like this. You want to remember the good, not the bad. You don't want to see what she looks like now. You don't want that to be your last memory of her. You want this to be your forever memory of her."

Snatching the photo from him, Helena spun and walked out of the clinic. The brutal Maine October wind immediately cut through her clothing. Wrapping her coat tighter around her body, she was grateful the paramedics at least thought to grab it for her when they knocked her out.

She hoped to wake from this nightmare soon. Memories of her sister flashed through her mind while she walked to their two-bedroom condominium on the compound.

Growing up, her sister was her best friend. While playing ring-around-the-rosey, their strawberry-blond curls would dance in the sunlight. Giggling at the overnighters between both sets of their friends echoed in her mind. Being only a year apart, their friend circle was interchangeable. Riding bikes through the neighborhood with their friends, playing games together on their dead-end street as kids until they were called home…things seemed so innocent.

Then came junior high and high school. Boys entered the picture and it messed up everything, but only for a little while. Eventually they found their way back to each other, and there was harmony in the home again.

Helena then headed to college. The world completely opened up for her. She was thrilled when Hope not only joined her at the same college, but also joined the same sorority.

It was at college in their room at their sorority house that the girls found out about the car accident. Their parents were on the highway, heading to see the girls when they hit a patch of ice on the road. It sent them sliding off the side of the road, over an embankment. The car flipped over and over again, crushing them in the wreckage. They were traveling with the three remaining grandparents in their family to see the college for parent's weekend. They all died in the wreck. In one fell swoop, their entire family was gone.

Tears poured down Helena's cheeks as she unlocked the door of their condo. She walked into their home, looking around. Dropping to her knees, she felt the weight of the events of the last several hours.

Curling into a ball on the floor, she lost herself in tears and memories of those she had lost while staring at the photo of her sister smiling back at her.

◈◈◈◈

"THIS ONE IS ADORABLE," Grace Matthews, a female nurse at the clinic, gushed over the newborn.

"What makes that one so special?" Ben Scott asked, while sitting at the desk working on reports.

She showed Ben the baby. "Have you ever seen a little one with curly red hair?"

Seeing the bright blue eyes and light-red wavy hair, he shook his head at the newborn. As the little girl sucked her thumb, Ben's heart broke for her. "That's the one they just lost the mother on, correct?"

"Yes. Poor thing. I wonder if she has any other family?"

Cocking his head to the side, Ben clicked his tongue. "You serious? You've worked here long enough to know how this will go for her. You know what kind of man Professor Roth is. With the mother out of the way, what do you think will happen to her?"

"Is this another one of them?" she asked, her fingers touching her parted lips. "It worked again?"

Standing, Ben walked over to get a good look at the baby. "How many are there now?" he asked, lightly rubbing her cheek with the back of his finger. "Have the blood tests all come back yet?"

"Well, this is one," she said, pointing to a little boy. "And those two over there are as well," she said, gesturing toward another boy and girl amongst the twenty babies in the nursery. "All three have the gene. The rest have all been tested, but these babies have the marker that the others don't have. Are you saying this one's blood test is already back?"

"Yes. It came in a few minutes ago. I don't know if Professor Roth knows it's back yet."

"Well, he knows about the other three," she said, looking at the baby in her arms. "He'll find out about this one in the morning. So far, only these four out of the twenty from this test set retained the gene. There are several still to be delivered, so time will tell if there'll be more. Professor Roth is supposed to start another lot soon. He may not, though, since he got it to work with this bunch."

"Do they know what they can do yet?" Ben asked.

"No. There's no telling when they'll find out."

Looking up at Grace, Ben said, "It's the first time they've gotten it to work in over twenty years. Can you imagine what that man will do to these little ones?"

"I'm afraid to find out."

"They look normal."

"They are normal," she said. "Ten fingers, ten toes, and human in every way."

"They're not if the experiment worked. They're next-level humans. Do you really think they'll treat these little ones like normal human beings? They're going to grow up in this clinic."

"What do you mean?"

Raising an eyebrow, Ben asked, "Have you looked at their charts? I know for a fact that one lost his mother in labor." He pointed to a little boy with dark-brown hair and dark-blue eyes. His eyes would more than likely turn brown in the next six to twelve months. The little boy was named Blake, according to the card on his clear plastic bassinet. "And as you said, the one you're holding lost her mother in delivery as well."

"I know, but weren't these just an accident? They wouldn't kill the mothers. Would they?"

"Do you really think it was an accident that those two, who happened to retain the gene, lost their mothers? I'm sure they somehow killed her mother and his. Why not take out the other two? With no parent to object, they can experiment on them at will."

Grace looked at Ben, her blue eyes wide. "This one's mother had a heart attack during delivery!"

Reaching down, he grabbed the chart and showed it to her. "Does a heart attack cause blood to come out of every orifice in the head?"

She scanned the notes before returning the chart to him. With the baby girl still in her arms, she asked, "Do you really think they're going to kill the mothers of the other two babies?"

His brown eyes cool, he sternly said, "I know they are. This is the first time it's worked, right?"

"Right."

"Do you think they'll just let these little ones go home with the mother's family as if nothing happened? That's if the mother even has family." With one hand on his hip, he paced. Running his other hand through his dark-brown hair, he then rested it on the back of his neck. "Let's think about this. They used Professor Roth's sperm to fertilize all the eggs. Being the father of these children gives him full parental rights. These mothers were all single, with little or no family."

"Wouldn't they just keep the mothers at the compound?" she asked. "The mothers signed the paperwork to do testing on them. There's no reason to kill them."

"They can't experiment to the extent I'm pretty sure they're going to take. The mothers are going to die. Mark my words. The mothers of the others will go shortly. They're going to turn these babies into lab rats."

The PA system crackled to life with alarm, "Code blue… postpartum room four. Code blue… postpartum room four."

"I'll bet that's one now who will suddenly die of mysterious causes," Ben said, daring her to challenge him.

Glancing toward the speaker and then back to Ben with a pained expression, Grace asked, "What can we do about it? We can't let them torture these children. They need to be kids."

Inhaling deeply through his nose, Ben let out a slow breath of air before he asked, "How many are there?"

"Four," Grace said glancing at the babies.

"Can you carry two?"

Narrowing her eyes, she asked, "What are you thinking?"

"What if we saved them? What if we got them out of here and raised them somewhere in another part of the country far away from all of this?"

"I don't know if I can carry two."

"Can you carry that one?" he asked.

Clutching the little red-haired baby girl to her chest, Grace nodded.

"I can get another one. I need my other hand in case I need to defend us," Ben said, grabbing the keys to his car and his backpack. He also grabbed their coats.

"We can't leave the other two."

"Outside of recruiting two others and potentially alerting them to our plan, I don't see how that'll happen." Walking over to her, he rested his hands on her arms and explained, "We can't save them all, but we can save these two. You take this one, and I can take another. We can go into the country and raise them, homeschooling them to keep them out of the system."

Taking only a moment to look down at the little girl, in a split-second decision, she looked back up at him and nodded.

"Do we know which ones are the strongest?" he asked.

"No."

"Okay. This is the other one who lost his mother shortly after delivery," he said, looking down at a boy two days older than the little girl Hope held. "He looks strong. The other two look strong as well. They may endure."

"What if they don't?"

"Then, we've at least saved these two," Ben said, and then scooped up the sleeping little boy. "Ready? We're going to have to be sneaky. Keep to the stairwells."

"Got it," Grace said, resolved to protect the little girl. "It's okay, little Holly. We'll protect you and get you out of here. You too, little Blake," she said, kissing his tiny head.

Ben reminded her, "This could be a very short trip if we're not careful."

"Then, let's be careful. We have little lives counting on us."

"Agreed. Let's go."

The pair left the nursery, heading directly for the stairwell. Running down the rarely-used stairwells, Grace prayed no one would use the stairs until they were gone. "How are we going to get out the front door?" she asked.

Ben opened the door to the first level. "We're not." Looking both ways, he pulled her by her arm toward the cafeteria.

A security officer stopped the pair. "Where are you taking those two?"

"We're taking them for testing for Professor Roth," Ben explained. "He wants a CT scan on them."

The security officer raised an eyebrow. "With your coats and bags?"

"We're dropping them off before we leave for the day," Ben explained. "That way the next nurses on shift only have to come pick them up when they're ready."

"Why aren't they in cribs?" the security officer demanded.

Confidently stepping forward, Grace explained, "They will be in cribs all of their lives. Both of these two lost their mothers during delivery. A little human touch at such a young age is encouraged, especially since they'll probably spend most of their young lives here. They need the physical contact for healthy development. Now, unless you'd like to explain to Professor Roth as to why these two were late to getting a CT scan completed, then I suggest you let us pass. Would you like to scan our badges?" she asked, pushing hers forward, careful to cover her name. When he shook his head, she put it back in her pocket. She then picked up the bracelet around the little girl's foot. "What about theirs? Would you like to scan theirs?"

"No. I'm good." The security officer waved them off. "Frankly, Professor Roth scares me."

"Fear is a healthy thing when it comes to The Professor," Ben said, pushing past the security officer, heading down the hall toward radiology.

Grace followed suit, not sure how they were going to get out now.

When they were out of earshot, Ben pulled Grace into an alcove. "Okay, we need to head back down there and out to the kitchen. That's the only door not monitored."

"How do you know?"

"I sometimes have to sneak in a little late." He blushed. "Sandra in Admin told me how."

"Do I want to know?"

He shook his head. "No. Not really."

"All right." She sighed. "So, how are we going to get them out?"

"They're sleeping. If they stay asleep, I have an idea," he said, glancing at a cart down the hall with metal doors.

"You can't be serious!" Grace said, appalled. "You want us to stick them in a dietary cart?"

"We have to! Come on! This is how we're going to get them out."

She huffed. "Fine! I can*not* believe we're sticking newborns into a dining cart."

"Shut up!" Ben hissed.

Grabbing her arm, he ushered her over to the cart and opened the doors. "Stay quiet, please," Grace said, kissing the little girl's head before she slid her into a metal pan in the cart.

"Stay asleep, little guy," Ben said, and then set the baby into a metal pan inside the cart as well. "Now," he said, closing the doors, "let's go."

Both talking like nothing was going on, the pair slowly walked the cart like they knew what they were doing. They headed into the kitchen, toward the back. Once through the kitchen, they took the children out of the cart and slid out the back door.

"Where are you parked?" Grace asked, tucking the baby under her coat as they walked briskly into the parking lot.

"Walk straight, and don't look back," Ben ordered, the baby boy tucked under his coat as well. Glancing over his shoulder, he said, "Walk faster."

Just as they got to the car, there was a ruckus inside the building, and an alarm went off.

"Put them in the gym bag on the floor," Ben instructed, unlocking the doors. Once Grace was inside, he handed her the baby boy and went to his side of the car.

"In a gym bag? You can't be –"

"Yes!" Ben hissed, tossing his backpack into the backseat as he got in the car. When they were both in, he locked the doors and started the car, praying it would not give him any difficulty. "Do it now!"

Grace gently set the children side-by-side in the gym bag, on top of Ben's gym clothes. Ben drove normal speed out of the parking lot toward the gatehouse. Grace had the bag tucked under her legs, with her coat draped over her legs so she would not have to close the bag, but it was still hidden.

"What's going on?" Ben asked the guard, who suddenly appeared at the exit gate, where he was normally posted only at the entrance.

"There's something about missing kids. You two don't have any babies in there, do you?" the guard asked, glancing into the vehicle.

Both laughed. "Why would we have babies in here?" Ben asked.

"There are two missing, so they're having us check everyone leaving," he explained.

"We work with them all day. The volume is deafening," Ben said. "Trust me, we need the break. I mean honestly! Does it sound like there are babies in here?"

"No. True. Just do me a favor and pop the trunk?"

"Sure," Ben said, pulling the leaver to open the trunk.

The officer glanced around the trunk before closing it. "Okay. Thank you. Have a good day," the security guard waved him through while he lifted the security gate arm.

As they pulled away, the facility went into lock-down. Alarms blared loudly, and the solid gates slammed shut behind them.

"Just in the nick of time," Grace breathed out, as Ben pressed a little harder on the gas. "Don't get pulled over."

"I know. I just don't want them to follow us," Ben said, continuously glancing at the review mirror.

Together, they raced out of town. Several towns over, they stopped at a store. Grace went in and bought two sets of everything they would need for the babies in cash. She purchased two car seats, two pack-n-plays, six sets of bottles, several cannisters of formula, several boxes of sizes one to three diapers, and a case of wipes.

Barely any room left in the car, they drove for a few days. Starting their journey in Maine, they made their way to Tennessee, where they abandoned Ben's car and bought a truck for cash. That is where both emptied and shut down their bank accounts as well. From that point forward, they paid cash for everything.

Stopping by Goodwill in Arkansas to pick up some clothes for themselves, along with some baby clothes of various sizes, they then loaded up the kids, and resumed their drive. Continuously looking over their shoulders, they made sure to take backroads as much as possible until they crossed into Texas.

"What do you think?" Ben asked Grace as they drove into a small, deep East Texas town called Willow Bend.

Grace nodded while looking around. "I think it's cute."

"We need to think of a back story. As soon as we walk in with two little ones, they're going to want to know all about them," Ben pointed out.

"True. Well," she glanced at the little ones asleep in their car seats in the back seat, "their birthdays are two days apart. We could say they're twins, born in between their birthdays on the 9th of October?"

"That'll work," Ben agreed. "What about our story?"

"What do you mean?"

"Where did the twins come from?"

"Oh!" she said wide-eyed. "I didn't think of that! Well, are we married? Are we dating? Are they ours or just mine?" she asked, putting her light-brown hair up in a ponytail.

Pulling into the parking lot, he thought through her questions. "Those are good questions." Turning the car off, he asked, "What if we're married? Are you okay with that?"

"I think that's the safest thing for the kids. If we find others and fall in love, we'll have a lot of explaining to do."

"There's always after they grow up," Ben offered. "Can you tolerate me for eighteen years?"

"Pretty sure I can," Grace said with a smile. Truth be told, she was attracted to him from his first day on the job at the clinic three years ago. Most of the women at work were enamored with him. How could they not be? He was charismatic, outgoing, strong, and confident in himself. Grace, on the other hand, was shy, confident in her knowledge, but humble in heart. Her only hang-up with him? While Grace was a Christian, she was pretty sure Ben was not.

"There'll be a steep learning curve for both of us, but if there are any medical issues, we have that covered."

"What about birth certificates?" Grace asked.

"Well, if you're okay being Hope Hunt, I have Holly's file here," Ben said, showing her two of the files he pulled from his backpack in the back seat.

Grace flipped through the files. "So, does that mean you're Noah Roth?" she asked. "That's who's listed as Blake and Holly's dad on their birth certificates."

Shuddering, Ben adamantly shook his head. "No. What if we change the names on the birth certificates? We don't want our names attached to anything, but we need to keep some of our identity so we don't slip."

"Well, we could go to downtown Dallas and get social security numbers so we can work?" Grace offered. "My family is from down here. My brother knows some shady characters in Dallas who can get him whatever he needs."

"What if we just use our real first names and agree on a last name? We can work under the table?"

"The birth certificates for the mothers are in here, along with their social security numbers," Grace said, shuffling through the paperwork. "They had to give the information in order to enter the program. I could be Hope Hunt. I could use her birth certificate and social security number to get a real job while you stay at home to care for the little ones."

"Is it safe to use? And are you okay with me staying home while you work?"

"If I only use it for work and stay in a small town, we should be okay. If issues arise, we can move. If I work, that means you'll have to keep the house clean and take care of the babies."

"I'm okay with that," Ben agreed. Leaning back in his seat,

rubbing his chin deep, he asked, "Are we just going to rent a house? How will we do that without credit?"

"What if we use a house that no one knows about?"

"You have that?"

"Well, my great uncle has a hunting cabin a few hours from here in Louisiana?" she offered.

"If it's in your family, and they suspect we're the ones who took them, trust me, they'll know about it."

"What if we keep that in mind if things get hot?" Grace asked.

"Good idea. Okay, are you ready? Our names will be Ben and Hope Hunt. Remember that. We're about to garner a lot of unwanted attention with two little ones."

"It'll be okay, Ben," she said, taking his hand. "Just remember to call me Hope, not Grace."

He instinctively went to pull his hand away until she shook her head. "Oh, yeah," he chuckled nervously, "we're married."

"Right. And my name is?"

"Hope Hunt."

"Well, we don't have a marriage certificate, so keep that in mind if we need that for anything. What will the kid's names be?" she asked.

"What if we keep them the same? That way the boy's name starts with a B like mine, and the girl's name starts with an H like yours."

"Agreed," she said.

"Good. So, married?"

"Yes. How long have we been together?"

"Let's make it five years?" Ben suggested.

"That'll work. Keep it simple."

"Where did we live before here?"

"The kids were born in Maine. That's where their birth certificates are from."

"If we stay close enough to the truth, we won't have to remember as much. Let's keep it to Maine," he suggested.

"Agreed."

"So, what brought us down here?"

She shrugged. "New life?"

"Sounds good. Let's do this. We'll use this as a test. If we flunk, then we move on to the next town."

"Let's try to stay here," she suggested. "It's a cute little town in the middle of nowhere."

"We'll see," he said, getting out of the car.

As they walked into the restaurant, they were pleasantly surprised by the friendliness. "Welcome! Aww! They're so cute! Are they twins?" the hostess gushed over the babies.

"Yes, ma'am," Ben said as he held Blake.

"Are y'all passing through, or do you live around here?"

"Just pulled in…literally," Hope (nurse Grace) explained. "We're looking for work and a possible place to rent if you know of anything?"

"Actually, we're looking for a server," the hostess said, hopeful.

Hope looked to Ben, who nodded. "Great! Do you have an application?" she asked.

With a grin on her face, the hostess handed Hope an application. "I'm Macy Bryant," she said, sticking her hand out for Hope to shake.

As she shook her hand, Hope said, "I'm Hope Hunt. This is my husband, Ben, and our two children, Blake and Holly."

"Welcome to Willow Bend! We'd love to have y'all be a part of our community! Would y'all like a table or a booth?"

"Booth would be fine," Ben said, "then we can put them on the seat next to us."

Hope tucked her hair behind her ear. "Great idea!" she agreed.

"So, where does the red hair come from?" Macy asked, showing them to their table.

"It's from my side of the family," Ben mentioned. Ben was six-foot-two. He had dark brown-hair, and dark-brown eyes. Meanwhile, Hope (Grace), was five-foot-seven. She had light-brown hair, and blue eyes. While she tried to keep her weight down, she could stand to lose a few pounds around the mid-section.

"Your server will be Serrin," Macy said. "Can I get you something to drink?"

"Water would be wonderful," Ben said. "It's hot down here. We're not used to this heat still in October."

"Where are y'all from?"

"Maine," Hope mentioned, scanning the menu.

"Bet it's cold up there in the winter."

"Brutal," Ben agreed, opening his menu.

"Well, if you don't like the cold, then you'll like it here," Macy said. "I'll get your waters."

While she was gone, there was a silence between the pair. They would periodically look up at each other every few moments.

After giving their waitress their order, Ben folded his hands in front of him and said, "We'll never be able to rest."

"I know. They're worth it, though. I'm only sorry we weren't able to get the other two out. Hopefully, their families will care for them, and the clinic won't do too much damage to them."

Sitting back in his seat, Ben crossed his arms. "You're serious?"

She looked up innocently. "What?"

Leaning forward, Ben quietly reminded her, "The boy? Adam? His mother will probably die soon. As for the girl? Deanna? It was her mom's room that was the Code Blue we heard just before we escaped with these two. We know what happened to Holly and Blake's mothers."

"Are you serious?" she asked, wide-eyed.

"You really didn't get a good look at their charts, did you?"

"I guess not. Maybe it was easier to pretend we worked in a fertility clinic instead of the actual clinic."

"They're going to test those poor little babies out of their childhood. I really wish we could have saved the others. Who knows how many others may be born?"

"We don't know. But," she glanced at the babies, "we saved these two."

"True. Okay, so do you really want to work here?" he asked.

"I think it would give me a chance to find out more about the town. Pretty sure whatever is going on in this town is discussed somewhere within these walls. It'll allow me to keep a pulse on what's going on. Also, we can't be in the medical field. Unfortunately, that could tag us. We need to not be who we were."

"Right. So, the first step is to find somewhere to live." Seeing their waitress coming with their food, Ben sat back. "That looks great!" he said, pleased.

Serrin placed their burgers and chips in front of them. "Is there anything else I can help you with?"

"Not unless you know someone renting a home in the area?" Ben asked.

"Actually, I do. My mother's friend does that sort of thing. I could contact her."

"It's a house, right? We're not picky, but we would rather not have an apartment."

"Yep," Serrin said. "Let me call her. I'll be back in a minute."

"Great! Thank you so much!" Ben smiled. "We really appreciate it."

"I get it," Serrin said. "My mom used to watch children. They get kind of loud. I can't imagine it would be any quieter times two."

Hope smirked. "It gets interesting when they go off at the same time."

Serrin rolled her eyes. "I can only imagine."

"When one goes off, the other isn't far behind," Ben added.

"It's my understanding that twins have their own language of sorts," Serrin suggested.

"They do. They coo at each other for hours," Hope said. "Say, Macy mentioned that you're hiring?"

"Yes. Are you thinking of applying?" Serrin asked.

"Looking for servers, right?"

"Yes."

"Well, we need a home first."

"I'm fixin' to give my mom a call while y'all eat."

"Thank you!" Hope smiled. When Serrin left, Hope leaned closer to Ben and said, "We can afford to rent a house on what we have together for about a year. Hopefully, I can make enough for us to keep it."

"What if we actually buy a house…in cash?"

Wide-eyed, Hope shook her head. "We don't have that kind of money!"

"Actually, we do if we buy a fixer-upper. I have all that money I inherited," Ben pointed out. "Also, I had quite a bit of cash I had been stashing away to buy a house of my own. That's what we got when I closed my accounts."

"Right. And I have the money we pulled from my account for the European trip and my savings."

"Between the two of us, we could get a fixer-upper with acreage. Then, with the money left over we could fix the house. We'll put it in your name since we have a social security number for Hope Hunt?"

"Do you know how to do all that home remodeling stuff?"

"In my off-time, I worked with a local organization to build homes for the homeless or low-income families. Anything I don't know, I'm pretty sure I can find a video online to get through it. With the little ones, I can do it while they're asleep."

"Are you sure? That's a lot of work!"

"If we want complete privacy, we're going to need to get a home where no one is near, with acreage. Once these two start to show any signs of what they can do, we need them to not be in public."

"I'll probably need a better-paying job if we're keeping all three of you home."

"Work this for a year, allowing you to branch out into the community…slowly."

"What about church? That's always a great way to get to know people."

"And, what if they show signs of what they can do while they're at church and we're not with them because they're in the nursery or their own class?"

"Good point," she said, sitting back in her seat, snacking on her chips. "Can I at least go when I'm off work?"

"I don't see a problem with that."

"And when they get older and get themselves under control, can I bring the kids?"

"I don't think that'll be a problem with that."

She grinned. "Thank you!"

Serrin walked up to the table. "I'm sorry. My mom's friend doesn't have anything right now."

"No problem. We've come up with a different idea. Do you know a reputable realtor?" Ben asked. "We'd like to buy a fixer-upper with some land."

"Oh, yes! Here ya go!" she said, pulling a ticket from her tablet. She scribbled the name and number of a realtor and handed it to him. "He likes a challenge."

"Great!" Ben accepted the paper, pleased. "Thank you!"

"Are y'all fixing to have some dessert?"

"No. This'll fill us," Hope smiled. "Thank you, though."

"No problem. I'll keep an eye on y'all in case you need refills on your drinks. Other than that," she placed the ticket on the table, "here's your check. Feel free to pay at the register near the door when you're ready."

"Thank you, Serrin," Hope said as Ben picked up the check. When Serrin was out of earshot, Hope asked, "Do you really think we can do this?"

"I think it's the only way we can do it. We need to do this without people learning too much about us."

"Can we really settle and feel safe?" Hope asked.

"We'll stay here until we don't feel safe. Any hint of someone possibly sniffing too close, and we'll pull out."

"Agreed," Hope said. Silently praying before she continued eating, she prayed for safety for the two little ones left behind and for safety and security for them as well. She knew it was wrong to take the babies, but she also knew what the clinic was doing was wrong. While her head was bowed, she prayed the Lord would understand why she helped take the children and that He would keep the innocent involved safe.

"If we take care of the moments, the years will take care of themselves." Maria Edgeworth

"This is going to take *a lot* of work," Hope said, looking around their new home.

The living room was the only room that was not in desperate need of remodeling. It looked like the people before them had a glorious vision of a massive remodel, started the work, but then realized there was too much. The good news about the property was that it was on ten acres, and the house was situated in the center of the ten acres, so they would not have to be concerned about neighbors seeing or hearing anything. Since the house was in the center, they would see anyone approaching the house.

"Well, with you working double shifts, I mainly need to worry about the little ones and the house." Ben shrugged. "I'll work while they sleep so they'll get used to the noise. Pretty soon, they'll sleep through it."

"This is true."

"It's more you that I'm worried about. Are you sure you want to pull double shifts in a restaurant?"

"I'm used to the long hours from being a nurse. I'm also used to working with difficult people," she said, rolling her eyes as she was cooking dinner. The babies slept in their carriers on the brown leather couch delivered the previous day.

As the infusion of fried chicken in the bottom oven, mixed with the delightful scent of fresh macaroni and cheese in the top oven, Hope cut the ingredients for a salad on the small make-shift counter. The counter was the top of a short bookshelf until the kitchen could be completed. It would be tricky, but having a stove and refrigerator, also delivered the day before, made things much easier.

"That smells amazing! I'm not sure you're going to be so happy about my cooking skills." Ben grinned sheepishly.

"Well, there are videos and recipes online on how to cook as well."

Ben laughed, shaking his head. "You're going to domesticate me yet!"

"It'll be fun trying!"

Holly started whining in her sleep for a moment before she suddenly woke up and started crying.

"It's that time," Ben said loudly over Holly's crying. "Better get the bottles going. Blake's going to join her in –"

Blake cut him off as he let out a loud yell and then immediately jumped into crying.

"In stereo!" Hope said, opening the fridge to grab two bottles. Tossing them in the microwave without a top, she warmed them up. She knew she would have to shake them very well so there would not be cold or hot spots in the formula. While she was not happy with this method, with two of them it would be difficult not to have everything pre-made and ready to go.

After a few moments, she pulled the bottles, topped them,

and shook them for thirty seconds before taking them into Ben, who had a child in each arm.

He looked up at her. "This is going to be fun, isn't it?" he asked, giving a half-smile as his forehead creased.

Her eyebrows rose. "Can you do this?"

Ben set the two screaming little ones each into a pack-n-play. He then turned back to Hope. Setting his hands on her shoulders, slightly bending his knees so he could look at her eye-to-eye, he confidently assured her, "I can do this. Give me the bottles and watch this."

Handing him the bottles, she turned back to the kitchen to finish the salad. As she chopped the fresh spinach, romaine lettuce, tomatoes, cucumbers, carrots, and green peppers, she kept an eye on Ben.

At first, he started the playlist on his phone. He made one with a list of classical music to play in hopes it would soothe the babies. Then he took a deep, cleansing breath, slowly letting out his air, psyching himself up. "I got this," he said aloud to himself over the screaming and crying children. "I can do this."

He picked up Holly and put her in the swing. Since Blake was the loudest, he would be the first one fed. Holly whimpered for a few moments before she settled herself, watching Ben and Blake.

When he picked up Blake, the little boy fought him until Ben got a little formula into his mouth. Once he did, Blake jumped at the chance to chug the precious, warm formula from the bottle.

"Don't do anything else," Ben said to Hope. "I need to juggle all of this myself."

"Let me go ahead and finish dinner. If we can have at least one decent meal a week when I'm home, I'll be happy."

Grinning, Ben agreed, "Fair enough. Thank you."

Turning back to the salad, Hope listened to the music while listening to Ben in the other room with the little ones. This was what she often imagined her married life to be like. A thought struck her. *Could this be what she had been looking for all along? If so, could she and Ben really form a family out of this situation? Would their family have love, or would it simply be out of convenience?* Time would tell.

❦❦❦

OVER THE NEXT FEW WEEKS, the house was in complete chaos. With the living room completed, Ben decided one of the bathrooms and the kitchen would be the next priority. They would sleep in the living room until they were finished. Each baby slept in a pack-n-play, while Ben and Hope slept on a blow-up queen mattress fully clothed. To Hope, it was a comfort to know he was close, but each kept to their side of the mattress.

Ben did an amazing job of juggling two newborns, remodeling the kitchen and bathroom, and keeping up with the cooking. He would cook in bulk and freeze the extra in meal sizes for two, leaving only a salad to make at dinner time. He would also pre-make bottles each morning, making sure there was enough for the first wake-up the next day as well.

In the meantime, Hope was working from eight in the morning until ten at night. She would come in and take a shower in a bucket. Then she would help with the eleven o'clock at night feeding, so she would be able to play with the kids a little bit before going to bed.

It took Ben a month and a half to do the entire kitchen and one of the three bathrooms. This allowed them to not have to take a shower in a bucket anymore…even taking a blessed bath once and a while! Having a beautiful kitchen, living room, and bathroom made Hope want to stay home even more.

Finally, about three months after they moved in, Ben sat Hope down on the couch to talk. "You can't keep pulling these shifts without a break. It will break you. You also need to bond more with the kids before they get too much older."

Tears filled her eyes as she glanced from him, to the babies, and back again. "I don't know how I can do that and we still be able to keep our heads above water."

"We didn't have to buy Christmas gifts this year since they were only a few months old. However, I promise you next year we won't be so lucky. I'm sure since the holidays have passed, you guys have slowed down."

"We have."

"Well, if you want to slow down a bit as well, I think it would be wise. We're both pushing our limits. Just because I don't have a set schedule doesn't mean it isn't hectic. I would love to have a day off here or there. What if you take off two days per week?" he asked. "One of those days will be my day off and one will be yours."

"I'll talk to Sam about it," Hope agreed, referring to the manager at the restaurant. "If we each have a day off, we can do with it whatever we want, correct?"

"Of course! Whoever's day off it is, the other has custody and responsibility for the little ones and the house. That way, it's a true day off."

"I agree. What if, for example, I want to do something as a group together…like a family?" she asked, hopeful.

"If that's what you want to do on your day off, then that's what we'll do. We both work our behinds off. We need to pace ourselves. We're also working so hard, we're going to miss a lot of their firsts if we're not careful," Ben said, glancing toward the door of the room with the sleeping babies. Each was in their own pack-n-play, fast asleep.

"I agree. I hate to ask this and possibly mess up our rhythm, but what are we?" she asked.

"What do you mean?"

"Are we a family?"

"Families don't look traditional anymore. This is a family in the heart."

She shifted nervously in her seat, tucking a portion of her hair behind her ear. "Um…okay."

"What's wrong?"

"Well, I just wondered what exactly we're doing here?"

"We're raising two babies," he said, furrowing his brow. "Why?"

"Okay. Fair enough." She gave up. Standing, she cocked her head to the side when she saw something floating in the kitchen. "Ben, what's that?"

"What's what?" Ben asked. Turning to see where she was looking, he followed her line of sight and slowly stood, cautiously walking into the kitchen. Once in there, he saw a bottle floating in the air by itself. He reached up and plucked it out of the air. Looking at it, and then around the kitchen, he turned back to Hope. "Which one is awake?"

Going to their room, Hope quietly opened the door to find Holly smiling at her, as she had ahold of her feet with her hands, rolling side to side.

"Was that you?" Hope whispered, picking up Holly out of her pack-n-play. Holly rested her hand on Hope's cheek. "You little stinker!" Hope said with a smile. "Let me take you to Daddy, and then I'll come back for your brother."

When she left the bedroom, she heard Blake stirring in his pack-n-play. Walking into the kitchen with Holly, she mentioned, "It was Holly."

"Hmmm," he said, pulling the bottle from the microwave, "seems her gift is telekinesis."

"You think?"

"I don't think a bottle simply floats through the air." Shaking the bottle, he then held it up so Holly could see it. "You want this?"

Holly reached for it, but Ben pulled it back. "If you want it, you have to get it yourself."

Holly's bottom lip jutted out as she started to cry.

"Nope. That doesn't work with me," Ben said. "If you want it, you have to get it. You know what I mean."

"Ben, she's too little for this," Hope said, rolling her eyes. "You can't seriously think she knows how to do this?"

"Give her time," he said confidently. Rattling the bottle near her, teasing her, he said, "Come on, Holly. If you want it, get it." When she pouted again, Ben told Hope, "Go ahead and put her on the floor on the blanket, and let's go get Blake."

"Isn't this kind of cruel?"

"Just watch," Ben said. They went around the corner toward the bedroom. As Holly went to get Blake up, Ben gently grabbed her arm to stop her. Shaking his head, he whispered, "Watch this."

At first, Holly was crying. When Holly noticed they still were not getting the bottle for her, she stopped for a moment, and then cried louder.

"Ben?" Hope whispered.

"Just watch. I have a feeling. Trust me."

Hope sighed. "Okay."

Watching around the corner out of Holly's line of sight, they saw her fuss and cry for another few minutes before she stopped and looked toward the kitchen where she could see the bottle on the edge of the counter. To Hope and Ben's astonishment, the bottle dropped from the counter to the floor before it rolled toward her, leaving a formula trail along the way. Reaching her hand out, the bottle rolled farther, until it rolled right into her hand. She picked it up and started drinking as if it was no big deal.

Wide-eyed, Hope looked at Ben. "How did you know?" she asked, dumbfounded.

"It was a feeling. Blake hasn't done anything yet. I'm sure he will soon. If she's showing signs, he can't be far behind."

"How do we teach a three-month-old to control telekinesis?" Hope asked.

"We don't...yet. When she can control it, then we'll work with her. Until then, we keep on our toes."

Shaking her head, Hope sighed. "What a weird family we have."

"Ohh, be careful. It may get worse. We don't know what Blake has in store for us."

"Or worse yet, if she has anything else in her."

Ben gasped as he covered his mouth. Then he confessed, "I hadn't thought of that."

"Well, stay on your toes. This is just beginning."

Nine Months Later – A Few Days Before Their First Birthday

"I'M SO glad we agreed we each get a day off," Hope said, sitting on the couch with her feet up. I'm going to church this morning. Do you want to come?"

"And bring these two with us? No way." Ben shook his head. "Holly's still out of control. Trying to keep her room clear of any and all things she could pull into the crib with her has been a nightmare! This gives new meaning to the term baby proofing a home."

Picking up Blake, with his toy in hand, Hope sat back down on the couch. "I wonder when they'll start walking."

Finished dressing Holly for the day, Ben stood her on her feet. "Not sure if we're ready for that yet."

"Dada...tookie?" Holly asked.

"Oh, I don't think so. It's too early for that."

Holly reached her hand toward the kitchen.

"Holly, I said no," Ben warned.

The lid of the cookie jar lifted itself off. Then it rested on the counter as if some invisible force set it there.

"Holly," Ben warned. "I mean it. No."

A cookie lifted from the jar and floated toward the living room.

Ben took Holly's hand that was reached out, and sharply tapped it. "I said no."

Holly's hand dropped, and the cookie dropped breaking apart as soon as it hit the floor. Turning back to Ben, Holly's bottom lip trembled as tears slowly crawled down her cheeks.

"Yes, I love you. However, no means no, Holly. Just because you can, doesn't mean you should."

Holly looked back toward the broken cookie on the floor. "Tookie." She pouted.

"I said no," Ben scolded. "Maybe later."

"Pay attention, Blake," Hope said, "No means no for you too."

Blake reached up and touched the side of Hope's face with his tiny hand. When he did, an image got shoved into Hope's mind so strongly, she struggled to understand what she was seeing.

The image was the four of them playing on the floor. Ben and Hope were singing *The Wheels On The Bus* song, as they each had one of the babies in front of them, moving the feet of the babies to the sound of the music.

As soon as she was able to focus on that one, another vision was thrust into her mind. It was of Hope making cookies. Hope felt herself making the cookies. She smelled the cookie dough mixture, as well as when the cookies were baking. The heavenly aroma of cookies baking permeated her every sense. She could almost taste them

"Um." Hope shook her head to clear it. "I think Blake wants me to make cookies. He also wants us to play on the floor. I think he thinks both would stop Holly from crying."

"What do you mean you think he wants you to do those things?" Ben asked, hugging Holly, who was still whimpering.

"Come here," Hope said. Ben scooted next to the couch with Holly on his lap. Looking up at Blake, Ben asked, "What's Mommy talking about, Blake?" Blake reached his hand toward Ben, so Hope and Ben switched kids. Holly leaned her head against Hope's chest while Hope wrapped her arms around Holly to comfort her. When she kissed Holly's head, Hope mentioned, "No still means no. Just because you're on my lap doesn't mean you get a cookie. I will cuddle you, but Mommy and Daddy will back each other up. No means no. Understand?"

Holly leaned her head against Hope's chest again, listening to her heartbeat, clutching Hope's shirt in her tiny hand.

Meanwhile, Blake was sitting on Ben's lap, leaning against Ben's upright, bent knees. "What's wrong?" Ben asked him. Blake smiled as he reached up toward Ben's face. When his hand made contact with Ben's cheek, Ben's mind was overcome with the scent of chocolate chip cookies baking in the oven while the vision of Hope and him playing with the kids on the floor played out in Ben's mind.

"Whoa!" Ben said, shaking his head. Looking toward Hope, he asked, "Chocolate chip cookies?"

"Tookie!" Holly grinned as she sat up and clapped her hands together. "Tookie! Tookie! Toooooookie!"

"No, Holly. Not right now," Ben said again.

When he said no, the toys on the floor slowly rose into the air and began to slowly bounce through the air on their own. Blake looked up and giggled, watching the toys floating around them. He reached his tiny hands into the air to attempt to touch them. "Mine," Blake said. Then he looked at Holly and pointed as he said, "Tookie? Peease?"

"Just because you two are being –"

"Ben?" Hope cut Ben off when a thought struck her.

"What?"

"Can we talk in the other room for a minute?"

"Fine." Turning to Holly, he warned, "If we come back out

and you have eaten a cookie, you will *not* get a cookie for the rest of the day. No cookie. Understand?"

Holly looked at him, batting her eyes.

"No cookie. We'll be right back," he said as the pair set the two babies on the floor.

Holly continued to play with the toys in the air amidst Blake's giggles.

When they were in the hallway, Ben asked, "What?"

"If we're going to train them to use their gifts, what better way than with positive reinforcement. Blake showed you what Holly wanted and how to stop his sister from crying. If Holly does something good, she gets a cookie. We can show her that by saying what Blake did and giving him a cookie."

"What can Holly do to get a cookie?"

"She can put the lid back on the cookie jar. She can also put the toys back on the shelf. The cookies are baby cookies that are good for them. They're not going to get the chocolate chip cookies they want, but they'll still get a cookie. Teach them the difference between right and wrong."

Crossing his arms, Ben argued, "They're only a year old."

"If we don't get a grip on them by the time they're two, we're in major trouble! Teach them now. We also need to start schooling them. We can use their gifts in positive ways while teaching them control."

"By *we*, you mean *me*."

"For the schooling, yes. That's the only way we can keep them at home. We need to homeschool them, and I need to work."

"True. Speaking of that, have you thought more about your manager's proposition of being trained as an assistant manager?"

"I have, but I wanted to talk to you. That will put me on salary. It may also mean more hours."

"As long as you have two days off a week, I'm fine."

"Yes. I already made that a clear stipulation."

"Okay." Glancing around the corner, Ben said, "So, Blake is a telepath?"

"I think so, but not sure to what extent. This is the first time he's ever shown signs of it. I wonder if he's done it with Holly yet, or if this is the first time he's ever used it?"

"That's something we'll probably never know. We just need to be aware she's telekinetic, and he's a telepath."

Hope shook her head. "Kind of hard to believe Professor Roth did this via DNA experiments."

"While you may have been there longer, I was a bit sneakier. I dove into the archives and did some research of my own," Ben pointed out. "I know the true extent of his experiments."

"What? How?"

Ben sheepishly admitted, "During my break times, I would go down and sweet-talk Erin in Records into letting me in there."

"Do I *want* to know how you did that?"

"Probably not. The point is…Professor Roth was doing this for more than twenty years before he finally got it right with the four babies. By messing with their genetic code, some of the babies weren't even viable. Some were born without parts. I don't even know how many were really lost or were aborted before he finally got some who were viable and showed the gene. And now, he's figured out the genetic code to create them," Ben said, gesturing toward the two little ones still playing on the floor.

During the time the pair were talking, the two babies had since rolled over and were rocking on their hands and knees. They watched as Holly pulled herself up on the couch, shifting from one foot to the other while she held onto the couch. Blake got up on his hands and knees, and then crawled over and mimicked Holly until he, too, stood with his hands on the couch. They both giggled as they beat their hands on the couch like they were hitting drums.

"I wonder if they can understand each other yet," Hope said.

"There are times where they almost seem to have their own language."

"Pretty sure they do. If nothing else, Blake probably puts thoughts into her mind like he did to us."

"True," Hope said, and then she saw Blake put his hand on Holly's cheek.

At first, Holly furrowed her brow, and then a huge grin spread across her face. A few seconds later, both burst out in laughter.

Leaning against the corner of the wall, Hope sighed. Then she said, "I'm glad they get along so well. This could have turned out pretty scary."

"Let's just hope they continue to get along."

"I don't think that'll be an issue. We get along as well."

Resting his arm over Hope's shoulder, as both were now visible to the two little ones, Ben smiled as he said, "We do. I'm glad to be raising these two with someone like you."

"Someone like me?" Hope asked.

"Someone who is sweet and understanding. Someone who isn't combative."

"True. You're not too bad yourself," she said with a smile.

⟐⟐⟐⟐

FOR THEIR FIRST BIRTHDAY PARTY, it was just the four of them. Some of the staff at the restaurant gave Hope grief for keeping the babies away from the rest of the world.

"Seriously, Hope," Serrin scolded, as Hope cashed her out for the day around four, "raising those two in a bubble is not a good thing."

"They're a handful to take out. There are two of them. They're usually going in different directions at the same time. Not really sure how poor Ben does it. I get a break here at the diner."

"Not sure how much of a break that is. Don't you miss them?"

"Of course I do. That's why I make sure to have two days off a week."

"You've been here for almost a year. Your one-year anniversary is coming up in three weeks. I never see you around town, nor do I see that handsome man of yours. Why do y'all keep everyone locked up?"

"They're not locked up," Hope said, rolling her eyes as she shook her head. While Hope counted the money in her head, she explained, "They play outside all the time. We even took them to the pumpkin patch the other day. We're selective on where we take them. Those kids will be raised in a quiet environment but will also be fully-functional in this world. Trust me, they'll be socially adept."

"What about their birthday party?"

"We had a quiet one a few days ago on their birthday. They dove into their cakes too! It was adorable!"

Truth be told, Holly picked up her cupcake with her mind and slammed it against the wall. She then took the other cupcakes, one after the other, and flew them all over the kitchen until Blake reached over and rested his hand on her arm. When he did, Holly got a serene look on her face and immediately calmed down. The reason for the temper tantrum this time? Holly wanted more than one cupcake, but Hope and Ben wanted to limit their sugar intake, and Holly did not agree.

Holly seemed to have a bit more of a temper, while Blake was happy-go-lucky and laid-back. Both were social in their own way. Blake had dark-brown hair and chestnut-brown eyes, while Holly had beautiful strawberry-blond hair and baby-blue eyes. Hope knew as adorable as the pair were now, they would be stunning when they got older. Hope and Ben would have their hands full.

⫘⫘

LATER THAT NIGHT, as the dinner rush was going on, the County Sheriff, Wyatt Reynolds, came in and sat down at the bar. As usual, the wait staff had their hands full, so Hope took care of him. "Evening, Sheriff. What can I get for you tonight?"

"How about the meatloaf and potatoes?"

"Sure. Comfort food day?"

"Definitely! This weather is wreaking havoc on the mental state of this town. It's eighty-five one day and fifty-five the next. This is crazy!"

"I'm sure!"

"On top of that, there's a full moon coming up tomorrow, *and* it's on Friday the thirteenth of all days. It's days like this that make me want to turn in my badge."

Leaning on the counter in front of him, Hope's heart broke. Wyatt was a forty-year-old man who was married to his job. His uncle was the Sheriff before him, and he was a great County Sheriff. Unfortunately, he was killed during a traffic stop that turned out to be a drug-running vehicle. There was another Sheriff between them, but that Sheriff did not do very well. So, when Wyatt ran, he won by a landslide. He has continued to hold that position for the last five years.

His rugged good looks helped his position, but so did his spotless record. His county had the most arrests for drug runners, which forced the drug runners to take a different route, one which went around his county. He also added more patrols to help clean up his county, which his constituents appreciated.

Since it was hunting season, he grew out his beard. While he had dark-brown hair, his beard was a mix of silver and dark-brown. When he grew it out, it made his green eyes pop. Over the last year, Hope found out he went to the same church as she did. Hope could not figure out why he was not already married.

"Oh, you don't really want to do that," Hope said, bringing

them both back to the conversation. "You love the job and the people of this county too much."

"This is true. I also wouldn't have the benefit of a discounted dinner, or you as my personal waitress," he said with a wink and a smile.

"That's only because I don't want to bog the others down with making sure you get the best food in the restaurant."

"Always lookin' out for me. Love that about you."

"Well, gotta look out for those who take care of this town," Hope said with a grin and a shrug. "Who knows? I may need you to fix a ticket for me someday."

"I highly doubt you would get a ticket. I haven't seen you break a single law since you've been here."

"Meh." She shrugged again. "I'll own the fact that I sometimes go over the speed limit."

"I'm pretty sure we all do. Just don't go more than five miles over the speed limit, and you should be good. Five you're fine, nine you're mine."

"That's what I usually do."

Leaning forward, he asked, "So, how come I never see your husband or those babies out and about?"

"Have you ever tried to corral twin toddlers? It's like herding cats! When Ben or I go shopping, as strange as it sounds, it's a break for us."

"Interesting. So, are they ever going to see the light of day?"

Chuckling, she explained, "They see the light of day all the time. They play outside on the playset. We just took them to the pumpkin patch the other day, too. When we can tag-team, it makes it easier."

"I'm sure! Do you have pictures of it?"

"Yeah, here," she said, showing him the pictures on her phone.

"They're adorable!"

"They are, but they also have their moments," she said on a

sigh. Then, with a smile, she added, "But I wouldn't change it for the world."

"I'm sure! You make a handsome family!"

"Thank you!" she said, accepting her phone back. She tucked it into her pocket.

"Are they going to go to school when they're old enough? Or Headstart?"

"No. They've already started homeschooling."

"At one?"

"Yep. We're doing colors first. They play a game where there is a piece of construction paper on the floor. They have to show us what color ball goes with what color paper. When they get a little older, they can play where they toss the color ball into the laundry basket where the matching colored piece of paper is taped. We also have that toy with the shapes on a hard, plastic ball. They have to get the shape into the right hole in order for it to go in, and we tell them what the shape is. And we read to them each night. Homeschooling isn't grilling them. It's teaching them with different learning techniques. They're exploring the world. Another example is the pumpkin patch. We picked up a pumpkin for the family." She smiled as she reminisced. "The kids had so much fun at the pumpkin patch. We played tag in the hay maze, with Ben carrying Blake and me carrying Holly. The next day we hollowed out the pumpkin, cooked the seeds, and carved a cool design in the pumpkin. Then we used canned pumpkin and made pumpkin muffins. The kids sat in their highchairs while we did a pretend cooking show, measuring and putting everything together. Of course, eating the muffins was their favorite part, but we taught them math by doing the measuring. Homeschooling is hands-on teaching. When they get older, it'll be a little more formal, maybe even implement some computer games for hand-to-eye coordination. We'll explore the woods around the house for Science. We will even do gardening and fun with Chemistry. We will take trips to places like Boston,

Washington DC, The Alamo, etcetera for History and Social Studies. We'll read books, and they may even write a couple stories for English. There is a myriad of ways to learn. In the meantime, we're keeping it simple."

"I've never heard it explained that way. That's actually really cool!"

"Thank you. Well," Hope glanced around the restaurant, "as much as I enjoy talking to you and about my babies, there are a lot of people in here. I'll get your drink and put in your order."

"Thank you. It has *truly* been a pleasure."

"Maybe come in when it isn't so crowded and we can talk more."

"I may just do that," he said with a smile as she disappeared into the kitchen. He enjoyed talking to Hope. There was a light about her, which drew him to her. But she was married. There was something about the pair that did not make sense, though. While they seemed to cuddle and play with the babies, in flipping through her phone, he did not see a single picture of just the pair of them. Then, in the pictures of them as a family, they did not touch or seem to be in love. He decided to see if he could find out more about the family. *Was it a marriage of convenience or love?* The thought of it being a marriage of convenience broke his heart for Hope. She was a lady full of love and deserved to have that love reciprocated. *Was she afraid to lose her children if she left him? What type of man was she married to? Was there abuse or neglect involved?* The detective portion of his brain kicked into high gear. It would be his mission to find out more about her and her family…mainly her husband.

A MATTER OF TIME

"Being deeply loved by someone gives you strength, while loving someone deeply gives you courage." Lao Tzu

Through the course of the next few months, Wyatt Reynolds did his best to find anything he could on Hope's husband, Ben Hunt. He pulled every string he knew to pull. He even called in his favors from those in the FBI and military he knew. The fact that he could not find anything, not even a social security number or birth certificate, made him not only more curious, but also more afraid for Hope and her children.

As he was going over the information in the files he had on his desk on Ben and Hope Hunt one morning, his secretary, Sherry Waters, walked in with his coffee. When he gave her a questioning look, she responded with, "This one looks deep. I've seen lines appear in your face overnight about this case. May I ask what's concerning you?"

"You may not," he said, accepting the precious elixir from Sherry. He knew she liked him, but he was not interested in her.

She was pretty, with her blonde hair and brown eyes. Her figure was delightful, but he did not appreciate her attitude most of the time, not to mention the fact that he did not trust her. She started about six months ago, and seemed to be more curious about his cases then in doing her job. Her unhealthy interest in his cases made him even more frustrated with her. He did not care that her secretary skills were excellent, or that he was the envy of the male officers under him. He was pretty sure they made up half the reasons for coming to his office just to see her.

Sitting in the seat in front of his desk, she suggested, "Sometimes it's good to bounce ideas, or have a fresh set of eyes on a case."

"Sherry, you're nice enough, but you are not an officer. I can't discuss cases with you, no matter how hard you push."

"I'm not pushing."

"Oh, really?" He raised an eyebrow. "I caught you in my office going through a file the other day. By the way, this is your final warning. If you pursue trying to get into my files one more time, I *will* fire you. Your job is to be my secretary…not my sounding board; not my confidant; not my conscience; not my second set of eyes or ears. You are *not* allowed in my office when I am not here, and you are *not* allowed to ask me about a case."

"I didn't mean to upset you."

"Yes. You did. I told you all of this months ago, yet you still pursue it. Stop asking. Stay out of my office. I appreciate the coffee, but I did not ask for it."

"My job is also to anticipate your needs."

"Thank you. I appreciate the coffee right now. A cup of coffee once in a while is fine, as long as I'm in here."

"Yes, sir," she said sweetly. Sitting forward in her chair, she asked, "Is there anything I can do to help?"

"Now that is a good question to ask. Thank you, but not at this time. I have to figure this out on my own."

Standing, she excused herself and left, leaving him lost in the pile of files once again. He was determined to find out who Ben Hunt was, and what he and Hope's marriage truly looked like behind closed doors. *Was she afraid? Is that why she works double shifts? Why doesn't she talk about Ben? She normally only talked about her kids when asked about her family, but not him. Was he holding something over her?* It was then he decided to sit down with Hope and talk to her.

Tapping the intercom to Sherry's phone, he asked, "Sherry?"

"Yes, sir?"

"Would you please contact Hope Hunt, and have her come to my office?"

"Yes, sir," she said, and disconnected the line. Getting on her computer, she looked up Hope Hunt's phone number. Noticing there was not a landline, she got up, went to his office, and knocked on the door.

"Enter."

"Sir, the Hunt's don't have a landline. Do you have Hope's cell number?"

"No. Call the restaurant, and put her through to me when she answers."

"No problem," she said, and went back to her desk. Her mind whirling, she dialed the number to the restaurant.

"Willow's Bend Diner."

"Yes, is Hope Hunt available?"

"Just a moment," the person on the other end of the phone said, and then set the phone down.

A minute later, Hope answered, "This is Hope. How can I help you?"

"Hope, this is Sheriff Reynold's secretary, Sherry."

"Yes, ma'am. What can I do for you?"

"He would like you to come by the office at your earliest convenience. There is something he wants to touch base with you about. By the way, what is your cell phone number, so I don't have to call the restaurant to get ahold of you?"

"No problem. I'll be in after the lunch rush. The restaurant will slow down for a few hours at that point."

"Great. And, your cell phone?"

"I'll give it to him directly if he still needs it when we're finished. I don't like to give it out."

"Yes, ma'am," she said, and hung up. She called the Sheriff via the intercom.

"Yes?"

"Sir, she said she'll be in after a few hours. She's waiting for the lunch rush to blow over."

"Thank you. I'll just head on over there in a bit so she doesn't have to venture this way."

"Yes, sir," she said, and hung up. Glancing toward the door, she rested her chin on her hand. Getting close to Hope and Ben Hunt had proven more difficult than anticipated. Even worse was every other police officer in the building let her do whatever she wanted, except the Sheriff...the one she needed to let her do what she wanted. She needed to do her real job.

⬤⬤⬤⬤

SITTING on the stool at the restaurant, Wyatt placed the bag with his files in it next to him.

"Afternoon, Sheriff," Hope said, suddenly appearing on the other side of the counter from him.

"Hello, Hope!" He couldn't help the smile that appeared on his face. "Thank you for giving me some of your time."

She furrowed her brow. "I thought I was supposed to come to your office?"

"I thought doing this here would put you more at ease," he said. "What if you get me my lunch, and then when you're ready, grab a soda and come have a seat."

"Sounds good. What do you want?"

"Honestly?"

"Your food…your choice. Do you need a menu?"

"No. Who is the chef today?"

"It's Miguel."

"Then enchiladas, please? Scott makes a great meatloaf, but Miguel does not. His enchiladas are amazing, though!"

"Is it sad that you know what to order by which chef is on?"

He grinned. "Probably, but it keeps my kitchen clean at home."

"True. Your regular sweet tea?"

"Yes, please."

"Great! I'll be back in a few minutes."

Wyatt knew he should have probably met with her in his office, but he did not want Sherry eavesdropping. At least in the restaurant, he knew Sherry would not be around.

⬧⬧⬧⬧

AFTER ABOUT AN HOUR of running around to finish the lunch rush, Hope finally sat down next to Wyatt with a soda in her hand. Using the straw, she played with the ice. "Okay. You've got me nervous. What's on your mind?" Hope asked.

"Hope, I need to be honest with you. Will you hear me out before you run away, or suddenly have something to do here? Can we talk and not be disturbed?"

"I told Macy to only disturb us if it's an emergency, or if it's something she simply cannot handle. She's a smart cookie and has been here longer than me. I'm pretty sure we'll have a few hours to talk."

"Want to go to a corner booth, out of the way?"

"Sure," she agreed.

They walked through the restaurant. While it was called a diner, the size was more indicative of a restaurant. A diner, to

Hope, seemed more quaint, more intimate. A diner had a bar, and maybe five to ten tables or booths. This restaurant had a bar section, along with about fifty tables. The Willow's Bend Diner was located just off the highway, so they got a lot of highway traffic. Also, anyone in the area who knew about it, considered it East Texas's best-kept secret. There was never a wait, and the food was better than one would get at home…even with Momma cooking. There was always some sort of heavenly scent in the air. It ranged from fresh-baked pies, to fresh rolls, to pot roast, meatloaf, fried chicken, enchiladas, sizzling fajitas, and pretty much anything in between. The chefs made killer twice-baked mashed potatoes, fried okra, fried green tomatoes, and chicken fried steak. Their signature dishes were their fried chicken, mashed potatoes and gravy, rolls, and fresh vegetables (depending on the season). Fresh sweet tea and fresh-squeezed lemonade was made almost every other hour due to the traffic. Hope got used to it after a few weeks, but those first few weeks were rough around her waistline.

They settled into a corner booth, where Wyatt pulled out a stack of folders and set them on the table. "You promise to not leave until you hear me out?"

"I made that promise at the bar, and I keep my promises," Hope agreed.

"All right, then. Here we go." He opened the first file, which was completely empty. He set it on the table in front of her.

Glancing from the file, to Wyatt, Hope shook her head, confused. "I don't understand."

"Hope, you need to tell me what's going on."

"With what?"

"This is the file I have with everything I could find on Ben Hunt. I have pulled every string I have from the FBI, to the police force, to even the military. He doesn't exist."

Hope gulped. Heart racing, she took a deep breath to calm herself before she said, "I still don't understand."

"Where did you meet Ben Hunt?" Wyatt asked. When she sighed, he explained, "Look, I like you. I'm pretty sure that's obvious. However," he held up his hand to stop her from talking when she went to open her mouth, "however, you seem to be married, but I can't find a marriage license. I can't find a driver's license. Heck, I can't even find a birth certificate or social security number for Ben Hunt. I can however, find a birth certificate for Hope Hunt, along with driver's license… and a death certificate," he said, opening another file, showing her the pictures of Holly's mother. "Now, who are you…and who is Ben? Are those your children? Tell me what's going on."

"If I tell you, can I trust you?"

"If you don't, then I'll have social services out within a half-hour, and you'll never see those children again. The two of you will also be arrested for kidnapping."

Hope let out a gasp as the color drained from her face.

"Look," he said, softer, "I don't like to threaten, but I also don't like secrets. I originally started looking into Ben, because I thought maybe he was hurting you, or he was holding the children over your head. When I couldn't find anything on him, I looked into you. None of this makes sense. You both act like nothing is wrong, but there is something very wrong. I haven't called anyone because I want to know the truth. I want to make my own choice here."

Hope sat back in her seat. With tears in her eyes, she dropped her hands into her lap. *Could she trust Sheriff Reynolds? Wyatt had been friendly enough, and had even come to her first. However, if she did not trust him, she may lose everything.*

"Talk to me, Hope," he said, reaching for her hand.

When their hands touched, Hope felt tingles shoot through her body. She looked toward Heaven for answers as she sighed.

"I need to know how to help you…if I can help you."

"If I tell you, do you promise to hear me out until I'm done?"

Hope asked, searching his eyes for a spark of hope there was a way out of this situation.

"Yes. I feel we owe each other the truth in this."

Hope sat up. She kept ahold of his hand, but under the table so no one would see. "I'm going to have to tell you something you may have a difficult time believing, but I pray you'll understand things from our perspective."

"I've pretty much seen it all up to this point in my career."

"I promise you haven't seen it all."

"What's that supposed to mean?"

"This is seriously like some science fiction movie, but I swear, as God is my witness, this is the truth. Give me a Bible, and I will swear it is the truth."

"Hope, I don't think you could lie to me if you tried. I'm kind of like a human lie detector. I know you're hiding something, but I don't know what it is. I also know you're a strong Christian woman. I've watched you here and at church. I know where your heart is in regards to our Lord and Savior."

"Then know what I'm about to tell you took a lot to make this choice, and it is the truth."

"Okay, go ahead."

"The babies are not twins."

"I don't —"

"Don't interrupt or I may lose my nerve."

"Fair enough. Go ahead."

"The babies were actually born two days apart, from different mothers. You see, up in Maine, there is a clinic run by Professor Noah Roth. He's been doing experimental research for almost twenty years up there on mothers and babies."

Wyatt's jaw dropped. "What?"

"He has been doing genetic manipulation experiments on babies for over twenty years." When he went to object again, she held her hand up to stop him this time. "Please?" she asked. When he nodded, she continued, "The mothers either didn't have any family, or the family situation was minimal. Up until a year ago, the experiments failed. However, he somehow found a way to make it work. Now, here's where you need to pay extra attention," she said, and looked to him to make sure he was following along. When he nodded, she continued, "There were four babies at the time we left the clinic who had the gene he was looking to produce. Two of the baby's mothers had already mysteriously died in childbirth. At the time Ben and I made a choice to rescue some of them, there was another mother who suddenly crashed. We had to make a decision…fast. We knew the babies would grow up to be lab rats. Their father was Professor Roth. The clinic used his sperm to fertilize the eggs. With the mothers dead, he would have free reign to do with them what he wanted. At the time, I was holding Holly. She had these big blue eyes, and this curly red hair. I couldn't imagine her being used as a lab rat! Ben and I decided we couldn't take all four. We figured we could get away with at least two of them, and save them, letting them be children."

"I see."

"Ben's real last name is Scott. My real name is Grace Matthews. The facility went into lock-down just as we pulled out. We were able to rescue two, but we know there were at least two more in that place."

"What…um…what is the genetic marker for?"

"In the simplest terms, it allows them to utilize more brain power than the average human. So far, Holly is telekinetic, and Blake is telepathic. Now, could you imagine taking them to the store?"

Wyatt chuckled as he pictured it.

"I mean, seriously! We would have a sudden overabundance of cookies and cereal in the cart, and we wouldn't have put it in there. At least by homeschooling, we can teach them to use their gifts in a way that won't get them noticed. I seriously cannot imagine what would happen if we actually put them in school for kindergarten…can you?"

Wyatt could not help but laugh at the vision in his mind.

"Wyatt, you have to understand. There are two babies right now who are probably being pushed beyond their limits every day, even though they are only a year old. Could you imagine Holly or Blake being put through that?"

"No. Not really."

"I gave you our real names, but please don't run them. They're probably flagged. If you run them, it will trigger the clinic to come down here looking for us."

"Even just a local check?"

"You don't understand how deep the roots Professor Roth has in the systems. He has an entire facility, along with a compound of condos where the mothers stay until delivery. He has more connections than even some of the higher-up politicians. He only needs to pick up a phone to make whatever he wants to happen… happen. He killed three out of the four mothers either during, or right after childbirth. And, I promise you that he will never spend even a minute behind bars for it. You probably triggered someone coming down as it is by researching Hope Hunt. We'll have to look over our shoulders for a while."

"How did he get this much power? How is he able to do this stuff without it being regulated?"

"It's all under wraps. He has the money. He also has connections to bury what's going on. You seriously have no idea!"

"I'm sorry. I don't know what to do here."

"If you run our real names, or make any other sort of search for us, the clinic, or Professor Roth will find out. When they do, I promise you they will bring down the force of black ops government so hard, it would make your head spin!"

Stunned, Wyatt asked, "Are you serious? How am I supposed to check your story?"

"I don't know what to tell you. Outside of them showing you what they can do –"

"Would you?" he asked, cutting her off.

"Can I?"

"I would think so."

"If I do this, will you trust me and not ever search again?"

Sticking his hand out for her to shake, he said, "Deal."

Shaking his hand, she half-wondered if she made a mistake. At this point it was either get arrested and the children go back to Professor Roth…or trust Wyatt.

⬧⬧⬧⬧

HOPE CONTACTED THE MANAGER. She got permission to leave for about two hours, as long as she returned before five for the dinner rush.

Driving out in Wyatt's cruiser made her uncomfortable, but at least she was doing something to hopefully help their situation. As they drove, Hope watched the landscape pass by the window, lost in her own thoughts.

Finally, a few minutes out from her home, Wyatt reached over and gently took her hand into his. When she did not pull away, he tried to comfort her. "I'm not going to hurt you or your family. I really do like you. I don't know how you feel about Ben or me."

When she looked over at him, she explained, "I like you, too. You make me smile. I'm not really married to Ben. We just said that so people wouldn't ask questions."

"So, you're not married?"

"No. We even have our own bedrooms. I work outside the home, because we had a social security number and a birth certificate for Holly's mother."

"So, her real mom's name was Hope Hunt?"

"Yes. Hope had a sister. However, as far as the sister knows, neither her sister, nor the baby made it through delivery."

"That's not good. So, you two escaped with the two babies, and are raising them outside of the clinic."

"Yes. I don't know if he knows where we are or not."

"When did y'all do this?"

"About a year ago. Holly wasn't even a day old."

"Okay. I'll keep an eye out for any shady characters snooping around for you. Here," he said, handing her his cell phone from his belt clip, "put your cell phone number in there, but put it under Grace."

"Anyone who knew my past, would know it was me."

"What's your middle name?"

"Ann."

"Then put it under 'Ann Reynolds.' That way if someone gets ahold of my phone and asks about it, I'll just tell them it's a relative."

"Good idea," she said, and entered it into his phone.

"Now, when we text, don't use names. I'll know it's you. Put my number in your phone too, so you know it's me who is texting."

"Thank you," she said, pulling his cell number off his phone, and entering it into hers.

As they pulled up to the house, Hope saw Ben look out the window with a confused look on his face, while wiping his hands off on a towel.

"Great," Hope said on a sigh.

When they got out, Ben stepped outside, closing the door behind him. "Hi, Sheriff. Hope, what's going on?"

"We need to talk," Hope explained, "inside."

"But –"

"I know. Just go inside," Hope said. "Trust me."

They went inside to a fairly clean home. The babies were

sitting in their highchairs, snacking on cereal. "I'm just preparing dinner," Ben explained.

"I don't mean to mess up your schedule. It's just that we need to talk," Wyatt said.

"Have a seat on the couch. As long as I can see them, I feel better," Ben said, taking the chair which allowed him to see the babies from the living room, while Hope and Wyatt sat on the couch. "Now, what can I do for you?"

"Actually, it's what I can do for you," Wyatt pointed out. "Please hear me out before you get upset at anyone?"

Sitting back in his chair, studying Wyatt, Ben reluctantly nodded.

"Okay," Wyatt started, "back a couple of months ago, I noticed things weren't lining up with y'all. When that happens, my senses start tingling, and my detective skills kick into high gear. So, I started to check you out."

Ben's eyebrows arched in surprise. "Really?"

"Yes. Want to see what I've found?"

"Sure."

Taking the file out of his bag, Wyatt opened it and tossed the empty file onto the floor.

Ben's heart skipped a beat. He gulped. "Um, it's empty."

"Correct. That's because you don't exist. So, I took this information, along with the information I had on Hope Hunt," Wyatt said, pulling out another folder, "and brought it to Hope. Here," Wyatt said, handing the file to a pale Ben, who flipped through it, landing on the death certificate. "You see, she's dead. So, I went ahead and sat down with Hope." Wyatt leaned forward to block Ben's icy stares toward Hope. "Now, before you go gettin' all upset, you said you would let me finish."

"Go ahead," Ben said coolly.

"I threatened to arrest both of you, and send those babies into social services if she didn't tell me what was going on."

Ben's jaw dropped. After a second, he closed it, but did not say a word.

"With that thought in mind, her choices were either jail and never seeing those babies again, or telling me what's going on. For the record, she chose the latter."

"Hope?" Ben said, heartbroken. "How could you?"

"Be quiet and just listen," Hope reprimanded him. "He knows. In order for him to not look into us any further, he only asked to see their gifts."

"That's it?" Ben asked, stunned. "You're not going to arrest us? You're not going to take the babies away from us?"

"From what I can tell, you're helping those little ones. To me, that's more honorable than turning them back over to be lab rats."

"Yes, sir," Ben said, finally able to breathe regularly.

"The only thing I ask is to see it for myself."

"Fair enough. This is the easiest way to get Holly to do hers." Ben got off the couch and went into the kitchen. Pulling out a cookie from the cookie jar, he held up two in the air. "Holly, do you want to get a cookie for you and Blake?"

A grin spread across Holly's face, and then she started bouncing up and down in excitement in her seat. Blake furrowed his brow before he looked back to Ben. Holly took a moment, and then she reached out with her hand toward the cookies. Ben let them go, and they floated across the room to Holly. As they got closer, Blake joined the excitement in bouncing up and down in his high chair.

Once she got ahold of them, she gave one to Blake.

"Well don't that beat all!" Wyatt exclaimed. "Can I try?"

Ben shrugged. "I'm sure she won't mind." When Wyatt stood beside Ben, Ben handed him two cookies.

"Okay, little one, do you want another cookie for you and your brother?"

Holly got excited again, and stretched her hand out. Wyatt

had his hands open with a cookie resting on each one. He watched in awe as the cookies lifted off his hands, and into the air. "Whoa!" he said, amazed. "That's scary, yet cool at the same time." He watched the cookies float all the way over to Holly before she handed Blake another cookie. When she did, Blake grinned.

"Tookies!" Blake said, excited, with a cookie in each hand.

Excited to see Blake happy, Holly joined in, "Tookies! Tookies!"

"Yes, you got your cookies. Go ahead and eat them," Ben encouraged.

"So," Wyatt crossed his arms, leaning on the counter, watching the babies eat their cookies, "what can the little guy do?"

"Go over to him and let him touch your cheek," Ben said.

Wyatt walked over and crouched in front of Blake. "Hi, Blake, I'm Sheriff Wyatt Reynolds. I've seen what your sister can do. What can you do?"

Blake set one of his cookies on the tray, and then reached up toward Wyatt's face. Wyatt leaned forward, so Blake rested his hand on Wyatt's cheek. When he did, Wyatt quickly pulled away. "What was that?" he asked, alarmed.

"Try again," Ben instructed. "Don't pull away this time."

"Are you sure?"

"Just do it," Ben insisted. Ben's body finally relaxed regarding the situation.

When Blake touched Wyatt's cheek, Wyatt flashed to earlier in the diner when he first touched Hope's hand. The tingling feeling electrified through his body, before the feelings he held for Hope washed over any other feeling. He wanted to pull away, at the same time he wanted to stay in the feelings. The feelings changed to a happy feeling as Wyatt saw in his head when Hope and Ben took them to the pumpkin patch. Blake took Wyatt through the feelings of the day in a matter of minutes.

Standing, it took Wyatt a moment to recover. "How'd he do that?"

"That's his gift," Hope explained. "He's telepathic."

"He first showed me feelings that happened when he wasn't in the area, and then when I wasn't in the area. Can these two do anything else?"

"The fact that they're doing it at such a young age, tells me they'll only get stronger," Ben explained. "We're teaching them to control their gifts, so when we do go out in public, they won't use them. The pumpkin patch was a trial run. We may take them to the store soon if we can trust them, but not by ourselves. We have to go together."

"Understandable. Can we talk in the other room so they can't hear?" Wyatt asked.

"It won't matter with Blake," Ben said. "He'll know regardless. There are no secrets in a house with a telepath. We might as well talk in here."

"Well, it's about the two of you," Wyatt said. Hope got off the couch, and went into the kitchen to join Wyatt and Ben. When she was standing next to the guys, Wyatt said, "While I don't mean to be a nosey Nellie, I gotta ask…what is your relationship?"

"We're not married," Hope said. When Ben looked cross at her, she said, "I'm making that clear, because I have an interest in Wyatt and he has one in me."

"How are we supposed to put on a face of being married if you two are meeting on the side?" Ben asked, upset. "What kind of example is that setting for the kids?"

"You and I are not married," Hope said sternly. "There is no true love in our relationship. We are two people raising two babies."

"How is that going to look?"

"I don't care how it looks."

"We can be quiet," Wyatt offered. "That way, as far as the

town is concerned the two of you are together. Here in the house, we will all know the truth."

"Do you know how difficult it is to teach children morals, along with the difference between right and wrong? How can we teach them this if there are relationships they need to keep secret?" Ben asked.

"You want them to think a marriage is just two people living together?" Hope asked.

"I want them to be safe. I want them to know the difference between right and wrong. I want –"

"You want all of that, but you don't understand that by stealing them from the clinic, their lives started off as a lie," Hope challenged. "At least we can show them, potentially, what a real relationship looks like. Our family is not the normal family by any stretch of the imagination."

"Not even close," Ben agreed.

"Then, while we teach them how to control their gifts, we can teach them how the world works as well?"

Ben rubbed his chin. "If we do this, how will it look?"

"I can keep our relationship on the down-low for a while… that is, if you're interested," Wyatt asked Hope, correcting himself halfway through his thought.

"Yes. I'm interested," Hope said. "Maybe we can go a few towns over to hide when we go out?" she suggested.

"I think we would need to go further than a few towns. I'm the County Sheriff. My face is all over social media. You don't want your picture all over social media. What if we go on 'dates'," he said, making quotes with his hands, "at my house. We can watch movies, cook, and do lots of things until you're comfortable with bringing our relationship public. My house is on twenty acres. I don't have any immediate neighbors, so no need to worry about that."

"We can try that, and here at the house as well," Ben offered.

"If the two of you progress, we'll have to talk about how this'll work."

"I appreciate it." Wyatt grinned. "While I know how I feel, I only have an idea of how Hope feels."

"Blake, can you show Wyatt how I feel?" Hope asked Blake. She went over to him and let him touch her cheek. When he did, she had the same feelings when their hands touched in the restaurant. "Yes. That's it. Can you show Wyatt?" she asked, pointing to Wyatt.

Blake reached his hand up toward Wyatt, who went over to Blake. When he did, Blake touched Wyatt's cheek. Hope watched as a broad smile formed across Wyatt's face.

"Exactly," Wyatt said. "I guess we've been having these feelings through the year?"

Hope nodded.

Ben looked over at Hope. He crossed his arms. "You've had feelings for him? For how long?"

"Several months," she admitted.

"Why didn't you talk to me?"

"I tried to talk to you about six months ago, but you brushed it off."

"Was that the whole what are we conversation?" Ben asked.

"Yes. I was trying to figure out where we stood. I was going to explain to you how I felt, but you didn't seem interested," Hope defended herself.

"I'm sorry. I had no idea."

"We never finished the conversation of what we would do if one of us wanted to date."

Ben shrugged. "I figured we would cross that bridge when we got to it."

"Well, we're to it," she said bluntly.

"We'll take it one step at a time. We knew it would only be a matter of time before something like this came up. At least it's with someone who's in a position to help us."

"I intend to do my best to keep your secrets a secret," Wyatt said. "I'm going to shred those files when I get back to the office tonight."

"I would actually feel better if you left them with us. I'll dispose of them," Ben said. "That way no one can get into your shredded files and put them back together."

"Who would get into my shredded trash?"

"Seriously?" Ben asked. "Is that a trick question?" Turning to Hope, Ben asked, "Did you not explain who Professor Roth was?"

"I did," Hope said.

Turning back to Wyatt, Ben asked, "And, you doubted what she said?"

"No. I just didn't think –"

Rubbing the back of his neck, Ben asked, "Have you had any new employees over the last year?"

"Of course. Every police station does."

"How many?"

"Two officers, a secretary, and three dispatchers."

"Do me a favor and check them out as thoroughly as you tried to check us out?" Ben asked. "One of them could be connected to the clinic."

"You think?" Hope asked.

"His roots run extremely deep," Ben reminded her. "I saw those files in records. If you saw them, you would be a lot more paranoid."

"I'll check them out on the down-low," Wyatt promised. "I'll also get back with you via Hope's cell as to the answer."

"No. Nothing electronic. Tell her face-to-face."

"You're serious?" Hope looked at him. "You think it's that bad."

"Hope, he killed three out of the four mothers only a few days after the birth of the children. I have no doubt the fourth was not far behind. Don't put anything past him." Resting his hands on Hope's arms, Ben pointed out, "He could be watching us right now. This isn't what he planned, but he may be using it as part of his experiment. He could be waiting until an appointed time to come get them."

Hope shook her head, distraught. "I don't-I don't know what to say."

Wyatt walked back over to them, and gave Hope a hug when Ben let her go. With his arms wrapped around her, she felt safe. "I won't know who to trust," she mumbled.

"Trust me," Ben said, "and, now Wyatt. Do not trust anyone else. I mean no one!"

ALL THE TIME IN THE WORLD

"In youth we learn, in age we understand." Marie Ebner-Eschenbach

Over the next several days, Wyatt did his best to dig up information on the new hires acquired over the last year. He cleared all the dispatchers, and the new officers. His secretary, and favorite person, is where he ran into a brick wall. Her social security number checked out, as did her birth certificate. There was even some background he was able to locate, but it only went back seven years. His next step would be to contact the references.

"Yes. I understand. She is a phenomenal secretary. I only wanted to verify her employment with you, and check to see how well of a job she did for you folks." Wyatt listened as the person on the other end gushed over her skills for over ten minutes. When he finally got a word in edgewise, he asked, "Why was it again that she left?"

"She decided she needed a fresh start."

"Really? That's exactly what the three other places I called said…almost word-for-word. Thank you for your time," he said, and hung up.

With the paperwork he had spread out on his desk in front of him, Wyatt shook his head. The mole was his secretary. He knew he did not like her. He thought it was only because she was nosey. Now, knowing what he knew about Hope, Ben, and the babies, he was certain she was the one he was looking for.

After a few minutes of looking at the paperwork before him, there was a knock on his door. He quickly shuffled the papers back into the folders, and shoved them into his bag. "Come on in," he said acting like he was studying a case file, instead of the files originally on his desk.

Sherry walked in and sat down in front of him. Crossing her legs, she also crossed her arms in front of her, studying him.

Wyatt huffed. "Can I help you?"

Leaning forward, she uncrossed her arms and rested her elbows on her knees.

Getting impatient, Wyatt snapped, "Sherry, I have a lot of work to do. What do you want?"

"I want to know why you're checking me out?"

"It's my right as an employer to check out whichever employees I want, whenever I want." Interlacing his hands in front of him, he squeezed them in order to keep himself under control. It was a trick he learned during his years on the force.

Returning the icy tone, Sherry explained, "I thought that was done at the time of hiring."

Now to the point of amusement, Wyatt sat back in his seat. He crossed his arms in front of him as a smirk appeared on his face. He was getting to her. "Do you have a problem with me excising my right as an employer?"

Narrowing her eyes, she warned, "You do not want to do this."

"Oh!" Wyatt chuckled. "You're threatening me now?"

"No. I'm only trying to steer you clear of potential trouble."

"I'll tell you what," Wyatt said, pulling out the file on her, "why don't you level with me, and I'll level with you?"

Sitting up straight in her chair, she rested her elbows on the arms of the chair. "What exactly do you mean by that?"

"Let's play a game. I'll tell you something I know, and you tell me something you know in return, and we'll see where that lands us."

"Sounds like a fair game," she agreed.

Noticing she was watching him like a cat watching a mouse, he knew he would need to tread carefully. "Okay, I'll start. Your references are bogus."

"Yes. They are."

"Why?"

"Because I wanted the job," she offered.

"If this is going to work, we need to be honest with each other, so try again. Why are your references bogus?"

Moving her hand to rest her chin on it, she said, "I don't know if I like this game."

"The choice is be honest, or you know where the door is."

Sitting up in surprise, she asked, "What does that mean?"

"Honesty, or you're fired."

"You can't do that."

Wyatt burst out in laughter. "Why not? You lied about your references. That's cause for termination."

Sherry narrowed her eyes. "Am I not proficient at my job?"

"Yes, but you still lied. Now, back to my original question of 'Why did you lie about your references?' If you choose not to answer this one more time, this conversation is finished…and, so are you."

A brief moment of surprise crossed her face, before she narrowed her eyes again, and said, "I don't do well with threats."

"I'm sure," he responded but did not say another word. He learned a long time ago, he who speaks first loses.

Clearing her throat, she sat up and said, "Okay, I'll play. My references are bogus, because of my real reason for being here."

"Which is?"

"If I'm honest with you, I would expect to be able to stay."

"Not necessarily."

Sherry clicked her tongue before she finally answered, "I work for a detective."

"For what purpose?"

"To locate two renegade employees."

"Really? Who?"

"I can't answer that."

"What company do you work for?"

"Marcos D'Angelo Detective Agency."

"What company are the people from?"

"Can't answer that."

"Okay. I can respect that," Wyatt said. Thinking it may behoove him to keep her close so as to know who the players are, he said, "Your turn."

"Who really is Hope Hunt?"

"That's not her name?"

"I thought we were being honest."

"I am. According to her social security number and birth certificate, that's who she is." Wyatt did not consider that a lie. The name and numbers matched, he only neglected to mention the death certificate.

"What about her husband, Ben Hunt?"

"Oh no." Wyatt shook his head. "My turn."

"Fair enough. Go ahead."

Leaning forward, he asked, "If I keep you on, do you promise to stop snooping around Hope and her husband?"

"That goes against my job."

"I'm giving you an opportunity for a better job. A safer job. If you stay here, you get regular hours along with benefits."

"That's tempting," she admitted.

"Do you like the area?"

"I do."

"Do you like your job?"

"Which one?"

"Either."

"I like the variety in the detective agency, but not the hours. I like the hours here, and the benefits are definitely a perk."

"It's also safer. Look, I'm going to be honest with you. You're not only a good secretary, but you're also super observant and a challenge – in a good way – to work with. Those are good qualities to have in a police station. I would sincerely like to ask you to stay on, but I need to trust you. I cannot trust you if you're still working for Marcos what's-his-face."

"D'Angelo, and you're serious?"

"Very."

"Well, to be honest, I have considered it. You're a good boss, and as you said, it's safer."

"Then?" he asked again.

"Can I have some time to think about it?"

"You can have until the end of the day. If you choose to stay here, you have to sign another non-disclosure statement, this time with your real name."

"Real name?"

"Yes, Alexandra Murphy."

She sighed. "You can call me Alex."

"Does that mean you'll stay?"

"Obviously you truly know who I am, so I'm busted. You're good," she said with a reluctant smile. "This is the first time anyone's actually found my real identity."

"Job's yours if you want it, Alex. Of course, you'll have to let everyone know your real name, but that'll blow over pretty quickly. Being a small town, you'll probably have a few weeks of people teasing you. Some may even go a little longer if they think they're getting to you. Otherwise, I'll stop them in their tracks if it'll help."

"It would."

"So, you'll stay?"

"Fine," she relented. "I'll stay."

"Wonderful! No need to go through orientation again. I'll have you fill out the hiring paperwork again. I'll take it down to HR myself so you don't have to deal with it."

"Can I ask another question?"

"Of course."

"Have you found out anything regarding Hope or Ben that I can take back to my current employer to satisfy him?"

Coming around the front of the desk, he thought for a moment before he said, "Can I trust you now?"

"Yes. I'm here."

"Okay. Yes, I did. They aren't really married. They're common-law married, so that's why there's no marriage license. That's what I wanted to talk to her about."

"I see. So, that's it?"

"Yeah. They're just really protective of their little ones." He smiled as he explained. "When she pointed out the idea of two toddlers running around a grocery store, I completely understood her perspective of keeping them at home. That's why they bought ten acres."

"Hmm. Okay. I really thought they were who we're looking for."

"Not sure who you're looking for, but that couple is as innocent as they come. They're just looking to raise their family in a friendly town."

She sighed. "Okay. I'll let him know to keep looking. I'm going to stay, though."

"Will you do me a favor and keep a look out for anyone who seems strange to you in town? Any new people? With the drug situation calming down, they may be looking to find a route through this area again."

"Sure."

"Great! I'll get your paperwork. I'll need your real identity for the paperwork." When she stood, he shook her hand and said, "Welcome aboard, Alex."

"Thank you."

"New life, new identity, new start. I think you'll like it here."

"I know I will," she said with a smile.

When she left for her office just outside of his, he knew he would have to keep an eye on her. His choices were to keep her there knowing who she worked for, or potentially have someone there he did not know. He prayed the false information he gave her was enough to throw whoever was searching for Hope and Ben off the scent for now. Keeping in mind they were still being searched for, he knew it would only be a matter of time before they were discovered.

⊄⊅⊄⊅⊄⊅

OVER THE NEXT FEW YEARS, Hope, Ben, and Wyatt relaxed in their new world. Wyatt and Hope would go to church, playing the best friends routine, and then have dinner with Ben and the kids afterward. Then as a group, they would go out together to do something fun. Having three adults helping to cover any accidents Holly may trigger helped immensely. After their afternoon adventure Ben would take the kids home, while Hope and Wyatt would head to Wyatt's house for their date night.

In the meantime, Hope and Wyatt's relationship grew stronger behind closed doors. They were a perfect match! They agreed on just about everything, especially with keeping the Lord in the center of their relationship. When they got together at Wyatt's house, the first thing they did was to do devotions, reminding them God was there with them, and they did not want to cross any physical lines in their relationship. They agreed when they first started dating to keep their relationship pure until marriage during their courtship. When he dropped her off for the night, they would kiss goodnight before she got out. Otherwise, they would hold hands and cuddle for the physical portion of their relationship. It was not easy, but Hope and Wyatt were both strong people. When one was weak, the other would be strong enough to sidetrack the other person.

Also, through the years, Alex became a valuable member of not only the police department, but also of the community. She went through a few rough weeks while making the transition from 'Sherry Waters' to 'Alex Murphy,' but to her it was worth it. No more looking over her shoulder. No more long hours. She fit into the town very well. Willow Bend took a little time to trust her, but once they understood her story, the trust process started.

◁▷◁▷

HOPE CLEANED the counter during her shift at Willow's Bend diner, when a man came and sat down. "Hello, Grace."

Hope froze. Heart racing, she turned to see who called her by her real name. She gasped when she saw her controlling ex-boyfriend sitting there looking at her.

She gulped. "Asher, what are you doing here?"

"Well, I was sitting at the newspaper looking for a community story, when I saw the cutest little kids running through a pumpkin patch on a website for a hay maze. Did you know they posted those pictures on their site? Well," he sat back in his seat crossing his arms over his chest, "while I sat there, I looked at the picture a little closer, and I saw you! Imagine my surprise. Here, I thought you were in Maine all this time. I had no idea you were here in my backyard. I wonder if your brother knows you're here?"

"You wouldn't," she challenged.

"Oh! I would!"

"No, you won't," Wyatt said, sitting next to him in his Sheriff's uniform.

Asher glanced from Wyatt's face, to his gun, and back again. "Who are you?"

"I'm Grace's boyfriend. If you don't want me to look deeper into you, I highly suggest you walk yourself out of this restaurant and forget you ever saw that picture."

"What if I don't?"

Wyatt leaned closer to him, as he asked, "Are you saying you're squeaky clean? Are you saying if I dig deep enough, I won't find a single thing? I have resources you never knew existed."

"Are you threatening me?"

"Nope," Wyatt said, sitting back in his seat. "I'm protecting what's mine."

Hope stood there in complete shock, unsure of what to do.

"She was mine," Asher argued.

"Was is the operative word there. She's mine now. If you have anything you want to say to her, you'll have to come through me. Now, there are many families in this fine establishment. Before we make a scene, I suggest you get amnesia as to the reason for your little visit, and do not return. I promise you that I will know the second you step back into my territory. That territory includes this entire county."

"Who are you?"

"The County Sheriff. I'm surprised you don't know my face. With as much research as you seem to have done, I would think my face would have popped up at some point."

"Really? Oh! Sheriff Wyatt Reynolds? You're Sheriff Wyatt Reynolds! We love getting stories about you and what you're doing out here!"

Wyatt leaned forward again, his face stern. "So, you're familiar with the fact that I run a tight ship?"

"Yes."

"Then you'll understand when I tell you that I will know if you step into this county again."

Asher put his hands up in surrender. "Yeah. Oh yeah. No problem."

"You need to set your sights on another lady. This one's taken. Have I made myself clear?"

"Yes," Asher said, getting off his seat.

"And, Asher?" Wyatt said Asher's name with a snide tone.

Asher turned back toward Wyatt. "What?"

"I mean it. Forget why you ever came out here. I will have my eye on you. Mark my words."

"I believe you."

"Good. Glad we have an understanding. Grace," Wyatt said quietly, not wanting those in the restaurant to know her real name, but also not wanting to tip her hand as to her alias, "please give Asher my meal, so he won't have to stop anywhere on the way home."

"Yes, sir. I'll be back in a moment," she said, and disappeared into the kitchen.

When the doors closed, Wyatt got out of his chair. He leaned with one elbow on the counter near where Asher stood. "Asher, I'm paying for your meal. That way you feel you didn't come out here for nothing. I do not want to see you here ever again. And do not tell her brother."

"Here," Hope said, bringing out his meal in a bag. She handed it to Asher.

"Thank you," Asher said, accepting the bag.

"Asher?" Wyatt said, as Asher went to leave. When Asher turned back toward Wyatt, he mentioned, "You may want to reconsider ever coming to any East Texas town. I'll let my fellow compatriots know all about you."

"Understood," Asher said, and left.

Only when the door closed did Hope finally breathe. She grabbed the chair nearest to her, hoping to not pass out.

"Are you okay?" Wyatt asked, not moving from his position. Sticking up for her is different than the hug he wanted to give her. He knew if he did, their secret would get out.

"I'm…I'll be okay," she said. "Thank you."

"No problem." Leaning closer, he quietly added, "I wish I could take you into my arms right now, but there are too many witnesses."

"I know. Same for me."

"You know this brings up an issue."

"What issue?" Hope asked.

"Actually multiple. One would be to talk to Schneider and get him to take the photos off his site of y'all."

"True," Hope agreed.

"Secondly, we got too comfortable. We need to have a talk with Ben and the kids about staying on alert. I'll talk to the other County Sheriff's about Asher…what's his last name?"

"Asher Billings."

"Well, Mr. Asher Billings is not going to be welcome in East Texas again if I have anything to say about it."

"Thank you. And I'll make you another meal…on me," Hope said. "It's the least I can do."

"I insist on paying for at least one of the meals."

"Nope." Hope shook her head. "Your money is no good here."

"Okay. But I'll only let you do that for tonight."

Looking at her watch, she said, "I'm off in about thirty minutes. Let me get the chef working on our dinners, and we'll take it all back with us. I think you're right. We need to stay more on our toes. We did get too comfortable."

⟐⟐⟐⟐

75

THAT NIGHT, the tiny group had a serious discussion on safety. After Hope and Wyatt explained what happened at the diner, they set a few precautions in place. No one is to be alone around town. Ben also set up a few closed-circuit cameras around the property, along with motion detectors that rang into the house. Finally, they taught the children about the safety word. If someone told the two little ones any of the adults sent them to get them, they were to ask for the code word. If the adult could not tell them the correct code, they were to scream and run. Holly had permission at that point to use her gift to defend herself and Blake.

◀◧◀◧

A FEW DAYS LATER, Ben, Wyatt, Hope, Alex, and the kids had a cookout on Ben's day off. That was his activity of choice.

"So glad y'all invited me," Alex said, bringing in a pasta salad to add to their meal. Holding up another bag she announced, "I also brought marshmallows."

"Great!" Ben grinned. "We can use them on the fire when it cools a bit. I'm so glad you came."

"I've heard about these great cookouts through the years. So glad to finally be a part of one."

"Well, if your dish is any good, you may just be invited to more," Ben said, taking the salad from her, putting it in the refrigerator.

After dinner, they relaxed around the fire. The kids roasted marshmallows.

Eight-year-old Holly caught hers on fire. "Pretty!" she remarked. "Look at all the colors."

Hope blew her marshmallow out. "Now, the key is to take off the burnt part. Here," Hope said, sliding the burnt portion off Holly's marshmallow. "Now have at it."

Holly pulled the gooey mess off the stick. "Mmmm!" she gushed. "This is great!"

"Oh! You're not done," Alex said, pulling out a box of gram crackers and a chocolate bar. "Watch this." Alex lit her marshmallow on fire. She blew it out, and then pulled off the outer coating. Afterward, she scraped the marshmallow onto half a graham cracker, covered it with a piece of chocolate, and then topped it with the other half of the graham cracker. When she took a bite, she moaned in pleasure.

"Can I try it?" Holly asked.

"Mom?" Alex asked permission from Hope. When Hope nodded, Alex nodded.

Holly jumped up and ran over and took a bite. "Oh my!" Holly said, wide-eyed, as she wiped a portion of marshmallow from her chin. "That's good!"

"That is something you can make as well."

"What if they split one?" Hope suggested.

"I think making mini ones would be appropriate," Alex agreed.

Alex made one for Blake and one for Holly. Then she handed one to each of the kids.

"I think you have a friend for life," Ben said with a smile. "Sugar is definitely the way to their hearts."

"Their smiles are the reward for me," Alex said, heart soaking in the love and sweetness of the moment. This was new to her, and she liked it. She wanted more. To her, she knew this was what a real family felt like. This was not how she was raised. She hoped to be included in more nights like this to learn more about love and family.

⟨⊕⟨⊕⟩⊕⟩

"ALEX," Wyatt called from his office the following Monday.

"Yes?" She poked her head into his office.

"I need you to put your detective skills to work for me."

"Sure!" Alex said, happy to be of value. "What do you need?"

"I need you to dig into an Asher Billings. He doesn't make me comfortable."

"Who is he?"

"He was one of Hope's ex-boyfriends. He came by the restaurant on Friday. You should have seen her face," he said, remembering. Alex came in and sat in the chair across from him. "She was terrified of him. Her face was pale and her hands were shaking. He was cocky until I set him straight."

Alex snickered. "I'll bet you did!"

"Will you look into him and figure out if he's really going to stay away."

"I'll do it off the books. That way it's not connected to you at all."

"That would be appreciated. Thank you."

"My pleasure," she said, and left the office.

Sitting at her desk, she opened her computer and searched *Asher Billings*. It turns out he was a journalist in the Dallas area. His column was on community events.

"Hmm," Alex thought aloud. The more she dug, the more she decided she not only did not like Mr. Asher Billings, but she also needed to make sure he never came back.

⬧⬧⬧⬧

ALEX WALKED INTO THE BAR. She did her homework on Asher Billings. She knew what he liked and what he did not like. She found out everything she could about him before venturing to Dallas to handle the situation. She could not have Ben, Hope, and the kids running. At this point, she knew they needed to stay right where they were. She liked Ben. She knew Wyatt liked Hope. She also knew it was the best place for all of them. When this Asher Billings came into the picture, it put all of them on edge. She needed them to relax around her.

Asher walked up to the bar after work and ordered a drink.

"Make that two," Alex said, holding two fingers up. "My treat."

"Why? To what do I owe the pleasure?" Asher asked.

Alex shrugged. "You look like a man who's had a rough week."

"I have," he said hesitantly.

"Would you like to have a seat and talk to me about it?" Alex offered, as the bartender set the drinks in front of them.

"You're here by yourself?" Asher asked.

Alex toyed with the ice in her drink with a straw. "Yep. I didn't have the best week either."

Asher sat next to her. "You tell me yours, and I'll tell you mine."

"Fair enough," Alex agreed. She made up an elaborate story about a horrific week, while continuing to order him drinks, as she nursed the first drink.

Within a few hours, she had Asher eating out of her hand. "Well, I hate to do this, because this has been refreshing after this week, but I have to go."

Asher grabbed her arm to stop her. "What about a nightcap?"

Alex debated it in her head for a moment, before she finally nodded. "I'm parked around the corner."

"Okay then!" Asher grinned. He could not believe his luck after his rough week.

He followed her from the bar. As they went out of sight around the corner, Alex slammed her arm into his neck. He hit the wall with such force, he saw stars. "Wh-what's going on?" he asked, alarmed.

"You are ruining things," Alex hissed. "I cannot have that."

"Wh-what do you mean?" Asher stammered. "I-I haven't done anything. I only met you tonight!"

"You may have only met me tonight, but I've been watching you all week," Alex said, pulling a knife from its sheath on the inside of her pants suit. Placing it on his neck, she growled, "You're messing things up with a family I hold dear. I don't take kindly to that. Hurt them once, shame on you. Hurt them twice, shame on me. I will not let you have another shot at them."

"What are you talking about?"

"You're going to have an accident," Alex said. His eyes widened as Alex continued, "You see, the bartender knows exactly how many drinks you had. After we left, you walked home, only to get mugged and robbed."

"You wouldn't dare!" Asher said. "Do you know who I am?"

"Ha!" Alex chuckled. "You're nothing but a spit in time. You're abusive to your girlfriends. I checked you out. Seems you've had a few restraining orders placed against you. That tells me it's a pattern. I'm going to do the world a favor tonight."

"This isn't right!" Asher objected.

"Neither is what you do to women. You have been warned not to come back to East Texas. I'm not giving you another shot at her," she said, and plunged the knife into his neck.

He dropped to the ground holding his neck. As blood poured over his hands to his neck, Alex pulled his wallet from his back pocket. Flipping through it, she found the money and pocketed it before tossing it onto his lap. Tapping his cheek as he looked up at her, she said, "Pleasant dreams. Maybe in the next life you'll be kinder to women."

He was gone by the time she reached her car. She was relieved to know she kept her family safe. *Family*. That's when she realized what she truly thought about Wyatt, Ben, Hope, and the kids...they were family. This was something she would protect with her life.

NO TIME TO LOSE

"Yesterday is gone. Tomorrow has not yet come. We have only today. Let us begin." Mother Teresa

Over the years, Wyatt, Hope, and Ben stayed on high alert. With no new people snooping around, they finally decided they were safe.

Holly and Blake grew into extremely attractive teenagers. Through the years there were struggles and mistakes out in public, but Ben and Hope were able to cover for them. Holly's early teen years were a nightmare! Even though she was home-schooled, she wanted to go to church and to town functions to meet other people. She was only allowed to go to things like the fair or Friday night football games if Blake was with her, or her parents accompanied her. This caused massive tension in the home. They knew if it got out what she or Blake could do, it would prove disastrous!

Holly, strong-willed and probably the more dangerous of the pair, grew more powerful over the years. When she wanted to, she and Ben would go out to the woods around their home to practice her strength and abilities. He did not want to push her, but he wanted her to know what she could do. He wanted her to be able to control herself, so she would not accidentally hurt someone.

A few days after their sixteenth birthday, Holly went to Ben and asked, "Can we go practice?"

"We can right after I get dinner going in the crockpot."

"Thanks," she said, sitting on the stool at the breakfast bar in the kitchen. "Dad, what's going on with Mom and Uncle Wyatt?"

"Why?" Ben asked, his heart picking up pace.

"Well, we know they're in love. We also know you and Mom aren't really married. When are they going to get married?"

"What do you mean?"

"We want her to be happy. We see her heart break when he has to leave her here on Sunday nights. Haven't they been patient long enough?"

Blake came around the corner, leaning on the doorway. He had grown to be both physically and mentally strong. His dark-brown hair was longer. He kept it kind of shaggy. He brushed his hair out of his brown eyes before he crossed his arms. His physique fit the standard of farm-raised East Texas bred boys his age. When they went out as a family, the girls in the area his age would grin, giggle, and swoon. He could feel their feelings. Learning a long time ago how to project feelings, he would project a calm feeling toward them, allowing him not to blush too badly. Whenever he blushed, his sister would give him a lot of grief.

Holly, to her credit, was gorgeous as well. She had slightly curly, strawberry-blond hair that reached to her mid-back in layers. Her baby-blue eyes stood out on her fair skin. Her athletic figure and strong features only attracted the boys, garnering nasty looks from other girls. She was a force to be reckoned with, but that did not deter the boys in town. They followed her, and tried to hit on her despite her quips to get them to stop. Blake could usually calm the situation if it got too intense.

Blake asked, "Yeah, when are you going to let them get married?"

"When am I going to…what?" Ben asked, taken aback. "Where's this coming from? What makes you think I'm the reason they aren't married?"

"Because I feel that from Mom," Blake explained. "She doesn't want to hurt you. She also doesn't want to cause issues for you, since you don't have a social security number. You both still have another five years to pay on the property, and she doesn't want to leave you short. They can live in Wyatt's house, but that will leave you in the cold. There's also a question as to what will happen with us?"

"You been reading her mind again?" Ben raised an eyebrow. "I know you have to practice, but you're supposed to ask first."

"Her mind swirls at night…especially on Sunday night," Blake explained. "It's too overwhelming to block it out."

"Why don't you ease her mind? Tell her as long as the house is taken care of for you, that you'll be fine. We'll stay here until we graduate, but she can see us whenever she wants to," Holly suggested. "When we graduate, you can start as a handyman, getting paid under the table so you won't attract the attention of the government. The house will be paid for, so you'll only have to be concerned with taxes, utilities, groceries…that sort of thing."

"The fact that you're both coming up with this stuff is disturbing," Ben said nervously, as he cut the vegetables. "You should be relaxing and enjoying your teen years, not trying to figure out your parent's love lives or livelihood scenarios."

"Speaking of," Blake started, "while you are both our parent in heart, we know we're not by birth. Care to share the real story?"

Ben topped the crockpot before slowly turning toward the pair. Leaning against the counter, he crossed his arms. "We've told you all along you're ours in our hearts. We love you as if you were ours by birth."

"That would require the pair of you to be in love," Blake said knowingly.

"Did you snoop?" Ben accused.

"Yes, but couldn't get details," Blake admitted. "That's why we're asking."

"Fine," Ben said in a sigh. Letting out a slow breath of air before he spoke, he arranged his thoughts. "You were both born in a clinic in Maine. The doctor who runs the facility is Professor Noah Roth. He's not a good man."

"What happened to our real parents?" Holly asked, excited to finally be getting answers, yet nervous at the same time.

"Professor Roth used his own sperm to fertilize the eggs implanted in the mothers. Once an egg was fertilized, there were experiments done on them prior to implantation."

"What kind of experiments?" Holly pressed.

"Genetic manipulation," Ben said to their horror. "Anyway, these experiments went on for over twenty years. Babies were born deformed, still-born, or only lived a few days…that is if they were carried to term." Seeing that the two were not phased, Ben asked, "Did you know this?"

"Parts of it," Blake acknowledged. "But please continue to fill in the details.

"Okay," Ben agreed. "Finally, about sixteen years ago, he was successful in manipulating the correct gene to produce the effect he was looking for."

"Us," Blake said in understanding.

"Yes. There were four of you at the time your mom and I were nurses in the newborn ward. Blake, you were born two days before Holly. Holly, your mother died during childbirth."

When he said that, Holly's jaw dropped. "Blake, yours died the day after your birth."

Blake looked at him, momentarily wide-eyed. However, he was distracted when the kitchen table and chairs slightly lifted off the ground. Blake walked over to his sister and took her hand into his to calm her down.

"Sorry," Holly said, realizing what she did, and gently set the table and chairs back down on the floor undamaged.

"There was a third mother who coded while we were there," Ben continued. "We knew with the mothers gone, and him being the father, Professor Roth would have free range to do what he wanted with the children. We didn't want you to grow up in a lab being pushed beyond what you should be doing, and probably tortured or abused. Unfortunately, we could only take two of the four."

"Oh!" Holly said, wide-eyed. "So, there are two more of us out there?"

"At least. If he could figure out which DNA strand achieved the results he was looking for, there may very well be more than that out there. There were also still several mothers from your test group who needed to deliver. We're not one-hundred-percent sure how many of you there are right now."

Holly gulped. "I see."

"So," Blake spoke up, "your position in the family was to care for us, as well as homeschool us in order to stop us from potentially exposing ourselves?"

"Yes. Also, I can't use my social security number, or I'll be found. It's not that I don't have one. It's that I can't use it. If they find me, they'll arrest me…or more likely I'll die a mysterious death like those mothers."

"Then, how is Mom working?" Holly asked.

"She's using your real birth mother's information," he said to Holly. "Your real mother's name was Hope Hunt. Your real name is Holly." Turning to Blake, he added, "Blake, your real first name is Blake. Your mother's real name was Brenna Charles. Chances are, both of your last names would have probably been changed to Roth, after Professor Roth."

"So, what's Mom's real name?" Holly asked.

"Her real name is Grace Matthews. She can't use it for the same reason I can't use my real last name," Ben explained. "My real last name is Scott. I know this seems complicated, but –"

"No," Blake shook his head, "it makes perfect sense. Does Wyatt know all of this?"

"Yes."

"How long has he known?" Holly asked.

"Since you two were about a year old."

"How long have they been dating?" Holly pressed. They were getting answers, so she wanted to get as much information as possible.

"Since you were about a year old. He found out the same time they chose to start dating."

"They've been dating for fifteen years?" Blake asked. "Seriously?"

"Well, I'm sure they want to go out with their relationship, but she has the concerns you've already explained," Ben said.

"Okay," Holly said, finally getting a full picture, "they've waited long enough. We need to find out from Wyatt if he wants to marry Mom. If so, I say we let them do it. We'll sort out the rest later. That way you're free you to date as well."

"Me?" Ben asked

"Yes, you. Alex?" Blake raised an eyebrow. Ben nodded. "You two have sacrificed everything for us. Let us give you the same gift. In the meantime, little sister and I will be especially careful…won't we?" he asked, putting his arm over her shoulder to keep her calm.

Holly nodded. "Yes. I agree."

"Well, your mom'll be home in a few hours. Being Thursday, she doesn't have to close," Ben said, looking at his watch. "Why don't we talk to her about it when she gets home. I'll text her and have her bring Wyatt with her."

Holly grinned. "Perfect!"

"In the meantime, let's head outside to practice," Ben suggested.

As the trio went outside, Ben's mind raced. *Would he and Alex be free to date when Wyatt and Hope came out about their relationship? Would Alex want to date him? He knew she was interested, and he was definitely interested in her. They had become great friends over the years. With a basis of a strong friendship. he knew they would make a great couple.*

When they reached the tree line, they took a good look around. Blake closed his eyes to see if he could feel anyone near them. Since he could not, they went deeper into the woods.

Over time, they discovered the power behind Blake. He could sense people in the area. He could even tell what they were thinking. He had to be careful when he used the searching skill, or he would get overwhelmed. His other gift was empathic. He could feel not only what others were feeling, but could also project feelings if he needed to in certain situations. The most useful skill he acquired over the years, was reading minds. This one took him a while to fine-tune. He was to the point where he could read a single person's mind in a crowd if he concentrated. He often practiced when they were in the store or on a family outing.

As for Holly, her skill grew in strength and intensity. Unfortunately, if she was extremely angry, she could almost create tornado-like effects. That is one of the main reasons why Blake rarely left her side when they were out in public. The other reason was the males in town had an unhealthy interest in her, just as the girls had an unhealthy interest in Blake.

When they would practice in the woods, Ben taught Holly to calm herself. She would often want to push herself beyond her limits just to see what she could do. Today's test would be one she was working up to for several months.

"Are you ready?" Ben asked, gesturing toward a medium-sized red oak tree.

"I think so. We're clear, right Blake?" she asked.

Taking a moment to close his eyes and concentrate on the area around them, he finally nodded. "Go ahead."

Closing her eyes, she imagined the root ball of the tree under the earth. Then, she opened her eyes, concentrating on the tree with her hands extended. Looking as if she were lifting something, she raised her hands. At the same time, the ground around the tree, and the tree itself, shook. Slowly, Ben and Blake watched as the tree lifted from the ground. Suspended in the air, the dirt continued to fall from the six-foot diameter root ball.

"Very good. Now, gently put it back, making sure to replace the dirt around it so it will continue to grow," Ben calmly instructed.

Feeling the weight of suspending the tree in the air, her face turned red from the strain.

"Slowly," Ben coaxed. "Come on, you can do it."

"I'm…trying!" Holly grunted.

Slowly lowering the tree, she then gently placed it in the ground. Once it was solid in the ground, she dropped to her hands and knees, breathing heavily.

Resting his hand on her back to let her know he was there, Ben said, "Excellent job, Holly! You did it! That was definitely not easy. When you recover, fix the dirt so no one knows what happened out here."

Holly nodded. She huffed and puffed as if she just finished a marathon.

Blake leaned against a tree near them in order to give her space. As he did, he sent a calming feeling toward her to relax her.

Taking a few minutes to recover, Holly then stood. She

walked over to the area where the tree was set down. Using her hands as if she were making a mess with paints while she stood up straight, she adjusted the dirt until it looked as if nothing happened. Some of the dirt was damp, so it was darker in a few areas. She understood within several hours, it would look as it did when they arrived.

"You did an amazing job!" Ben said proudly, giving her a hug. "Well done!" Turning toward Blake, he added, "And thank you for calming her. I know when you do that."

Blake nodded in acknowledgment. Then he asked Holly, "You okay? That took a lot out of you."

"It did," she admitted. "But," she grinned, "I did it!"

Giving her a high-five and then a hug, Blake congratulated her, "Well done, little sis!"

Rolling her eyes, she said, "Great! Now that you know you're older than me, you're going to hold it over my head. Aren't you?"

"Always. I'll always look out for you, too."

She hugged him again. "I don't mind."

"You want another challenge, or are you done for the day?" Ben asked.

Looking at him, she debated in her mind for a few moments. "Is it still clear?" she asked.

"Yes," Blake said. "There's no one anywhere near us."

"What are you thinking?" Holly asked Ben.

"Well, we had a rough storm last night, so there are a lot of loose branches and debris around here. You've tested your strength. What if you test your flexibility? Pick up as much as you can and organize it into piles," Ben suggested.

"That would be a challenge," Holly agreed. "Yeah, I'll do it."

"Blake, stand behind her. She may need you to organize the chaos."

"Got it," Blake said, standing behind her.

Holly scanned the area to get an idea of the amount of debris.

She took a couple deep breaths. Slowly letting her air out, she stretched her hands out toward the woods.

Tree branches of all sizes, along with uprooted underbrush, suddenly lifted, hoovering around five feet off the ground. Getting stuck in one section where three trees collapsed on each other, she held up what she had, and lowered that section. Then, she floated everything, collecting it into a simple pile just outside the tree line.

Turning back toward the tangled section, she used her fingers as if she were manually manipulating the tree branches in order to untangle them from each other. When she freed one tree, she floated it near the tree line and set it down. Then, she turned back to the two still tangled trees, and worked on them. Finally, she untangled the pair and floated the two trees at the same time, toward the first one. She gently set them down so they would not tangle again.

Sweat dripping from her face, she rested her hands on her knees, trying to catch her breath. She finally stood with her hands on her hips. "Okay, that was fun but a definite challenge."

"You both have grown so strong, and I'm proud of the way you are and who you are. I don't regret any choices we've made over the years," Ben said. "You are amazing young people."

"We had great influences," Holly said. "I know we haven't been the easiest."

"Raising two babies the same age is a challenge, but worth it."

"Thank you," Holly said, giving him a hug.

"It was honestly my pleasure." Taking a step back, he said, "So far, we've been lucky. I'm pretty sure it has a lot to do with Wyatt keeping an eye out."

"Has Mom texted back yet?" Holly asked.

"Yes. She's bringing Wyatt with her when she gets off work at six tonight. Since she opened this morning, she gets off early today. Sam's closing."

"Great!" Blake smiled. "We can sit down and talk over dinner."

"Just don't ambush them. You two," Ben said, pointing at them, "have probably been talking about this for a while. The rest of us are just now getting into the conversation."

"True," Blake acknowledged. "We'll be kind."

"Also, no projecting or mind-reading," Ben warned. "We want to have an honest conversation with honest statements and feelings."

"Yes, sir," they said in unison.

"Okay, let's head back inside," Ben said, resting his arms over the shoulders of the teens while they walked toward the house.

⽔⽔⽔⽔

LATER THAT NIGHT AT DINNER, after everyone sat down and prayer was said, Holly was the first to speak up, "We had a long talk with Dad today about something, and we wanted to talk with you two about it as well."

"Really?" Hope said, feeling her pulse pick up. "What's it pertaining to?"

"Our pasts and your future," Blake explained.

"In talking with all of us tonight, I've laid down some ground rules," Ben clarified. "They're not allowed to use their gifts."

"This must be big," Wyatt said, looking at the three of them.

"I have to tell you it makes me nervous," Hope admitted. "If that's a requirement, then it's huge."

"It's complicated," Blake conceded.

"Okay." Hope let out a slow breath of air. "Go ahead."

"Well," Blake started, "first, I need to start with a confession."

Hope smiled. "Uh-oh."

"Yeah." Blake's face flushed in embarrassment. "You see,

with my gifts, I need to practice in a sneaky way. I don't mean to be rude. It's if I don't use it, I'm afraid I'll lose it. Holly can practice by rearranging the room. If I practice, I end up violating someone's privacy. In this case…yours," he explained to Hope.

"Oh really? And, what did you learn?" Hope asked.

"A lot, actually. Every Sunday night, you come home devastated that you have to leave Wyatt," Blake said. "That's heartbreaking."

"It's what we have to do."

"We don't want you to do that anymore. If the two of you want to get married, we want you to do so."

Hope's jaw dropped, as her face flushed.

"I don't mean to put anyone on the spot. I just –"

"We," Holly corrected, cutting Blake off.

"Right. We just want you to be happy. You see, Dad explained everything that happened surrounding our births, and everything after."

"Everything?" Hope squeaked out.

"Everything. We know," Holly said, reaching across the table, taking her mom's hand into hers. "We also know the sacrifices you both have made to give us this life. We want you to be happy as well."

"So, we came up with a solution…if you want," Blake offered.

"What's that?" Wyatt asked.

"Wyatt!" Hope said, panic taking over her every thought.

"Can I calm her, so she can focus?" Blake asked Ben. When Ben nodded, Blake sent calm feelings toward Hope. He watched as her body relaxed. "There," he said, satisfied. "Now that you're calm, here's our solution."

"If the two of you want to get married, please do so," Holly said, letting Hope's hand go. "We'll stay here with Dad, but you can have us whenever you want."

"We can do holidays here if you want, so it'll make life easier," Ben suggested. "We'll just keep your room as it is, so you two have a place to stay here."

"I appreciate that," Wyatt said, "but how are you going to keep ahold of the house?"

"That's part of the solution," Blake stepped back into the conversation. "There are only five years of payments left on the house. So, Mom, if you keep making the payments until we graduate, Dad will keep up the house and homeschooling us. Once we graduate, he'll start an under-the-table handyman business. He'll only have a year or so of payments left."

"We could just pay off the house," Wyatt suggested. "You really don't have that much left on it."

"Let me see if I understand what you're proposing. I'll still be working to keep up the bills, but you'll still take care of the daily needs and homeschooling needs of the kids?" Hope asked.

"Yes," Ben agreed. "That will also free me to date as well. At that point, you two can out yourselves to the town if you want."

"What are they going to say?" Hope asked.

"Who cares?" Wyatt waved her off. "It'll just give them something else to talk about, other than ranting about the police. Who knows? It may even make Mrs. Appleton finally smile. She's always giving me the stink-eye, but she likes you," he said to Hope.

"Are you okay with marrying me, knowing it's not my real identity?" Hope asked.

"As far as the world is concerned, you are Hope Hunt. No one has found you so far. I think it's safe, especially since a marriage license is kept in-state. Your license and identity have been Hope Hunt for over sixteen years, and they haven't said come to town yet. Alex and I have kept a close eye out."

"What does she know?"

"Nothing. I made something up when she pushed. That was a long time ago, though. She's become protective of me over the years. Of you, too. She likes you. She's not too sure about Ben over there, though."

Ben laughed. "What do you mean?"

"She can't figure you out. To her, you're a puzzle. She doesn't like a puzzle she can't figure out."

"Why is she trying?"

"Because, my man, she likes you!" Wyatt explained.

"No way!" Ben waved him off. "I mean…I like her, but I wasn't sure if she liked me."

"Why do you think she hasn't dated? Don't even think for a minute she hasn't been asked out. I'm pretty sure she's figured out we're together," Wyatt said, pointing to Hope and himself. "She's trying to figure out why you two are still together," he said, pointing toward Ben and Hope. "Pretty sure the whole town wonders that. They love y'all, yet all y'all pull back when it comes to relationships and they know it. Pretty sure the youth of the town want the two of you to come to church in a big way," Wyatt said to Blake and Holly.

"I know they do. They ask me every week at church," Hope said.

"You think we can handle it?" Holly asked.

"What if something happens?" Blake asked.

"Stay beside your sister." Hope shrugged. "Holly, control yourself. You two are old enough. Starting you in a youth group will help ease you into the whole social skills department. We know what you're capable of. Maybe see how it goes with church service for a few weeks?"

"You'd miss Sunday School for us?" Holly asked.

"I would, but I don't think I have to," she said, glancing at Ben.

"What does that mean?" Ben asked, surprised to find himself in the middle of a conversation regarding church.

"Well, they're sixteen. We need to teach them to drive, so they can get a license. If you bring them to church until they get their license, it would be appreciated. If this is going to work, we're going to have to work together."

"I can do that," Ben consented. "But don't expect me to come in. It'll be bad enough being the talk of the town. If I ever set foot in that church, they'd probably shame me to an early grave."

"Technically, I'll be the one shamed due to a supposed affair," Hope pointed out. "We'll move in together once we're married. They don't know we've been dating for fifteen years."

Aghast, Wyatt asked, "Has it been that long?"

"We turned sixteen a few days ago," Holly said. "So, yes."

"Wow. Time flies! I feel like we've had all the time in the world to figure this out, and we've wasted so much of it," Wyatt said, shaking his head. Turning to Hope, he asked, "Hope Hunt, slash Grace Ann Matthews, would you finally do me the honor of being my wife?"

"I would love to!" She grinned. Then, looking around the table, she asked, "Are you all sure?"

"Please…and, thank you," Blake said. "You break my heart every Sunday night. This way we know you'll be happy."

"Also, Dad'll be happy because he'll be free to date too," Holly added. "We're not as much trouble as we used to be. We're older and getting more independent."

"We'll work on that independent part," Ben said. "Don't be so quick to grow up. You have time. We still need to get you more under control. And you," he said to Blake. "You need to watch whose mind you dig into. You may find stuff you won't like."

Blake rolled his eyes. "I find that all the time."

"Makes my job a lot easier," Wyatt pointed out to everyone's laughter. While on some family outings, Blake told Wyatt what someone was planning, so he had officers tail them until they started to commit the crime and arrested them right before it happened.

"I may ask Alex out on Sunday after I drop you two off at church," Ben said, thinking how to go about asking her out.

"I'm one-hundred percent sure she'll say yes," Wyatt encouraged.

"What do I say when she asks about you?" Ben looked to Hope.

Hope shrugged. "We're going to be getting married soon, so just tell her Wyatt and I are together. If she asks how long, tell her just for a while."

"She may push," Wyatt warned. "She's a bit nosey."

"That's okay. I can handle her," Ben said confidently. "I actually like her too. I really hope she says yes."

Hope grinned. "I think you two would make a great pair!"

"So, when will you two get married?" Holly asked Hope and Wyatt.

"Sooner than later, as far as I'm concerned," Wyatt said, giving Hope's shoulder a gentle squeeze.

"When can we do it?" Hope asked.

"We can go to the Justice of the Peace whenever you want," Wyatt suggested. "Remember, he's one of my golfing buddies. He'll do it tonight if you want."

"How will we get the license?" Hope asked. "And, don't we need to wait for twenty-four hours after getting it?"

"What if we plan on doing it next Sunday after church?" Wyatt asked. "I'll have Sara-Beth from records come in tomorrow morning to get the license, and then we'll talk to Pastor after church on Sunday. He'll probably want us to do counseling or something first."

"Why doesn't he just ask us questions?" Hope asked. "After fifteen years, we know pretty much everything we need to know about each other."

"I would think so. I'll talk to him, and fill him in on stuff without giving out too much information."

"Can I be the maid of honor?" Holly asked.

Hope smiled. "Of course!"

"And, you two can both be my best man," Wyatt said to Ben and Blake.

"Won't it look weird if we're supposedly married for over fifteen years?" Ben asked.

"We'll keep it to just us. No one needs to know anything else," Wyatt suggested.

"I think that'll work," Ben agreed.

"Definitely!" Blake grinned.

"Hope?" Wyatt asked. "Do I have your permission to talk to Pastor?"

"Yes. Just be cautious about the information. And do your best not to lie."

"I can't lie to a Pastor. I can omit the truth to other officers, or to Alex, but not to a pastor. There's just something not right about that. That's like lying to Jesus. I can't do it."

"Just do your best."

"I will," he said, and leaned over, giving her a kiss on the top of her head. "I love you, darlin'."

"Love you too," she said with a shy smile.

"Then it's settled!" Holly clapped her hands together in excitement. "We start church this Sunday, and you're getting married next Sunday?"

"Yes," Hope said decisively.

"Great!" Blake grinned.

"So, hate to break the mood, but what did you think when your Dad told you your backstory?" Hope asked.

"Well, you've told us all along we're not your children by birth, but were by heart," Blake said, starting to eat the delicious roast beef, mashed potatoes and gravy, and green beans on his plate. "I also knew part of it, and told Holly what I knew. We've chatted a bit off and on through the years, and have pieced a lot of it together."

"Hearing the actual story itself gave me goosebumps," Holly

admitted. "I can't imagine all you went through. Everything you guys gave up just to raise us."

"I would do it again. I'm sure Ben would as well," Hope said.

"In a heartbeat," Ben agreed.

"Well, I, for one, am grateful the Lord led you down here. We'll do our best to protect your secret, but the fewer people who know, the better," Wyatt said.

"Agreed," everyone said in chorus.

BEFORE THEIR TIME

**"In the end, it's not the years in your life that count. It's the
life in your years." Edward J. Stieglitz, M.D.**

"You two going to be okay?" Ben asked Blake and
Holly as he pulled into the church parking lot.

"This is just church service. We'll be fine," Holly
said. "Now, when we first venture into Sunday School, that may
be a completely different scenario."

"This is true. Blake?" Ben asked him.

"Oh, I'm good." Blake waved him off. "If I get bored, I'll
just start reading minds. If it gets tense, I'll make it calm."

"This is true." Ben chuckled. "Okay, you guys wait around
while Hope and Wyatt meet with the pastor afterward. Then
we'll get together for our regular Sunday afternoon fun."

"What are we doing today?" Holly asked.

"Well, it's October. Pretty sure we can find something to do.
Maybe I'll plan for a bonfire tonight? That way we can relax.

Blake can play the guitar, and we'll roast some marshmallows," Ben suggested.

"That sounds great! Wait until I get home and I'll move all the wood for you," Holly said, leaning forward to kiss him on the cheek. "Love you, Dad."

"Love you too, pumpkin," Ben replied.

Blake wrapped his arm around him from behind in a hug. "Love ya too, Dad. See you in a bit."

"Sounds good. Love you too, Blake."

When they got out of the car, they saw several teens hanging out on the front porch of the church waiting for the service to start.

"Great. Here we go," Blake said on a sigh.

"Mom texted. They're just inside the doors," Holly encouraged. "We only need to get through."

"Fair enough."

Walking up the stairs, they saw a couple teens stand up. Blake did not care for what he read in the two of the boys' minds toward his sister, so he leaned over and quietly said, "Stay to my left near the wall. The boys have hormones raging."

"Gotcha," Holly said, walking to his other side, glancing in the windows as an excuse to be to that side of him.

"Hi!" one of the girls said with a huge grin as she looked at Blake doe-eyed. "I'm Lindsey Kemp," she introduced herself, sticking her hand out for each of them to shake.

As they each shook her hand, they introduced themselves.

"I'm Blake Hunt," he said.

"And, I'm Holly Hunt."

"We've seen you two around town, and heard of you, but have never had the pleasure of actually meeting you. I'm Megan Kaufman," she said, shaking both of their hands.

"I'm Shawn Shanks," he introduced himself, shaking their hands.

"Hey, there! I'm Colby Simmons." He shook each of their hands.

"Tanya Holland," she said, shaking their hands.

"And last, but certainly not least, I'm Mac McConnell," Mac introduced himself as he shook each of their hands.

"We're never going to remember all those names," Holly confessed. "It'll take us a few times."

"So, you plan on coming back?" Mac asked. Mac was about six-foot tall, slightly shorter than Ben. The guys all seemed to be around six-foot tall. Mac's dark-brown hair, was shorter and curly, but current in trend. It was a good compliment to his hazelnut-brown eyes, and medium-toned skin color. To Holly, with his skin tone, it looked as if he tanned well in the summer. His fit build told her he was athletic.

"Our mom has been coming here for years," Blake explained.

"Who's your mom?" Lindsey asked. Lindsey looked to be close to the same height as Hope, which was five-foot-seven. Holly was pretty sure she was a cheerleader with her perky attitude and huge smile. Her long, curly, blond hair hung to her midback, and her baby-blue eyes made her almost look like a doll.

"You're showing your intelligence quotient today," Tanya said, shaking her head. "Their last name is Hunt…as in Hope Hunt? The one who's been coming here forever and works at Willow's Bend?"

"Oh! Awesome!" Lindsey smiled. "I didn't connect you guys."

"Yes, you did," Tanya insisted. "Hope told us this morning they were coming." While Lindsey narrowed her eyes at Tanya, Tanya just rolled her eyes. Hope liked Tanya's attitude. She seemed more real than Lindsey.

Tanya stood about the same height at Holly, which was five-foot-ten. Holly was relieved to meet another girl the same height as her. While she enjoyed being tall, height had its disadvantages as well…especially a few years ago when she towered over the boys in town. Tanya had dark-brown, straight hair, which hung just a few inches past her shoulders. Her bright-blue eyes stood out against her medium skin tone. Holly studied people everywhere they went. People fascinated Holly, but frustrated Blake.

"Ladies, ladies, let's not give our visitors a bad image of our group," Shawn said, almost parting the two girls to get to Holly. "After all, we want them to come back."

Shawn stood to about the same height as Mac, with an athletic build. His shorter blond hair reminded Holly of boyband style. His face had chiseled features, and his eyes were a really cool bluish-gray. Holly thought he could pass as a model, if she did not already know he was a team roper from the rodeo. Over the last few years, when the rodeo was in town, she saw Shawn and Mac on a team. Shawn was the header, to Mac's footer. Whenever she saw him, his eyes had a mischievous look in them. To Holly, he seemed used to girls throwing themselves at him…she did not need Blake's gift to sniff that one out.

"Thank you," Blake said, stepping slightly in front of Holly, shaking Shawn's hand again.

When he did, Shawn felt Blake's arm. "Wow! You got some muscle, dude. Do you play football?"

"Nope. I'm homeschooled."

"Is that why we never see y'all in school?" Megan asked. Megan looked to be a couple inches shorter than Holly. She had ginger-colored, straight hair that hung to her mid-back. Her hair accentuated her blue eyes, which also stood out on her medium-framed, fair skin.

"Yes," Holly answered. "We've been homeschooled all the way through."

"Are y'all fixin' to come to school at all?" Colby asked. Colby, from Holly's best guess, looked like he enjoyed sports. In watching football over the years, she would place him as a receiver, due to his lean body type, which matched his six-foot-two frame. She saw him at a few of the games. He caught her eye. His medium-brown hair was kept neat, which allowed his chocolate-brown eyes to stand out even more. Holly liked his laid-back demeanor. She hoped her initial assessment of him was accurate.

"Nope," Blake said. "Dad's going to homeschool us all the way through."

"Shame! We could use a guy like you on our football team," Shawn said.

"Can you throw?" Mac asked.

Blake shrugged. "I don't know. I've never tried."

"We're all on the team," Colby explained. "We just lost our quarterback because he moved to Houston."

"I'm captain of the team," Shawn clarified.

As soon as he said that, Holly heard Blake's voice in her mind, say, *Of course you are.*

She had to stifle the giggle as she pressed her lips together. That was a new trick Blake had not shown her yet.

Knowing he was able to read her thoughts, she thought, *Be nice. They're trying.* Her head spun toward Blake when he burst out in laughter.

"What?" Shawn frowned, looking around to see what they were laughing at.

"Nothing," Blake said. "Just felt my phone go off in my pocket for the fifth time in less than a minute. Pretty sure Mom's looking for us."

"Oh! Service must be getting ready to start," Lindsey said, looking through the windows. "Yep. Better get inside. Can we talk more afterward?"

"I don't see why not. Our mom's meeting with Pastor afterward, so we'll be hanging out for a little bit," Blake explained.

"Y'all are welcome to sit with us," Tanya offered.

"Maybe next time," Holly said. "With this being the first time, Mom wants us to sit with her."

"Speaking of Mom," Blake said, pulling his phone out of his back pocket. He waggled it in the air.

"Right. Well, great to meet you all. We'll see you afterward?" Holly asked.

"Definitely!" Colby said with a smile.

As they went inside, the teens went one way, while Holly and Blake went the other. They saw the teens sit in the back of the sanctuary, while their mom and Wyatt sat about half-way back, on the opposite side of the sanctuary from the teens.

"Thank you," Holly said. "There are some I'm comfortable with, while others I'm not."

"Let me guess?" Blake said quietly. "Not comfortable with Shawn, but comfortable with Colby?"

"Yes. Neat trick, by the way. How did you do that?"

"Do what?" he asked, confused.

"You spoke in my mind. You said, *Of course you are*. I heard it."

"You did? I didn't do that on purpose! Nice!" He grinned. "Another trick. I'll practice that during the service."

"That's why I responded. Did you hear the response?"

"Yes. I also felt your feelings…theirs too."

"Social situations with teens will be interesting from now on," Holly said, as they neared their mom.

"Yeah. We may have been here all of our lives, but we didn't grow up with them. We're fresh meat in a small town," Blake pointed out.

When they got to the aisle where Wyatt and Hope were, both stood and gave them a hug.

"I was wondering where you two were," Hope said, as they sat down to the left of Hope, with Holly right beside Hope, and Blake on the other side of Holly.

"Did you really text Blake five times?" Holly whispered to Hope.

"No," Blake said. "Only once."

"You lied?" Holly asked, wide-eyed.

"I had to give a reason for my laughter. Speaking of which, how in the world did you keep quiet if you heard my comment?" Blake asked.

"Don't know. Could have been that calming effect you were projecting."

"Practicing your skills in the real world?" Wyatt asked quietly.

"Yes. Also learned a new trick," Blake said. "Seems I can not only read minds, but put thoughts into other's minds. I thought something, and Holly heard it in her head."

"Interesting," Hope said. "Be careful with that, or you could send the wrong message to the wrong person."

"I figured I would practice that one to sharpen it, especially since I didn't know I could do it until now."

"Good idea. In the meantime, be careful with your thoughts," Hope suggested.

"Noted," Blake said, and then sat back as service started.

Through the morning service, Blake and Holly felt relaxed. Blake did not even have to do anything to keep Holly calm for the first part, he felt it from her. From the worship songs sung, to the choir singing, to the reading of the Bible, everything had a feeling neither experienced. Being the first time they were in a church, everything was new to them.

When Pastor Wilson got up to speak, both Blake and Holly were taking notes, while reading the Bible app on their phones. He spoke on The Last Supper, since they would be doing communion afterward. Pastor Wilson talked about Jesus telling His inner circle that one of them would betray Him. He also told Peter that he would deny Jesus three times before the rooster crowed the next morning. Judas would be the eventual betrayer. This accusation from Jesus cut Judas so deep, he left the supper. He went straight to the temple, where he received thirty pieces of silver to identify Jesus in the Garden of Gethsemane.

While Judas was at the temple, the remaining apostles and Jesus headed to the Garden of Gethsemane to allow Jesus to pray. While He prayed, Jesus asked the apostles to stand guard.

When Jesus prayed, He asked God if there was any other way to release Him from the burden of the sacrifice to please show Him. If not, Jesus would willingly make the sacrifice.

When Jesus went back to His apostles, He found them sleeping. Heartbroken and upset, Jesus woke them and reprimanded them, before going back to pray again. While Jesus was praying the second time, the men from the temple came, accompanied by Judas. A fight broke out between the guards and the apostles. During the fight, Peter cut off the ear of one of the guards.

When Jesus got to them, He replaced the guard's ear, and then told His apostles to calm down. Judas went to Jesus and gave Jesus a kiss on the cheek, signifying which one was Jesus.

When Pastor said that, both Holly and Blake looked at each other, then back to Pastor, stunned. *He betrayed Jesus with a literal kiss on the cheek?* Holly thought.

Cretin, Blake thought back.

Holly shook her head, as she started reading ahead while half-listening to Pastor talk about the crucifixion. The horrors she read made her angry. She looked up on her phone what a cat-o-nine-tails was. That's what they beat Jesus with, all the way down to the bones in His back.

Calm down, little sister, Blake thought into Holly's mind.

How can you sit there so calmly? This really happened! I'm even finding it online. What I can't figure out is why people are just sitting here as if it's an everyday occurrence? she responded.

Blake reached over and touched her arm, letting a feeling of calm wash over her. When it sunk into her core, she noticed the hymnals in the row they were in slowly dropped back into their slots.

"Oops!" she whispered.

"It's okay," Hope whispered to her. "We'll go more into the story after church. I'm sure there are a lot of questions."

"You have no idea!" Holly whispered back.

"You lifted the hymnals about three inches," Hope pointed out. "Pretty sure I have a decent idea. Good thing we're the only ones in this aisle or we may have some explaining to do. Try to take notes, but stay calm."

"Yes, ma'am," Holly whispered back.

Holly did pay attention. After a while, she did not even notice that Blake left his hand on her arm through the entire message. She was so engrossed in the story, she almost forgot where she was sitting and that others were around her.

Pastor Wilson told the story of how, once they finished beating him with the cat-o-nine-tails, and Jesus was near death, they placed a purple cloak on Him. Purple, back in the day, signified royalty. They were making fun of Him, calling Him King of the Jews. Mocking Him.

Once the blood was dried, they tore it off His back, opening all the wounds once again. To Holly's horror, Pastor Wilson told of how they basically played a lottery to find out who would get the cloak. She could not believe what all they did to Him!

Also, through the night, a couple of the apostles went to the courtyard to see if they could find anything out on Jesus. When they were there, Peter was recognized. They accused him of being one of the followers of Jesus. Peter denied this not once… not twice…but three times…and then the rooster crowed. At that time, Peter looked up to see Jesus being taken through the courtyard, looking directly at him. Peter's shame overpowered every essence of his being. Jesus was right in His prediction. Heartbroken, Peter left.

The next day, they made Jesus attempt to carry His own cross through the streets, all the way to the Mount of Golgotha. With the shape His body was in, He could not finish the journey, so they pulled another from the crowd to finish the journey carrying the cross.

Once to Golgotha, they nailed Jesus to the cross with three-inch spikes by His hands and feet. Any time Jesus wanted a breath, He would have to push up with His feet, putting even more pressure on the spike through them.

During this time, those around Jesus mocked Him. The soldiers placed a sign above His head which said, 'King of the Jews.' They placed a three-inch thorn crown on His head, and pressed it down.

Also, there were true criminals to His left and to His right. One joined in, mocking Jesus, while the other scolded the man, and told him to be quiet. He said that was in fact, Jesus, the Son of the Living God. Jesus responded to the man who defended Him, that he would be in paradise with Him on that day.

In the meantime, Jesus's mother, Mary, was at the cross with John, one of Jesus's apostles. Jesus, even though He was being tortured to death, thought about not only the man on the cross next to Him, but also about His own mother. He charged John to look after her, making sure she would be taken care of after this was over.

Holly's heart broke. Blake pushed even harder the calmness Holly needed in order to stay under control.

With tears in her eyes, Holly whispered to her mom, "Is this all true?"

Her mom only nodded in response as she gently tapped Holly's hand.

"What is wrong with these people in here? Why are they not as upset at this as I am? Those kids we met earlier? A couple are even over there whispering and giggling."

"I'm sorry. Not everyone has as sensitive a heart as you do," Hope whispered. "Let your brother keep you calm."

Sitting back in her seat, Holly took several deep breaths to clear her heart and mind. Inside, she wanted to wake those people up! Pastor's words should have touched every soul in that building, but they only acted as if it was a story they heard a million times, and were desensitized to it.

She felt Blake's calmness wash over her. Holly was grateful for Blake. She understood without Blake, the church could have been turned upside down. She knew she would not have been able to keep control of herself. Blake also relied on her to help where needed. Her gift was used in a completely different way than Blake's, but they looked out for each other and complemented each other. They were a pair.

Finally, Pastor Wilson talked of when Jesus died, the veil was torn from top to bottom in the temple, and a darkness fell over the land. Jesus's last words were, *"Father, forgive them, for they know not what they do. It is finished."*

Tears poured down Holly's cheeks. Blake fought his own tears in order to keep Holly under control.

Pastor Wilson continued to tell of how they buried Jesus in a cave. He said those in power rolled a heavy stone in front, and placed guards in front of it so the apostles could not steal the body of Jesus. Throughout Jesus's life, He said He would die and be raised from the dead three days later. Those in power were afraid Jesus's apostles would steal His body in order for it to look like He was raised.

Well, three days after His death, there were three women going to place oils and spices on the body of Jesus. When they got there, the guards were passed out, the stone was moved with an angel sitting on top. The angel declared, *"He is not here, for He has risen!"*

The women ran back to the apostles as fast as they could, and returned with Peter and John. John got there first. When Peter got there, they were stunned to find the area just as the women described it. Fearing what would happen, they ran back to the others to tell them.

Jesus appeared multiple times over the next few days. One of those times He spoke directly with Peter, and asked Peter if he loved Him. Peter responded that indeed, he did. Jesus then told Peter to feed His sheep. Jesus did this three times, therefore negating Peter's denial of Jesus.

The heart of Jesus is what spoke the strongest to both Blake and Holly. This Jesus was tortured and killed, yet came back from the dead. And, when Jesus could do anything He wanted, His choice was to not only forgive one of his closest friends, but to also appear to over 500 people, and then give the precious gift of the Holy Spirit to His apostles.

Why did Jesus do this? Why wasn't He mad at Peter? Why did He bother to show Himself to over 500 people? Why did He care so much for those who left Him to die? How could someone in His inner circle actually betray Him like that? Holly thought to Blake.

Relax. We'll talk to Mom and Wyatt afterward. I'm sure they'll be able to answer whatever questions we have. Just write them down. I really need you to calm down, though. It's taking a lot out of me to keep you under control.

I'm sorry.

Don't be sorry. Just get a grip.

Holly nodded as she went back to listening to Pastor Wilson.

The pastor told how the precious gift of the Holy Spirit was given to not only the apostles, but also to those who chose to follow Jesus – Jews and Gentiles alike.

Can we really get this Spirit he's talking about? Holly thought to Blake.

Blake nodded. He did not know for sure, but keeping Holly under control for over thirty minutes was exhausting. Knowing the teens would be over after service was finished, he knew he needed to keep some in reserve to deal with them.

The pastor then went on to explain communion, and what it was about. After the deacons passed out the grape juice and crackers, one of them prayed. Pastor then read I Corinthians

11:23b-24, "*The Lord Jesus, on the night He was betrayed, took bread, and when He had given thanks, He broke it and said, "This is My body, which is for you; do this in remembrance of Me.*"

Once he finished reading, everyone ate the crackers who had them. Afterward, another deacon prayed. Then Pastor read 1 Corinthians 11:25-26, "*In the same way, after supper He took the cup, saying, "This cup is the new covenant in My blood; do this, whenever you drink it, in remembrance of Me. For whenever you eat this bread and drink this cup, you proclaim the Lord's death until He comes.*"

After he said that, everyone drank the cup of grape juice. Then, Pastor said another prayer before dismissing them for the week. Once he did, everyone stood to leave. Some stayed to talk to others, as many filtered out to gather their children or catch people they needed to see.

"Okay, I want to introduce you to Pastor before we go talk to him, please?" Hope said to Blake and Holly.

They nodded and followed Hope and Wyatt to the front to meet him.

"Pastor Wilson, this is my son, Blake, and my daughter, Holly," Hope introduced them.

"Well, I've heard a lot about you. So glad to finally meet you," Pastor said with a smile.

"Pleasure to meet you." Blake smiled, shaking his hand, pleasantly surprised Pastor was genuine.

"Glad to finally meet you as well," Holly said, shaking his hand.

"I hope you found our church family friendly?" Pastor asked.

"We did. We met some of the other teens on the way in," Holly explained.

"Oh! Well," Pastor smiled, "I hope they behaved themselves."

"They did."

"Good."

"Are you still good to take some time to chat?" Wyatt asked.

"Definitely! If you could give me about fifteen minutes to say goodbye to people, I'd be happy to sit down with y'all," Pastor agreed.

"Great! Well, you two can go talk to the teens if you want. We'll catch up with you after we're finished with Pastor," Hope suggested.

"I don't think they're going to give us an option," Blake said knowingly, as he glanced at the crew slowly walking toward them.

"Go have fun. We'll meet you out front when we're finished," Hope encouraged. It was her desire for them to connect with other teens so they would want to come to church again.

"Hi," Shawn said, looking directly at Holly.

"Hey," Holly responded. Then she turned to the girls, and said, "Nice to see you again."

"We were wondering if y'all wanted to come with us to the diner for a bit?" Tanya asked. "If you want, we'll drop you off at home afterward?"

The teens looked to Hope, who nodded. "Then you guys don't have to wait around for us," Hope said. Digging through her purse, she pulled out two twenty-dollar bills. She handed Blake and Holly each a bill. "Please have them home by four. We have family dinner together."

"That's sweet!" Lindsey gushed. "I love that!"

"We do, too," Holly agreed. "And will do."

They each gave Hope a kiss on the cheek before taking off with the teens.

"So glad they've already connected with a part of the youth," Wyatt commented, watching the group leave.

"I just hope they behave themselves. I'll text Ben to let him know," she said, pulling out her cell phone. When she texted him, she expected an immediate response, but did not receive one. Shrugging, she said, "He must be busy working in the workshop."

"Probably. He's usually with the kids, or working on cleaning, cooking, or whatnot. Let him enjoy his peace. He'll check his phone when he gets a break. When we're done with Pastor, we can go out to eat as well."

"Won't that be crashing in on the kids?"

"It'll give them an excuse in case they want to leave early," Wyatt countered. "They're not used to being around kids their age."

"This is true," she said, nibbling on her nails as concern set in. "They're not normal children. I hope Blake can keep Holly under control."

"You guys need to teach her to keep herself under control. Blake may not always be around when she needs him."

"We do. However, you have to remember that she's a female teenager. Emotions and hormones are out of control. We can't afford for her gift to get out of control."

"Speaking of that," Wyatt said, "the hymnals?"

"I'll talk to her about that tonight. You have to remember she's never heard anything like this before. I wasn't allowed to talk about Jesus or the Bible with them. Ben wants nothing to do with that."

"The hand that rocks the cradle," Wyatt said on a sigh. "Let's just hope we're getting the message to them soon enough. If anything happens to them before we can sit down with them to talk about what they heard today, you'll never forgive yourself."

"I know. They've been protected up until now. I always thought there would be time. Lord willing, we can talk to them tonight."

"Let's hope so. Here comes Pastor. Time to face the music."

"How much are you going to tell him?"

"Almost all of it. I'll leave out the gift part. We'll tell him they are both of your children, and instead of living apart and raising them, you raised them together. Now that they're getting older, everyone has decided to move on. I'll also tell him we've been dating, but keeping to ourselves until marriage."

"Are you going to tell him for how long?"

"Yep. While I understand the importance of keeping their true lives safe, I'd rather not lie to Pastor as much as possible."

"Agreed," she said, as Pastor walked up to the couple.

"Ready?" Pastor asked. When they nodded, Pastor gestured toward his office.

As they sat down, Wyatt took Hope's hand into his, and said, "Pastor, there are some things we need to fill you in on, and hope there's something you're willing to help us out with."

⬥⬥⬥⬥

WITH EIGHT IN the group of teens, they had to split up. Because Blake and Holly did not want to be separated, they went with the girls in Lindsey's royal blue Jeep with a black hardtop. The rest of the boys rode together in Shawn's hunter green and silver F150.

"So, we know you've lived here pretty much since birth, but we don't know much about you," Lindsey pointed out, as they pulled out of the church parking lot.

"Care to share a little?" Megan asked, hopeful, from her place in the passenger's seat.

"Well, we were born in Maine," Blake started.

"And, we're homeschooled," Holly continued, "which is why you probably don't see us around town much."

"While we're homeschooled, we usually go out on a family outing at least once a week. Where we go depends on the season," Blake said.

"And, you already know our mom works at Willow's Bend," Holly added.

"And our dad works at home. He's also a handyman," Blake said. "Once we graduate, he's thinking about going into business for himself as a handyman."

"Interesting," Tanya said, from her place on the one side of Holly in the back seat, while Holly sat between Blake and Tanya. "You don't usually find the man in the relationship staying at home."

"The house our parents bought when we moved here was an extreme fixer-upper." Blake shrugged. "In order for them to fix it, Dad had to stay home to do the work."

"Oh, that makes sense."

"Yep. Then he went ahead and stayed home to homeschool us, as he progressively makes improvements on the house," Blake explained.

Pulling into the Willow's Bend parking lot, Lindsey said, "Well, I'm glad y'all came today, and were able to come with us out to eat."

"It's good to get to know others our age," Holly said.

"Are you two twins?" Tanya asked, while they got out of Lindsey's Jeep.

"We were born in October," Holly said, not directly answering Tanya's question. "We just celebrated our sixteenth birthday recently."

"Are you guys planning on getting your driver's licenses soon?" Tanya asked.

"Eventually," Blake said, shoving his hands into his pockets as they walked toward the restaurant.

Meeting up with the guys, they headed into Willow's Bend Diner. Once seated in a booth, Blake and Holly made sure to sit on one end, with Holly on the actual end. Everyone opened their menus.

The others looked up at Holly when she immediately set her menu down without looking. "We tend to get the same thing every time we come," she explained.

"Oh, yeah. Your mom works here." Colby nodded in understanding. "So, what do you two normally get?"

"I get the fried chicken, salad, and green beans," Holly said.

"And I get steak, mashed potatoes, and green beans," Blake said, setting his menu down as well. "Neither of those items depends on the chef. Either one is good with both of those meals."

"Good to know," Shawn said. "So, what do you two like to do when you're not homeschooling?"

"We work on homework, gardening, etcetera," Blake said.

"What else?"

⟁⟁⟁⟁

WHILE BLAKE and Holly were being interrogated by the teens, Hope and Wyatt had some explaining to do of their own.

"What can I help you out with?" Pastor asked.

"Well, would you please hear us out before you say anything?" Wyatt asked.

"Fair enough. I can do that," Pastor agreed.

"We would like you to marry us."

"Umm, hold on." Pastor put his hand up. "I thought Hope was already married."

"Not really," Hope admitted. Then she explained, "You see, the kids are ours. Instead of having to answer for not being married, Ben and I pretended to be married. Ben and I have our own rooms, and have never had sex. We were living in the house together in order to give the kids a stable home life instead of shipping them from one parent to another."

"I see," Pastor said, processing what they were telling him. Then, turning to Wyatt, he asked, "How long have you known about this?"

"Since the kids were one," Wyatt said. "That's also when

Hope and I started dating. And, before you ask, we have not had sex either. We're waiting for marriage."

"Yes, we've been dating for fifteen years," Hope jumped back into the conversation. "Then the other day, the kids told us to go ahead and get married. With them being sixteen, they don't need me as much. They want both Ben and me to be happy. Blake is the one who knew it broke my heart every day to come home and leave Wyatt," she said, grabbing Wyatt's hand to hold in support. "Now, with their blessing, along with Ben's, we'd like to get married."

"Fifteen years, huh?" Pastor asked.

"Yes," they said in unison.

Then, Hope added, "I think we've waited long enough. We would rather you marry us, because you mean the world to us. If you don't want to, we understand, and will go to the Justice of the Peace."

"I think we've waited long enough," Wyatt reiterated. "So, will you marry us?"

"I have some questions I would like you to answer before I say yes or no," Pastor said. "Starting with, are you two in love? If so, what does love mean to you?"

"Yes, we're in love," Wyatt said. "To me, love is a commitment."

"I agree," Hope said. "Love, to me, is also commitment. We're going to have those days where we won't get along, but our love will pull us through."

"And, on those days, our marriage vows, along with our commitment to the Lord, will enable us to sit down and talk about the issue," Wyatt said. "Compromise may be in order to get us through what we don't agree on."

"Having said that, we also believe in the Chain of Command in our relationship. Wyatt will be the head of our family. He is responsible to the Lord for any choices we make as a family," Hope explained.

"Good. The next questions are, have you ever had a fight? If so, what does that look like?" Pastor asked.

"Yes. We have," Wyatt said. "And when we do, we don't let it get heated. We table it, cool down, and then come back together in order to talk it out."

"Another good answer." Pastor nodded in approval. "Just a couple more questions."

⟐⟐⟐⟐

"So, you all have learned a lot about us," Holly pointed out. "Now it's time for us to learn about you."

"I'm an open book," Lindsey said.

"That's probably because you can't keep a secret," Tanya shot, looking sideways at Lindsey. "Or your mouth shut."

"Easy, you two," Colby said, as he sat between them. Looking to Holly and Blake, he added, "These two don't always get along."

Smiling, Holly said, "We don't always get along either. I think that's what happens when you bond with someone."

"Good point," Colby agreed.

"So, tell us about yourselves," Blake asked, repeating Holly's question.

"I'll start," Shawn said. "I'm on the football, basketball, and baseball teams. I also run the hundred, four-by-four-hundred, the four-by-one-hundred, and I run hurdles."

"So, athlete?" Holly asked.

"Yes. Do the two of you like any sports?"

"We've been to many football games in town on Friday nights," Holly pointed out. "We also tend to watch football on TV, as well as basketball."

"We go more for the exciting sports to watch," Blake explained. "As for us actually playing, we've never tried any."

"We need to get the two of you in school so you can be on the football team," Shawn said to Blake.

"Oh, doubt that will happen. We can always check with Mom and Dad to see if they're okay with it, but I highly doubt it," Blake said.

"You said y'all don't live in a bubble," Megan said, "but I see a lot of sheltering going on."

"We don't mind it," Blake said. "We go out all the time as a family. Staying out of public schools is partly our choice, and partly theirs."

"You're willing to stay in the bubble?" Lindsey asked, furrowing her brow.

"We like the peace and quiet," Blake said.

"So, you don't ever want to come to public school?"

"We're okay with homeschooling," Holly said with a shrug. "It's nice to spend extra time with our mom and dad. If we were in public schools, we wouldn't have that time."

Linsey huffed. "If you're okay with it, then stay home."

"We're going to get our friends through church," Blake explained. "Think you can handle it?"

"I can," Megan said quickly.

"Me too," Shawn said.

"I can as well," Colby said. "It'll be nice to have new people in the group."

"As long as we can be friends, I'm okay with only seeing you on Sunday," Tanya pointed out. "Public schools aren't for everyone."

"But what are you going to do when college comes?" Lindsey asked. "You'll be thrown in over your heads."

"Why would you think that?" Holly asked. "We can get along with anyone of any age. It's not like we've had a deprived social life. We've just had one containing more adults than teens."

"Interesting," Colby said. "Personally, I'm curious as to what homeschooling looks like. What do y'all do all day?"

"We do our school work," Blake said, as the server brought their food. While the server set the food in front of each person, Blake continued, "Also, like we said earlier, we do gardening and help our dad with some of the housework and repairs."

"Sounds like fun," Tanya said. "So, there's a lot of flexibility."

"Yes. We seriously aren't locked up all day," Holly explained. "We get our daily school work finished around noon, depending on when we start. We have most of the day to do hands-on, practical work."

"That's pretty cool," Shawn said. "Definitely unique."

"It's not unique, but it is pretty cool," Blake said, "We get to do a lot more than most our age."

"Let's pray before the food gets cold," Megan suggested.

After prayer, they dove into the food. It was quiet around the table for several minutes. Finally, Mac said, "Let's get back to our get-to-know-you session. Shawn and I do team roping. Along with that, I also play basketball, football, and run track – same runs as Shawn."

"I am in the choir, do drama, and do UIL for academics," Tanya explained.

"Brains and beauty," Blake said, and she blushed.

"I'm in choir and love to do art – drawing is my forte," Megan chirped in.

"More like you've won multiple awards for your drawings," Colby pointed out. "She's also a genius."

"I did receive awards for art, and my intelligence quotient is higher than average," she admitted as she looked down, knowing her face was bright red.

"Humble too," Blake observed.

"She is also a whiz on the computer," Tanya pointed out. "Could be categorized as a hacker if pushed to do so."

"They're workarounds," Megan defended herself.

"You both are great with computers," Mac added. "I would classify them as hackers, but they use their powers for good."

"We try," Tanya acknowledged.

"I play football and run track," Colby explained. "I'm a receiver on the football team, and run four-by-one-hundred; four-by-four-hundred; the four-hundred; and the one-hundred."

"Won trophies in state for a few of those," Mac added.

"Like it," Holly said, which garnered a huge smile from Colby.

"Since I didn't get to finish mine," Lindsey inserted herself, "I am a cheerleader at school. I also run track – sprinter as well, same as Colby. I picked those two, because they don't conflict with each other."

"Good choices for all of you," Blake said. "They seem to fit your personalities."

Just then, Holly's cell phone rang. "Excuse me," she said, getting up, "I need to answer this." Heading outside to hear better, she answered the phone, "Hi, Mom."

"Hi, honey," Hope said. "We're just about done here. Do you want us to pick you up?"

"How soon are you talking?"

"In about fifteen minutes?"

"Hmmm. We just got our food. We'll have them drop us off, if that's okay?"

"Sure."

"So, what did the pastor say?"

"He'll marry us. He had a lot of questions, but in the end, I guess we satisfied him."

"So, when are you getting married?"

"Tonight. We pushed the issue, because we figured we waited long enough."

"Do you have everything you need?"

"I'll have everything I want when we pick you two up. Pastor will meet us at Ben's in a few hours."

"Okay. Come on over and get us. You've got too much to worry about, and need our help."

"Great! See you in about fifteen minutes."

Heading back inside, Holly asked the hostess to get the check for her and Blake. Then she headed over to the table. When she sat down, she said, "That was Mom. She's going to pick us up in about fifteen minutes. There are some things we have to do at home."

"Oh." Lindsey pouted.

"We'll be back next Sunday," Blake said, finishing up his meal.

Holly quickly finished hers as well. She did not want to take any home with them. "I'm really glad we met y'all," Holly said, as the waitress gave her their check.

"We're glad we met you as well," Lindsey said. "Are we gonna see you on Wednesday night?"

"Possibly," Holly said. "We won't know until Wednesday."

"You should see us next Sunday, though," Blake added.

Shawn smiled. "Great!"

"Can we put in a request to go out to lunch again next Sunday after church?" Megan asked.

"I think that can be arranged," Holly agreed.

"We go every Sunday after church," Tanya explained, looking at Blake.

"Next time, we would love to have you sit with us during church?" Shawn asked, hopeful.

Holly shook her head. "We enjoy sitting with Mom and Wyatt."

"We don't bite," Mac said, tongue in cheek.

"It's not that," Blake said. "We just enjoy spending time with our parents."

"What if after a few weeks you alternate?" Tanya suggested.

"See if you like sitting with us? We don't mind having custody of y'all part of the time."

"That may be a possibility," Holly relented. "But," she looked at her watch, "we need to work our way out of here. We need to pay our bill and get ready to meet them. They'll be here any minute."

They all said their goodbyes before Holly and Blake left the table. Paying for their lunches and leaving a tip with the hostess, they headed outside to wait for Hope and Wyatt.

THE APPOINTED TIME

"Life is inherently risky. There is only one big risk you should avoid at all costs, and that is the risk of doing nothing." Denis Waitley

*A*s they walked out, they saw two other kids their age. Both were leaning against the wall as if they were waiting for someone. Blake tried to read their minds, but he was blocked. *Something's off,* he pushed the thought into Holly's mind. When she did not say anything back, he whispered near her ear, "Something's off."

"What do you mean?" Holly whispered back.

"Nothing's off," the boy said aloud.

Hearts racing, both Blake and Holly looked at the pair in shock.

Blake gulped before he asked, "I'm sorry, are you talking to us?"

"Yes," the girl said, standing. She stood a few inches shorter than Holly. She had dark-auburn hair, which complimented her dark-brown eyes. She had her hair pulled back in a tight pony-tail. With her pale skin, her dark make-up made her features stand out.

"What did you say?" Blake asked.

"I said that nothing's off," the boy said again. He stood slightly taller than Blake. His medium-brown hair was longer on top and super short on the rest of his head. He seemed to be studying Holly with his baby-blue eyes, the same color as hers. He had the same build as Blake.

"Why did you say that?" Blake pressed.

The boy shrugged and said, "Why so defensive? We're just a couple of teenagers, like you."

"Not if you heard what I said," Blake pointed out. "I whispered that to her."

"Your sister?" the girl asked. "You whispered it to your sister?"

"What does it matter to you what I said to my sister?" Blake asked.

"You'll find out soon enough," the girl said. She and the boy turned to leave.

"Who are you?" Holly demanded.

"Someone you once knew," the girl said over her shoulder as they continued slowly walking away.

"Do we let them leave, or do we press it?" Blake asked Holly.

Holly thought for a moment before she shouted after them, "Wait a minute!"

The other pair stopped about five feet from the edge of the building, turned toward the two, and waited.

As Holly and Blake neared the pair, Blake grabbed Holly's arm to stop her. "No."

"Why?" Holly asked. "Don't you want to know?"

"It's a trap," he said, finding several minds to read around the corner, and nothing he heard was good.

Holly narrowed her eyes at the pair watching them. "Who are you?" she demanded again.

"I told you," the girl said. "We're someone you used to know."

Holly glanced over at Blake, who shook his head. Holly and Blake turned to leave when six guys rushed around the corner toward them. Holly spun around, and with a wave of her arm, threw all of the guys to the ground on their backs. Waving her other hand, she threw the guns they were holding away from them by about ten to fifteen feet.

The pair of teens looked at her, momentarily stunned.

Holly and Blake bolted for the restaurant. Just as Holly put her hand on the door, Wyatt and Hope pulled into the restaurant parking lot and honked. Blake and Holly looked at each other, and then ran for the car. The guys on the ground scrambled for their guns.

Just before Holly ducked into the car, she saw the girl swipe her hand, and the guns all reached the hands of the guys on the ground. As she got into the vehicle, Blake shouted, "Go! Fast!"

"What's going on?" Wyatt demanded.

"I said GO!" Blake ordered.

Wyatt spun the tires as they sped out of the parking lot. A couple of the guys got shots off toward the car.

"What did you two do?" Hope shouted.

One of the bullets shattered the back window. Blake yanked Holly down and covered her. "GET US OUT OF HERE!" Blake growled, unable to control his own emotions, let alone Holly's, as both Holly and Hope screamed when a few of the windows shattered.

Wyatt sped down the street, keeping an eye on the rearview mirror. Hope bent forward, covering her head, while the pair in the back kept their heads down. Seeing a van and a car speed out of the restaurant toward them, Wyatt turned toward the police station at a high rate of speed. He got on his phone, "This is

Sheriff Wyatt Reynolds. We're currently being pursued by two vehicles that have already taken shots at our vehicle. Requesting back-up immediately. We are en route to the station." After giving dispatch the information, Wyatt hung up the phone, and then pressed his foot down further on the gas.

"What's going on?" Hope yelled.

"We'll sort it out at the station," Wyatt said. Continuously glancing in the mirror, he drove as safely but as quickly as he dared. "Until then, stay down."

The two vehicles continued to pursue theirs, matching their speed. Wyatt thought they would overtake their car a few times. He finally let out a sigh of relief when he pulled into the police station. There were three cars with lights on guarding the station, while two more took off after the two vehicles tailing their car.

Wyatt threw the car into park. "We need to make a run for inside the station. We're safe here, but we still should run."

"Yes, sir!" Came from the pair in the back.

"Are you okay?" Wyatt asked Hope.

"No. This is not okay," Hope said, shaking.

"Are you hurt?"

"No."

"Good. Let's get in there."

They quickly scrambled from the vehicle, running into the Willow Bend Police Station. Wyatt identified himself and showed his badge. They were then shown to a vacant office. Initially, they tried to get them to go into an interrogation room, but Wyatt knew there could be cameras in there, and insisted on an office.

Once in the office, an officer got Hope and Wyatt a coffee. He grabbed Holly and Blake each a water bottle, and then left them to talk.

"Okay, spill it!" Wyatt said, still on edge, pacing the office as they spoke.

"We really aren't sure exactly what happened," Blake

confessed. "We walked out, and something just didn't seem right. For some reason, I couldn't read the minds of the pair of teens out there waiting."

"What do you mean?" Hope asked.

"When we walked out, there was a guy and a girl out there," Holly explained. "Blake told me something didn't seem right. Well, he actually whispered it to me."

"She didn't hear me push the thought," Blake added. "I told her something seemed off."

"Right! Then the guy said nothing was off," Holly said.

"He heard you?" Hope asked. "How close were they to you?"

"That's the thing. They were more than twenty feet from us. He shouldn't have heard a thing," Blake pointed out. "The girl also said we once knew them. We've never seen them before in our lives."

A thought suddenly hit Hope. Keeping quiet about the thought, she asked, "What happened next?"

"They went to leave, so Holly called after them," Blake continued. "But I knew there were several men around the corner. It was a trap."

"Then what happened?" Wyatt asked.

Blushing, Holly confessed, "I know I'm not supposed to use my gift in public, but I threw the men one direction and their guns in the other. I needed to give us a way out."

Resting her hand on Holly's, Hope assured her, "That's okay this time. You did it to save your life and the life of your brother. You gave us time to get away."

"Who were they?" Holly asked. "We don't know very many people. And, I'm certain we've never met them."

"Did they say their names?" Hope asked.

"No. Why?" Wyatt furrowed his brow. "Do you know something?"

"I'm wondering if they're the other two?" Hope suggested.

"Other two what?" Blake asked.

"If you recall the story, there were four of you at the time we took you two," Hope reminded them. "Those two might be the other two from the clinic."

"She did move the guns with her hand. She may have the same gift as me," Holly said. "But how did they know where we were? It's not like we were at home."

"Home!" Hope said, horrified at the thought that plunged into her mind. She thrust her hand into her purse for her phone, and then feverishly dialed Ben's number. "Come on! Come on! Come on! Answer!" she pleaded to the incessant rings from Ben's phone. When it went to voicemail, the color drained from her face. "You don't think…?"

"Is Dad okay?" Blake asked.

Standing, Wyatt said, "I'm going to send a couple uniforms out there. You guys stay here."

When the door closed behind him, Blake again asked, "Is Dad okay?"

"I don't know, honey," Hope confessed. "He didn't answer his phone earlier. I don't know how, but I think they've finally found us."

"Why now?" Holly asked. "We've been here for years."

"Usually we're together," Hope said, half to herself, half to them. "Maybe they were waiting to separate you from us? Your dad was at home, Wyatt and I were at the church, and you two were at the diner."

"To what end?" Blake asked.

"I don't know. I'm calling again," Hope said dialing his phone.

When someone answered, relief flooded Hope's face, before she gasped. The voice was not Ben's. "If you want him back, come home now…without the Sheriff." After he said that, the line went dead.

"We need to get out of here." Hope shoved her phone into her purse. "They want us to go to the house without Wyatt."

"Why?" Holly asked.

"I think they want us," Blake said. "They're using Dad as leverage."

"Do they know what we can do?" Holly asked.

"They have more than likely been watching us for some time, so I would say that's a strong possibility," Hope said.

"We also know the boy has super hearing, and the girl is a telekinetic like me," Holly said.

"How are we going to get out of here?" Blake asked.

Hope got up and went to the door. She barely opened it enough to see into the office area. She could see Wyatt at the dispatch center talking to the officers over the radio. His back was to them. She noted where the other officers were located throughout the floor they were on of the station.

Closing the door, she said, "Holly and I will go to the bathroom. Blake, you find your way to the snack machine. When you catch a moment to go, get out of the station. We'll meet you outside. Go to the park next to the station. Wait for us there."

"I don't think it's a good idea to separate." Blake shook his head. "I can't warn you, and Holly can't protect me."

"He's right," Holly agreed. "We're stronger together."

"Okay, we'll all go to the vending machine," she said, grabbing her purse.

They went out the door talking about food. If any officers saw them, they would think they were going to the vending machine for snacks. Holly and Blake pretended they disagreed on which snack to get.

"No. I don't want chocolate," Blake said. "I want chips."

"We can only get one," Hope said.

"Chocolate. I'm on edge," Holly explained. "We need chocolate."

"I hear that a lot from people on edge," an officer said, chuckling, as he was working on a report at his desk.

"Kids these days." Hope shrugged. "Offer them a snack...."

The officer chuckled again before returning back to his report.

"Snack machine is there," Hope whispered. "The door is about ten feet away. We need a distraction once we're there."

"Can I?" Holly asked.

"As long as it isn't obvious," Hope said.

Finally in front of the machine, Holly went to the one side so she could see the two male officers behind the desk. Meanwhile, Hope and Blake continued to talk.

Seeing the officers joking, but keeping an eye on the three of them, Holly formed a plan for the officers. She moved a pen so it rolled off the desk. The officer picked it up and set it back down on the desk. She rolled it off again, along with the other officer's pen.

"Geez! Is the station suddenly tipping?" the one officer laughed as he picked up both pens and set them back on the desk.

Holly rolled both pens again. One fell, and the officer bent down to get it, while the other officer tried to catch the other pen. When he slammed his hand down, Holly pushed the registration book onto the ground with both officers.

"Now," Holly whispered.

The trio ducked out of the station, and walked swiftly as they could to the park to the right of the station. Ducking behind a set of trees, they looked back to see several police officers run out of the station searching for them. Just then, Hope's phone rang. She reached in and turned the ringer down before looking to see who was calling. She did not want to alert the officers as to their position.

Unfortunately, it was Wyatt. "Oh, he's not going to be happy," she groaned, shoving her phone back in her purse.

"Take the battery out," Blake said. "Unless you pull the battery, they can still trace it."

"True," she said, and then pulled the battery from her phone. Shoving it into her purse, she asked, "Can we move yet?"

"Not yet," Blake said, focusing on the police officers in order to throw them in the opposite direction they were located.

"How are we going to get to the house?" Holly asked. "Wyatt drove us here."

"We'll get there any way we can," Hope said. In reality, she had no idea how they were going to get there. All she knew was they needed to get to the house in order to help Ben.

"Mom?" Blake said, concerned.

She looked up at him from searching her purse for her keys. "What?"

"I can distract everyone but Wyatt. He knows what I'm doing."

"We're not supposed to take him with us."

"We may not have a choice," Blake said.

"What do you mean?" she asked.

Blake pointed toward the police station. When Hope followed his line of sight, she saw all the officers going in one direction, while Wyatt purposefully walked the opposite toward them.

"Oh no," she groaned. "He's relentless."

"He loves you," Holly pointed out. "You would do no less."

"Fine," Hope huffed. Stepping from around the tree, Wyatt took only a moment to see her.

A smile quickly formed when he saw her, but it was immediately replaced with a look of concern. Jogging up to them, he asked, "What in blazes are y'all doing out here? Half the station is looking for the three of you!"

"I called Ben's phone when you were gone," Hope explained. "The person who answered said for just the three of us to go to the house. We aren't allowed to take you with us. They'll hurt him."

"What do you think they're going to do to you three? They may have already killed Ben. Knowing what I know about this clinic of yours, pretty sure they'll kill you and take the kids," Wyatt said to Hope. "Why do you think they don't want me with you?"

"I don't want you to get hurt," Hope said, hoping he would understand her heart.

Placing both hands on the sides of her face, Wyatt explained, "Where you go, I go. We may not be married legally, but to me you are my wife. Should anything happen tonight, I want you to know you are my true love." He then kissed her on the top of her head. "I love you Hope…or Grace. You are still you, no matter what I call you."

"I know, I just –"

"Trust me. This is what I do."

"Fine," she relented. "They called and said we were to go alone."

"To the house?"

"Yes."

"Okay. C'mon," he said taking her hand.

The group walked back into the police station. Wyatt called the officers back in, and then explained the dilemma regarding Ben. He assigned eight officers to head to the house in different directions. They were to leave their vehicles out far enough not to be seen, and walk toward the house from each direction in pairs. In the meantime, Wyatt would be in the back seat with Blake, with Hope driving, and Holly in the passenger seat.

The entire drive there, Holly nibbled on her nails. It was a nervous habit she had since childhood.

"Please don't bite your nails," Hope said.

"Can't help it."

"Holly?"

"Mom," Holly said, rolling her eyes. "You concentrate on driving, please?"

"Fine."

"How did you fight the urge to go the opposite direction?" Blake asked, a few minutes from the house.

"What?" Wyatt asked, as he sat on the floor of the back seat.

"I made everyone go one direction. How were you able to fight the urge and come in our direction instead?"

"Because I know you. I figured Holly did the pen trick, so you must have made everyone go that direction," Wyatt explained. "Trust me, there was an urgent need for me to go the opposite direction. Every fiber of my being wanted me to go the same direction as the other officers, but because of that, I knew I needed to do the opposite."

"So, you still felt propelled, right?"

"Yes. Why?"

"I know church took a lot out of me. I wanted to make sure I was still up to full strength," Blake said.

"You're fine. I'm not going to lie to you, your Dad may be another story."

"We haven't been able to get ahold of him all day," Hope said. "We called him before we talked to you guys at the restaurant. He didn't answer then either. We just figured he was in his shop or something."

"I would stick with the or something portion of that," Holly said. Suddenly feeling a rush of peace and calm, she turned to Blake, and said, "Save your strength. I need to be on edge."

"Fair enough," Blake said, crossing his arms. Leaning back in his seat, he added, "As long as you are clearheaded as well."

"I am. I know what I have to do," she defended herself.

"Which is?" Blake pressed.

"Get Dad. If he's not there, do as much damage as I can to hurt those who took him."

"Holly!" Hope said, appalled.

"They waited until we were away from him to take him. They waited until we were separated from the youth group kids and you two to try to take us. Both of those were in broad daylight. I promise you they won't be kind once we get there," Holly explained. "We're in the middle of nowhere out here."

"You can't hurt them," Blake said.

"Oh, I can hurt them," Holly countered. "I just won't kill them."

"Even though we've only been to church once, we know *thou shalt not kill* is in the commandments. I'm pretty sure that's a biggie," Blake added.

"It is one of them, yes," Hope said.

"And self-defense or defense of one we love is a viable reason to use this gift given to us," Holly countered. "Pretty sure God won't be angry if I defend you, Dad, Wyatt, or Blake."

"Just don't kill them," Hope asked.

"I won't…at least not on purpose," Holly corrected.

"Let's hope you won't have to hurt them," Wyatt said from the back seat.

Hope agreed, "That's my prayer."

⟐⟐⟐⟐

As they neared the house, Holly's nerves were more on edge. She understood Blake's desire to calm her. That was his assignment since they were little. However, she was certain this was what her dad was preparing her for all her life. All those training sessions in the forest of lifting trees, debris, etcetera. All those days of building strength one day, and yet turning around the next day learning control by picking up light things. He had her do technical building, as well as heavy lifting to make sure she could control her gift however she saw fit.

In the meantime, Blake's challenges were different. He would push all sorts of feelings with varying degrees of difficulty. There were also days where Ben would have Holly go into another room and he would test Blake by having him write down things Holly and Ben said to each other, and some things they thought about. They would then get together to confirm it. Blake was correct every time. Ben would push the distance between them, even to the point of one at one end of the ten acres and one at the other, and he still got it correct.

When Ben taught each of them to use their gift when they were younger, he made it into a game. One of Holly's favorites was moving the balls into the correct basket without touching them. Another was when Ben would let her cut loose with her gift, and Holly would make their stuffed animals dance in the air to the young Blake's delight. Blake, would play out stories in Holly's and Ben's minds that Holly created. Holly loved Blake's creativity and imagination in directing the scenes.

This situation, however, is nothing like they've ever faced before, and that put Holly on edge. She knew she had the stronger gift. She also understood the other girl had the same gift as hers. She hoped she would be the more powerful of the two. If the two were matched too closely, Holly might come out on the losing end of this…and so would her family.

A RACE AGAINST TIME

"Once you choose hope, anything's possible." Christopher Reeve

s they pulled into the driveway, the house was eerily still. As a matter of fact, there were no lights, no wind, and no movement anywhere.

The hairs on the back of Holly's neck stood on end. As she rubbed the back of her neck, she commented, "Something doesn't feel right. I mean, nothing about this situation is right, but something is very wrong."

"You're right," Blake said, looking around. "It's usually windy in October. It's dead still. This is like when a tornado comes through, only there's no green."

"Exactly!" Holly said, relieved he understood.

"What do you see?" Wyatt asked.

"Nothing. Absolutely nothing," Hope said, half to herself. Coming to a stop in front of the house, she put the car in park. "I don't want to go in there, but I know Ben needs us."

"He's not there. If he is, I'm being blocked like I was at the restaurant," Blake stated.

"How does someone block you from hearing their thoughts?" Hope asked.

"I don't know. They did at the restaurant, too. It was only for the two of them. I heard the guys with the guns."

"Okay," Hope said, taking a deep, cleansing breath. "Let's go."

Opening the door, Hope put her foot out. Hearing a crack in the distance, she stopped with her foot slightly outside the car, and froze. Seeing the pair from the restaurant walk out of the woods, she gulped. "Um, friends of yours?" Hope squeaked out.

"The two from the restaurant," Holly breathed out.

"You two take care of them. Hope, wait in the car until they're done. If those two are neutralized, we can all go inside together," Wyatt said from the floor of the backseat.

Hope brought her foot back inside the car and closed the door. "Agreed."

"Our turn, brother," Holly said, and the pair got out of the vehicle.

Splitting the distance, the two pairs of teens met in the middle. Blake was the first to speak. "Who are you?"

"Your brother and sister," the girl explained. "You know, the two left behind? We didn't get to grow up in this sweet little town, being homeschooled by mommy and daddy."

"What are your names?" Holly asked.

"Oh! I guess we didn't properly introduce ourselves earlier," the girl said. "My apologies. I'm Deanna and this is Adam. It seems we have the same father."

"You grew up in the lab," Blake said in understanding.

"Yes. And, you did not," Deanna said. "We waited until the appointed time to finally get the chance to meet you."

"Where's our dad?" Holly asked.

"Father is waiting for you in Maine," Adam said.

"No," Holly corrected, "our dad is Ben. Where is he?"

"No, he's not," Adam said. "Your dad is the same as ours."

"No." Holly crossed her arms. "Our dad is Ben. Our father is Professor Roth." Noticing the slight surprise on their faces, she continued, "Yes, mom and dad told us about the clinic. They told us everything. You two are not a surprise to us either. We're surprised you weren't here earlier. Now, where is our dad?"

"He's on his way to face the penalty for his actions," Adam said.

"What does that mean?" Blake asked, taken aback.

"He's on the way to the clinic to answer for taking the two of you so long ago. Your mom is about to face the same fate," Adam said, nodding toward the vehicle.

Holly and Blake turned to see several men with guns come from around the house, aimed right at Hope. Holly went to swipe them back, but Deanna threw Holly and Blake to the side in opposite directions.

Seeing Holly and Blake fly through the air, Hope threw her hands in the air in surrender. "Do not move," she ordered Wyatt. "The kids will need you to help them find us. Remember the clinic in Maine. Pretty sure that's where they're taking us."

"You're going to what?" Wyatt went to get up.

"Stay down!" Hope growled. "The kids need you!"

With that, she got out of the car. Closing the car door, she then put her hands in the air. Holly and Blake watched in horror as she got down on her knees. She was immediately surrounded by the men with the guns. She did not resist. She simply interlaced her hands behind her head, and allowed them to pull her up, zip-tie her hands behind her back, and lead her to a van around the corner.

"No!" Holly shouted, anger taking over. Holly shoved the van away from the men, who turned and pointed their weapons right at her.

"I suggest you control your temper," Deanna said calmly, "before it gets messy."

Narrowing her eyes, Holly stood, fists to her side.

"Holly, no," Blake pleaded. Due to the day's events, he knew there was no way he could control Holly's emotions as intense as they were at that point.

Holly picked up every man at least ten feet into the air. When Deanna went to stop Holly, Holly threw both her and Adam across the field. She was not taking chances with the two of them. Unsure as to the extent of either of their gifts, she sent them each into a tree, knocking them out.

While Holly was making sure to knock the pair out, one of the guys in the air got his gun up, and shot her in the leg. The searing pain sent her back off her feet, and she screamed as the guys all dropped to the ground with a thud.

The guys scrambled to their feet, grabbed Hope, and sped out before anything else could happen. Meanwhile, Blake ran over to Holly. He pressed on her thigh to stop the bleeding. The officers ran out of the woods, several running for the unconscious pair next to the trees.

Wyatt scrambled out of the car and ran for Blake and Holly, while on his phone calling for more police and an ambulance.

"No!" Blake shouted when Wyatt was part-way to them. "Go after Mom!"

Wyatt hesitated only a moment, before running back to the car to chase after Hope and the van full of gunmen. Kicking up a cloud of dust as he spun his tires, he peeled out of the driveway.

A female officer ran up to Blake and Holly. "You're going to be okay. There's an ambulance on the way." She pulled a handkerchief from her pocket and pressed it onto Holly's leg. "Don't move."

"Wasn't planning on it," Holly moaned, laying her head back onto the ground.

"How did you do that?" the officer asked. "That was amazing!"

"Not now. Talk to the Sheriff later," Blake said, keeping an eye in the distance on the unconscious pair. Turning back to the officer, he mentioned, "You may want to warn your friends over there that the girl can do the same thing Holly does, and the boy has his own gifts."

"Really?" the officer looked at him, stunned.

"Just warn them. I need to go check the house to see if Dad's there."

"Wait a second. Hey, Barnes!" the officer called to another. When he looked up, she waved him over. Once he was close enough, she asked, "Will you clear the house? Ben Hunt still hasn't been accounted for. Reynolds has gone after Hope Hunt."

"Got it," he said, and grabbed two other officers before going into the house.

"I want to go in too," Blake said.

"No. I don't think that's a good idea."

"I *want* to go in," Blake said, and pushed the thought into the officer's mind.

"Sure. Go ahead. There are a few others in there. You should be safe," the officer agreed.

"Go ahead," Holly said to Blake. "I want to know what's in there too."

While Holly stayed where she was, she kept an eye on the pair in the tree line. The officer with her warned the officers with the pair they were dangerous, so they handcuffed them even though they were unconscious. Holly could hear the ambulance in the distance coming their way.

As things settled outside, Blake took a deep breath before he pushed open the door. He was not prepared for what he walked into. The belongings in the home were tossed or broken. In the kitchen there was a large amount of blood all over their white tile flooring. In the dining room, there was a dining room chair coated in blood, with cut zip-ties on the floor.

Blake stared at it in horror, while one of the officers shouted, "Clear."

"Good," Officer Barnes said, as he stood in the kitchen watching Blake. "Are you okay, son?"

Blake shook his head, unable to tear his eyes away from the chair.

"Maybe we should get you outside?" Officer Barnes said, resting a hand on Blake's shoulder. With his other hand on Blake's arm, he to tried to turn Blake away. "You really shouldn't be in here. It's a crime scene."

Blake glared at the officer as he pushed the thoughts he could stay.

"Well, if he stays on the couch out of the way, he shouldn't be too much trouble," the officer in the kitchen suggested.

Officer Barnes released Blake. "Agreed."

Blake slowly moved to the couch, unable to look away from the chair. "That's a lot of blood."

"Yes, but not as much as you think," the officer he found out later was Officer Simmons, said.

"Right," Officer Barnes, said, "it is a fair amount, but not as much as it looks."

"It looks like they were painting the kitchen and dining room with his blood," Blake remarked. "Is he still alive with that amount gone?"

"With the amount here, there's no way he died from exsanguination," Officer Simmons pointed out. "I've seen crime scenes with a lot more blood where the victim still walked away."

"Okay," Blake said, and concentrated on reading their minds. From what he could tell, the officers were more confused than anything, waiting to see what the crime scene people said.

Hearing the ambulances pull up for Holly, Deanna, and

Adam, Blake scanned the scene in front of him more in-depth from his seat on the couch. That's when he saw it. There was a card tucked under the table on the floor.

Glancing at the officers, Blake shoved a thought into their minds.

"I'm going to go see if the others need help," Officer Barnes said. "With the way those other two behaved earlier, they may need the backup. Blake can watch the scene. Right?"

"Yep. It's not going anywhere," Blake agreed.

"I agree. Let's go," Officer Simmons said, and the three left.

"Finally," Blake said aloud to himself when the door closed behind them.

Going into the dining room, he was careful not to step in the blood. Reaching the table, he crouched down and picked up the card. It was a plain white card, containing only Professor Noah Roth's name, along with the address of the clinic.

It was as if The Professor knew Blake would be the one to find the card. Tucking it in his back pocket, he headed outside to ride with his sister in the ambulance to the hospital.

⊲⊕⊲⊕⊲⊕⊲⊕

BLAKE SAT in the waiting room of the hospital while Holly was in surgery to get the bullet out. While he was waiting, Blake pulled the card out of his pocket and looked at it. As he shifted it in his hand, he noticed a watermark in the lower corner. Tilting the card in the light, he saw a microchip embedded in the card. It was coated with white, so it was difficult to initially see.

He used his fingernail to dig around the microchip. After about fifteen minutes, he finally freed it from its casing. Taking a picture with his phone of the address of the clinic, he then threw the card in the trash.

Remembering Tanya and Megan were brilliant with computers, he debated for several minutes before he called Tanya using

145

Holly's phone. Holly got her number on the way to the restaurant.

"Hello?" she answered her phone.

"Tanya, this is Blake."

"Blake! Oh, my word! Are you okay! We were in the restaurant and saw people shooting at y'all, and then chasing the Sheriff's car!"

"Holly got shot, and is currently in surgery."

"We'll be right there!"

"Wait! Can you bring your computer with you? I found a microchip, and I want to know the information on it."

"Yes. I'll make sure to tell Megan to bring hers too. She's better than me. We'll be right there."

"Thank you. I'm in the waiting room. Hey, have you seen the news today?"

"No. Why?" she asked cautiously.

"They got my mom and dad. Wyatt took off after the van that grabbed Mom. I haven't heard from him yet. Pretty sure it would make the news."

"Uh…yeah. I'm sure it would. And, no. I haven't. Let me call everyone and we'll be right there."

"Thank you," Blake said, and hung up. Looking at his phone, he debated a few moments before he finally called Wyatt's cell phone.

"Hey, Blake," Wyatt answered.

"Did you get her?"

"No. I lost them when they were in Louisiana. I called ahead, and the state police met them at the border. A few stayed back to escort me. They tracked them via helicopter while the state police gave chase. They almost got them, until they lost them in some woody swampy area. I'm sorry."

"Holly's in surgery. The youth group kids are on their way. I found some things you'll need to know about."

"It'll take me a good forty-five minutes to get there. Can you tell me now?"

"No. Not over the phone."

"Got it. Okay. I'll meet you at the hospital as soon as I get back into town."

"Thank you," Blake said, and hung up. Sighing, he looked around. This sitting around was not working for him. He huffed as he crossed his arms in his seat. Knowing it would be at least twenty minutes before the rest of the group got there, he closed his eyes and starting reading minds out of pure boredom.

⧫⧫⧫⧫

WHEN TANYA WALKED in with the same group from lunch, Blake stood with a smile. She ran over and hugged him.

"I'm so happy you're in one piece," she said. "How's Holly?"

"She's out of surgery and in recovery," he explained as Megan and Lindsey also gave him a hug. "The doctor said everything went fine. He said she would have to stay here for three days in order to make sure there is no infection, but otherwise she should be okay."

"And your mom?" Megan asked.

"Lost," Blake said.

"Lost, as in gone?" Lindsey asked.

"No. Lost, as in the police couldn't catch them before they lost them in the swamps of Louisiana."

The words hung for a moment before Mac asked, "When can we see Holly?"

"She'll be in recovery for a bit longer, and then they'll move her to a room. That's when we can go up."

"What shape is she in?" Shawn asked.

"They shot her in the thigh," Blake explained. "She's more

angry than anything. She got distracted. That's when they got her."

"What exactly happened?" Colby asked. "We saw the guys with guns shooting at y'all. Speaking of which…why?"

"Well, that's a really long story." Blake's face flushed. "I'm not sure what I'm allowed to tell you."

"What happened to those men at the diner?" Lindsey asked. "They went flying through the air as if they were pulled by strings."

Face flushed again, Blake looked down at the ground in hopes of controlling his blushing.

"Who did that?" Megan asked. "How did who do that?"

"Well, I guess you'll know soon enough," Blake relented. Nervously rubbing the back of his neck, he admitted, "Holly and I have, um, gifts."

Shawn narrowed his eyes at Blake. "What does that mean?"

"Well, it's a genetic manipulation thing," Blake explained.

"What does *that* mean?" Colby asked.

"Okay, let's sit down. This will take a bit to explain." Blake gestured to a spot in the waiting room where there was no one else. Once everyone was settled close to Blake, he explained, "Okay, there's a clinic up in Maine…"

⟡⟡⟡⟡

"AND THAT BRINGS you all up to date," Blake said, finishing his story.

"Wow!" Mac shook his head. "Is this for real?"

"It's quite a story," Shawn said. "How do we know it's the truth?"

Blake's eyebrows arched in surprise. "Why would I make that up?"

"To try to impress us?" Shawn offered.

"Blake Hunt?" the nurse called.

"Right here," Blake said as he stood.

"She's in a room. If you would follow me, I'll take you to her," she said.

The group headed up in silence as they wrapped their brains around Blake's story.

HOLLY WAS AWAKE, but groggy when the crew walked into her room. "Hi guys," she said weakly.

"How are you feeling?" Colby asked, shoving his hands in his pockets as he stood next to her bed. The guys were on one side, and the girls were on the other.

"Had better days," she admitted.

"Heard an interesting story about you," Colby mentioned.

"Oh really? What would that be?"

"About a clinic, what you both can do, and about your siblings," he clarified.

Holly's eyes widened, and she quickly sobered. Looking to Blake for answers, she asked, "Why?"

"Because of what they saw at the restaurant," Blake defended himself. "Also, because we need them." He held up the microchip. "Speaking of which?"

"Oh yeah," Tanya said, taking it from him. She got Megan's attention, and the pair went over to the couch to work on their computers.

"Thank you," Blake said. Turning back to Holly, he asked, "How are you feeling now?"

"As I said, I've had better days," she repeated.

"So, is what he said true about you guys?" Mac asked. "Can you really move stuff with your mind?"

Holly's face flushed uncontrollably as her heart monitor took off. "Yes."

"Can you show us?" Shawn asked.

Holly looked around the room. "My head is a bit groggy, so it'll have to be something small." Seeing the girls working on the computer, she slowly raised them in the air, three feet off the couch where they sat with a computer on Megan's lap.

Tanya grinned. "Oh! This is wild!"

"And a little disturbing," Megan added.

"What?" Shawn turned toward them. Jaw-dropped, he said, "That is so cool!"

Exclamations of surprise were heard from the rest of the group, until Holly softly set them back down on the couch.

"Remind me to never get on your bad side," Mac said. "If that's small, I would be curious to see what you consider big!"

"You know, a vehicle, massive trees, semi-trucks, etcetera," Holly said nonchalantly.

"You can do that?" Colby asked.

"Yes," she admitted.

"Not sure if this is cool or scary," Lindsey commented under her breath.

"I think it's cool," Colby said. He winked at Holly, who smiled in response.

"Can you show us what you do?" Lindsey asked Blake.

"Okay," Blake said, thinking. "What about this?" He used his gift to allow a feeling of giddy. Everyone started giggling.

"Why are we laughing?" Tanya asked, cracking up.

"Honestly! Why?" Colby asked, laughing.

Blake immediately shifted to somber, and people started crying.

"I'm assuming this is you?" Shawn asked, wiping a tear off his face.

"Yes," Blake said, and then replaced all feelings in the room to peace.

Relief flooded everyone's body at once.

"That's sort of not cool," Megan said. "You can seriously control our feelings."

"It helps, especially when Holly's temper flares," Blake explained.

"He's helped me many times," Holly said.

Just then, there was a knock at the door.

"Come in," Holly called out.

"Well, how do you rate?" a male nurse said, chuckling, as he walked into the room. "You have several people already at your beck and call before I can even get your chart sorted."

Holly giggled. "They're from the youth group."

"I see. Then, if y'all are good, I'll let you stay in here. Don't get too rowdy though, or I'll have to ask you to keep it down to two or three."

"Yes, sir," Blake agreed. "By the way, I'm Blake, her brother," he said, shaking his hand.

"Trent," he said. "I'll be looking after her for today until seven, and tomorrow. I guess the plan is to release her the day after that if there are no signs of infection."

"That's what I heard," Blake said.

"My counterpart, Heather, will have her through the night for tonight and tomorrow night. She's nice, but a bit of a stickler. She's a mom of six, and makes sure her patients follow the rules just like her kids. She has what I call a mom brain." Trent smirked. "She treats everyone like her kids."

"Good to know."

"Where are your parents?" he asked, looking at the chart. "I see their names, but not their signatures on anything."

"That's, um…" Blake's voice faded, as he shoved his hands in his pockets. "You'll probably have to talk to Sheriff Reynolds regarding that."

"Is that why there are two police officers outside her room?"

"Yes."

"She looks innocent enough." Looking at Holly, Trent asked, "What did you do? Rob a bank? No. Wait! You murdered someone?"

Holly smiled. "No."

"She did knock two other people out," Wyatt said, coming into the room. "Pretty sure she won that battle."

"That's debatable," she said, looking down at her leg.

"Oh, I don't think so," Wyatt said. "I've already seen the other two. You're in much better shape."

"Okay. Since you're in here, I'm fixin' to scoot. I'll be at the nurse's station if you need anything," Trent said, and then left the room.

When the door was closed behind him, Blake turned to Wyatt. "They know everything."

"Who?" Wyatt asked.

"Everyone in this room," Blake said. Feeling the anxiety skyrocket, he sent a calm feeling to Wyatt.

"Thank you," Wyatt said, knowing Blake did it. "Um, why did you tell them?"

"Because we need their help."

"And, we already saw part of it at the restaurant," Shawn pointed out. "We really weren't going to let him get away with not telling us."

"We can be pretty persuasive when we want to," Linsey added.

"I would say you're more like nagging and annoying," Tanya said, as she and Megan were working on the computer. "Pushy even."

The guys stifled their laughter for Lindsey's sake. Linsey glared at Tanya. "Be nice."

"Actually, that was me being nice."

"Ladies," Mac said. "Let's not show our ugly side today. We have some things we have to figure out, starting with how to find their parents."

"True that," Colby said. "If it were me, I would be seriously freaked out!"

"We are," Blake said. "Trust me. I'm doing my best to keep a lid on the emotions in this room.”

“I can’t imagine that’s easy,” Wyatt snickered as he glanced at Tanya and Lindsey.

“No. It’s not. Maybe I’ll go grab a coke,” Blake said walking toward the door. “I need a break.”

“Can I walk with you?” Tanya jumped up from the couch. “I could use a coke too.”

“Wanna grab us some snacks while you two are down there?” Shawn asked, handing her several one-dollar bills. “Whatever you want to get. Pretty sure it’ll get eaten.”

“No problem,” she said, accepting the bills. When the door closed behind them, Tanya asked, “Wanna share some of that?”

“Some of what?” Blake asked, while they headed downstairs to the cafeteria.

“Those emotions. You may be able to suppress other’s emotions, but not your own.”

“What do you mean?”

Stopping, she stood in front of him with her arms crossed. “I mean I can feel what people are feeling. Not in the way you do, though. I can feel when people are angry. I can feel when people are upset. And, you are both angry and upset right now.”

He nodded in agreement.

“Good,” she said going back to his side so they could resume walking. “Nice to know you won’t lie to me.”

“I will avoid telling you things, but I won’t lie.”

“That would be a lie of omission.”

“I think of it more as protecting you,” Blake clarified. “I probably shouldn’t have told you all about our gifts, but I didn’t feel right not telling you. We’re heading into a mess. I may have to enlist your help, but from here.”

“That may not be up to you,” Tanya said.

“You guys can’t go with us. For one thing, your parents would definitely not approve.”

“This is true, but we want to help.”

"Help from here. I'm going to be worrying enough about Wyatt and Holly. I don't want to worry about the rest of you as well."

"Are we safe here?" she asked.

"What do you mean?"

"With what we know, are we safe?"

"I would think so. Well, I would hope so."

"Then, is leaving us behind a good thing? From what you told us, they could very well use us to get to you."

"I don't think so." He shook his head. "I'm pretty sure Professor Roth is doing this to get us back under his control."

"So, you think he'll keep them alive if you two turn yourselves in?"

"I don't know."

"Do you think he'll take them out anyway if you go?" she asked.

"I don't know the answer to that either."

"Is there a happy medium in this anywhere? If you guys go up there, they'll have you. They may still kill your parents."

"We'll have to wait until Holly's healthy enough before we go," Blake explained. "She's the stronger of the two of us. We'll need her if we have any chance of pulling this off at all."

"Do you have time to get her healthy before you guys leave?"

"We don't have a choice."

"It'll literally be days before she gets out of here. Then, she'll still not be up to full strength. You'll need her at full strength," Tanya said.

"Guess it's going to be a race against time."

"Kind of sounds like you're already on borrowed time."

"We are," Blake agreed.

"Then, I think we need to make sure to pray a lot!"

"Please, and thank you."

"Are you guys Christians?" Tanya asked.

"Not sure what that means?"

"You heard Pastor this morning in church. If you were to die today, and went to the gates of Heaven, what would you tell God when He asks you why He should let you into His Heaven?"

"I, uh, haven't ever thought of it, to be honest," he said, as they walked up to the vending machines.

"Why not?"

"Because while Mom told us a little, Dad asked her not to. She was pretty cryptic when it came to Christianity."

"Interesting. Well, do you have any questions?"

Putting money into the machine, Blake worked on buying several bags of chips before moving to the soda machine. "Yeah. Actually, I do. God is supposed to be a God of love, right?"

"Yes."

"And He's supposed to look out and take care of those who are His, correct?" Blake asked.

"Yes."

"Then why didn't He stop those men from taking my parents?"

"Ooo! Good question," she said, with a sly smile. "The answer to that would be sin."

While he liked Tanya's smile, his concern was for his parents at that moment. "What do you mean?" he asked, handing her the chips as he got them out of the machine.

"Well, when Adam and Eve sinned –"

"Who are Adam and Eve?" he asked, cutting her off.

"Oh dear! You really haven't been to church before, have you?" she asked.

Blake just shook his head as he moved to the soda machine.

"Okay, well, way back in the beginning, God created the world. After He created the planet itself, along with the vegetation, animals, sun, moon, and stars, He then created man, naming him Adam. He loved Adam, and even let him name all of the animals. He and Adam had a close relationship. After a little while, he noticed Adam was lonely. Yes, he had the animals, but in looking at all the male and female animals, God saw when Adam noticed there was no female for him. So, God put him to sleep. He used one of Adam's ribs to create a woman. Once Adam saw her, he loved her and looked after her. She was his. He named her Eve. While they had a close relationship, Adam and God still had a close relationship as well. Everything was good.

"Well, long before all that happened, there was an angel in Heaven named Lucifer. He was a powerful angel. Not only did he think he was better than God, but he also got other angels to follow him instead. When God found out, He kicked all of them out of Heaven.

"Fast-forwarding to the time of Adam and Eve, Lucifer saw the relationship of the trio. He also saw where God gave Adam and Eve access to everything on the land, except for a single tree. Lucifer knew he could use this to his advantage," she said, as they started back toward Holly's room. "You see, God told Adam he was not to eat any fruit from that tree. It's called the tree of *Knowledge of Good and Evil*. God knew once Adam ate of that fruit, Adam would be somewhat like Him. At that point, Adam only knew good. God knew as soon as Adam ate, he would know evil, and death would be inevitable. Satan, also known as Lucifer —"

"Now that name I've heard before."

"Good," she said with a smile. Knowing he was paying close attention, she continued, "So, Satan twisted Adam's warning to Eve about the tree, and he got Eve to eat the fruit. Then, Eve got Adam to eat the fruit, and they both knew they were naked."

"Naked?"

"Yes. They didn't realize it prior to that point, because they didn't know any better. Now, because Adam was naked, he was ashamed to meet with God, and hid when God searched for him."

"What did God do? Isn't He supposed to know everything?"

"Oh, He knew! And when He found Adam, He asked about it. Adam finally admitted to eating the fruit, but blamed Eve – the woman God gave him. When God turned to Eve, she blamed Satan, who at that point, was in the form of a snake. Neither took full responsibility for their actions."

"I see. That's disappointing."

"God thought so too, so He cursed them. Eve was cursed to have pain during childbirth. Adam was cursed to work for food. The snake was cursed to always live on the ground, able to be crushed underfoot."

"Got it, but –"

Tanya put her hand up to stop his objections, knowing what he was going to ask. "Bear with me a minute. You see, once that happened, they were tossed out of the garden – which is now guarded by angels with flaming swords. And once they ate, sin entered the world. Their one son even killed their other son out of jealousy. If you hear of Cain and Able, they were Adam and Eve's sons. Cain killed Able, but that's another story for later. Now back to your question. Sin is the culprit. At no point did God want people to become puppets. He gave us the curse and gift of free will. That free will can be used for good or evil."

"Kind of like our gifts?"

"Yes. Exactly like your gifts," Tanya said with a smile, loving that he was into what she was saying. "According to you, Holly and that other girl both have telekinesis."

"Right," he agreed.

"Well, Holly uses hers for good, while the other girl uses hers for evil. That evil is what took your parents. That evil is what got Holly shot while she was trying to do good. While your mom and dad did good by rescuing the pair of you from the clinic, it was still stealing. They kidnapped you."

"Professor Roth killed our mothers. Ben and Hope didn't want us to grow up as lab rats."

"Exactly. And, God is using this situation to make sure you are both on the good side of this, despite the circumstances. The gift is not good or evil. It's the person and heart behind the gift which makes it good or evil."

"I actually see your point," he said, as they got to the room.

"Good. We can talk more later if you want," she offered.

Pushing open the door, over his shoulder, he mentioned, "I would like that."

BUY TIME

"Life is 10% what happens to us and 90% how we react to it." Dennis P. Kimbro

Over the next few days Holly got better but also incredibly bored. She would make things dance in the room just to pass the time. She relished the time when the kids from the youth group came. Colby and Tanya would get there a few hours before the remainder of the group. This gave Holly and Colby, and Tanya and Blake some time to talk and get to know each other on a deeper level.

Any other time, Blake stayed in the room with Holly. He took a shower in the room, ate there, and slept on the couch. He was not going to let anyone get to Holly without a fight.

Wyatt was also in and out during that time. He kept a pulse on any news regarding Hope or Ben. He prayed his sources would come through with something…anything. He wanted some kind of sign that his love and his friend were both okay. In the meantime, he worked his normal hours, stopping in Holly's room at lunch and dinner time. It made him feel more connected to Hope to look after the pair.

"Well, your friends are still in here. They're heavily sedated, so they won't be able to use their powers until Holly's up to full strength enough to stop Deanna from using hers," Wyatt said, coming into the room. "Wanna hear some more interesting news?"

"Sure. It's obviously not about Mom or Dad, or you would have burst into the room," Blake pointed out.

"This is true," Wyatt agreed. "It's about Alex."

"Murphy? Dad's friend? What's going on?" Holly asked.

"Don't know. She didn't come in Monday morning. When I called, I got a disconnected message, so I went to her home. It was empty. It looked like no one ever lived there. Not even any mail."

"What do you know about her past?" Blake asked.

"I know she used to work for some detective agency. I can't remember the name at the moment, but she left that job to come here. She even had to go through a rough transition just to stay."

"She may be connected to the clinic." Blake rubbed his chin, thinking. "You said she started shortly after we got here."

"Correct," Wyatt said. "However, I called her on her duplicity."

"Did you check out the detective agency?" Holly asked.

"I did." Wyatt nodded. "When I talked to the detective over the phone, he confirmed she worked for him."

"What's the area code on the phone number?" Blake asked. "Do you remember?"

"I can find out after lunch," Wyatt offered.

"Maybe see in which state the agency is supposed to be in," Blake said. "That'll be enough for me."

"Done. I can call you when I get back to the office."

"Yeah. Just call the room here. Our cell phones are more than likely being tracked," Blake pointed out.

"I'll bring you both new phones when I come back tonight. In the meantime, hand me the ones you have."

"But the youth group kids only have our cell phone numbers," Blake objected.

"Text them. Have them call the room number." Wyatt put his hand out for the phones. "We can explain more tonight or tomorrow, whenever they come next."

"Okay," Blake said, and sent out a group text before handing Wyatt both his and Holly's phones.

"Thank you," he said, pulling the batteries from the phones before shoving them all into his backpack. "This way you're both off-grid. I have to keep mine, since mine's connected to my job."

"Do you think Mom and Dad are okay?" Holly asked.

"I honestly don't know. I hope so."

"We need to go to the clinic," Blake said. "That's where they are."

"I understand," Wyatt said, "but we need Holly up to full strength."

"That's not going to happen any time soon. I'll be on crutches for a few weeks at a minimum," Holly reminded him.

"But your head will be clear, right?" Wyatt asked.

"Yes."

"Good. When you're not on pain meds anymore, we'll wake your counterparts. Until then, I don't want them up," he said. "They're a dangerous pair. We know what she can do, but aren't one-hundred-percent certain as to what he can do. We know he has excellent hearing, but what else can he do?"

"That's a good question," Blake said. "I would be curious to find out what all he has in his arsenal."

"Actually, you may be the one who can find out," Holly pointed out.

"What do you mean?" Blake asked.

"Yeah. I don't follow," Wyatt said.

"Blake reads minds. Hello?" Holly reminded them. "Have him read their minds."

"Ooo! That would be interesting," Wyatt considered it. "What do you think, Blake? You up for it?"

"Sure." Blake shrugged. "I'm curious as to what's going through their minds."

"I'll arrange it," Wyatt said. "I want to be there for it. Give me a little time."

"I'll be right here," Blake gestured around the room. "As long as she's here, I'm here."

"Great! In the meantime, I have to get back to work," Wyatt said. "See y'all later." When he left, he closed the door behind him.

Once the door was closed, Holly asked, "Are you okay with that?"

"What? Reading their minds?"

"Yes."

"Sure. Why not? We may be able to find some useful information. In the meantime, I'm hoping with them in our custody, we're buying time for Mom and Dad."

"Me too," Holly said, nibbling on her nails. "I want to be strong enough to shut them down for good once we get there."

"Holly, do you think we're the only ones?"

"What do you mean?"

"He did it successfully four times, right?"

"Yes."

"Do you think he repeated the experiment? Do you think there are more like us out there?"

"I don't know. That's a good question. You may be able to find that out when you probe around in their minds."

"Let's hope it doesn't scar me for life!" Blake said with a smirk.

Holly smiled. "Pretty sure you can handle it."

"Meh. I can handle pretty much anything thrown at me, with the exception of losing my family."

⟐⟐⟐⟐

THAT NIGHT, Blake pushed Holly in the wheelchair while Wyatt walked beside them. As they headed to the room with Deanna and Adam, Wyatt mentioned, "The number for the detective agency is out of Maine. You don't have to tell me. I know what that means."

"She was with the clinic," Holly said.

"Yep."

"I don't know." Blake shook his head. "I didn't get that from her. She was all-in here."

"You think she was originally with the clinic, and when they grabbed Ben they grabbed her too?" Holly asked.

"It's possible," Wyatt acknowledged. "Blake, are you sure you want to do this? Not sure I would want to poke around someone's brain."

"It's the only way we'll get information from them. I promise you they won't give it up willingly," Blake pointed out.

"Fair enough," Wyatt agreed. Walking up to the room, where there were four police officers guarding the door, Wyatt acknowledged them as the trio went into the room. With him being the Sheriff, they obviously knew who he was, so they let him through. "Well, glad they're resting well," he commented, as Deanna and Adam were each in a bed, heavily sedated.

"Not sure how well they're resting, but they are drugged," Blake countered.

Wyatt gestured toward the two sleeping in the beds. "Well, do your thing."

"I'm right here," Holly encouraged. "I'm keeping a close eye on them as well."

"That would be appreciated," Blake said, standing beside

Deanna's bed first. Taking a deep breath, he rested his hands on both sides of her head. He closed his eyes to focus and sort through the myriad of memories.

⸺⸺⸺

DARKNESS. Screams. Yelling. Berating. So many traumatic memories. It took Blake a few minutes before he could focus on a single thought…

"You know what you need to do! Why do you choose not do it?" Professor Roth demanded of four-year-old Deanna.

Deanna's bottom lip trembled as her big brown eyes looked up at him. "I'm sorry, Daddy."

"You are sorry!" He snarled. "You need to do this! Do it now or you will regret it!"

"No. I'm tired," she whined. "I want to stop for the day."

"You want to stop for the day? Really? You know what happens when you refuse me."

"Please, Daddy? I'm tired."

"I don't have time for this. Put her in solitary and let her think about whether she wants to cooperate," Professor Roth said as he waved her off. "Make sure her rabbit is not with her!"

"Yes, sir," the nurse said, as she took the hand of the little girl. "Come on, Deanna."

Deanna took her hand, and they walked down the long hallway. In a gray sweatshirt, sweatpants, and a pair of hospital socks, the little girl clutched her stuffed rabbit for dear life. The bunny was her lifeline. He was her relief during those hard days. The bunny knew her thoughts and feelings. He comforted her while she cried. He sat on her lap while she read. Each child did not have much, but each one had a precious stuffed animal that was theirs, and theirs only. That was the one thing they did not have to share.

As they passed the kid's bedroom, Deanna stopped and looked in. "I want to be with the others."

"I'm sorry, but your Daddy has a different plan," the nurse explained. "He wants all of you to be strong. You will get the others in trouble if you don't do what The Professor wants you to do next time."

"What do you mean?" Deanna asked, horrified.

Kneeling in front of her, the nurse explained, "He sees the bond you kids share. If you're not careful, and do what he wants, he'll use that against you. He'll hurt them to make you do what he wants. You don't want that, do you?"

"No! Why would he hurt them? I'm the one getting into trouble!"

"He knows who is close in that room. He's well aware of just how close you and Adam are to each other," she said, glancing into the room.

There were three sets of twin-sized beds on one side of the room, and four on the other. Each metal bed had white sheets, blankets, and a single pillow. The girls were on one side, and the boys were on the opposite. At the far end of the room was a table for coloring, along with a shelf containing blocks, small cars, crayons, coloring books, and books for reading. Each child had one stuffed animal precious to them. Otherwise, there were no other stuffed animals. There were no dolls. There were no decorations on the walls.

"He sees a lot more than you think," the nurse continued. "Mark my words: he will use the others to make you cooperate. Focus, and do what he wants you to do." Standing, the nurse took Deanna's hand and tugged her down the hall again.

Looking in as they passed the door, Deanna saw Adam and Eddie laughing as they played with blocks, building the tallest building they could; Gemma and Freya coloring at the table; and Charlie and Isabelle reading a book on Isabelle's bed. Deanna longed to be in there with the other kids.

Deanna and the nurse walked down the hall, before they walked down three sets of stairs. To Deanna, the further down they went, the darker and more stifling it felt. As they walked into the hallway after the three flights of stairs, Deanna felt like she was suffocating. She experienced these rooms more than she wanted. She cringed as they walked into a hall lined with five metal doors on each side…no windows. Stopping, Deanna planted her feet. She knew where they were. This was a punishment she endured frequently.

"No, honey. Come on. We're almost there," the nurse coaxed.

"I want to go back to the room," Deanna insisted. She clutched her bunny while pulling away from the nurse.

"Come on, Deanna," the nurse coaxed. When the nurse tugged on her hand again, Deanna dropped to the floor, unwilling to walk. The nurse picked Deanna up by the wrist and dragged her to the door.

As they stood in front of door number four, Deanna realized her plan was not working. So, she scrambled off the floor while the nurse got the door opened. Once the door was open, the nurse chased Deanna. Catching her, she carried Deanna to the room, with Deanna kicking and screaming.

As they stood in front of the door, Deanna looked up at the nurse with her big brown tear-filled eyes. Her ponytails looked disheveled after the struggle. "Please, no," she begged, clutching the bunny. "Please don't put me in there."

"I'm sorry," the nurse said, setting the little girl down in front of the room. There were no windows. The walls were metal, painted orange, and the floor was concrete. There was a commode in the corner with a small sink next to it. Other than that, the six-by-six-foot room was bare. Food would be delivered three times a day via the tiny door at the bottom of the metal door. A tray would be slid into the room. The only light in the space, was a single bulb in the ceiling in the center of the room. Dismal was a kind word for it.

Thrusting Deanna into the room, the nurse grabbed for the rabbit. Deanna held onto it with both of her hands and a tug of war ensued over the bunny.

"You can't have it!" the nurse yelled. "Your Daddy said no!"

"I want it!" Deanna shouted.

"No!"

"Yes!"

The nurse let go of the bunny, and Deanna fell backward, hitting the ground hard. She momentarily let go of the bunny to stop herself from sliding. As soon as Deanna let go of the bunny, the nurse grabbed it. Deanna screamed, "No! Mine!" She scrambled to her feet to get to the bunny. The nurse looked sympathetically at her briefly before she ran out of the room, slamming the door behind her. Deanna froze when she heard the lock click into place.

"Whew!" the nurse said, breathing heavily. She clutched the bunny as she leaned against the door.

Hearing the small voice screaming and crying as she pounded her little fists on the metal door, the nurse hung her head and slouched her shoulders. She knew little Deanna's hands would be bloody from pounding on the door. Knowing Deanna could move the sliding locks with her mind, the nurse secured the padlock before she left. She could not help the tears that crawled down her cheeks while she walked away.

⬥⬥⬥⬥

"Give me back my bunny!" five-year-old Deanna said, pulling her bunny away from Freya.

Freya tugged on the stuffed rabbit. "No! I want to play with it!"

Deanna thrust her hand forward, shoving Freya back without touching her. Once Gemma saw that, she came to the defense of her twin sister. Gemma shoved Deanna back several feet without touching her. All three girls had the gift of telekinesis.

Once Freya got to her feet, she ran over and pushed Deanna, jerking on the stuffed bunny. "Gimme that!"

"No!" Deanna shouted.

Gemma got up and physically shoved Deanna. "Leave my sister alone!"

"She's my sister too!" Deanna yelled back. Feeling backed into a corner, Deanna yelled, "Leave me alone or you will get in trouble!"

"She's my twin!" Gemma said. "Don't hurt her!"

"She tried to take my bunny! It's mine! Not hers! She has a koala!"

"Gimme!" Freya said, grabbing for Deanna's bunny again.

"Stop it!" Isabelle shouted, running between the three, trying to make peace. "Freya, that's Deanna's."

"Not your fight!" Freya snapped, and shoved Isabelle against the wall. When she did that, Charlie jumped up to defend his best friend.

When Charlie jumped up, Eddie and Adam ran over to help as well. The mound of children pushing, hitting, yelling, and shoving made it difficult to distinguish who was who.

When Charlie, Eddie, and Adam tried to separate them, the girls waved their hands, throwing the boys through the air in various directions. Charlie hit his head on the wall, actually cracking the wall. He slid down, leaving a trail of blood on the wall. Slouching, Charlie was unconscious by the time he got to the floor. As Adam slid down the hall, he curled up into a ball on instinct. When he stopped at the door, his behind is what hit, cushioning the blow. He quickly scrambled up and hit the alarm button on the wall. Eddie flew through the air, landing on the floor a foot before the staircase. The momentum propelled him through the open door, sending Eddie bouncing down the staircase.

The nurses and security arrived quickly after the alarm went off. However, the damage was done. The three girls were sent into isolation. Adam was checked out and released.

Charlie and Eddie went into the hospital portion of the clinic. Charlie had brain damage. After that, he started having seizures and his nose bled whenever he used his telekinesis.

Eddie broke his back. He woke with no feeling below his waist. Eddie was unique among the kids. While he was born with the gene, there was no visible gift that surfaced. Unfortunately, his mother died at childbirth, so Professor Roth raised him with the other children. Now, with Eddie in a wheelchair, this just added another element that made Eddie different from the other children. He went through several surgeries before he could return to the room, permanently in a wheelchair.

From that point forward, the other kids looked after both Charlie and Eddie. As a group, they saw the damage their gifts could cause, so it initially made them anxious to use them at all. They made a promise among each other to not use them against each other ever again. They also promised to do their best to protect Eddie and Charlie.

To them, their Daddy was mean, but they had to do what he wanted or face the consequences. They were pushed and tested frequently. While Eddie joined them when they did school work, during the trials as the kids called them, Eddie simply observed.

⟡⟡⟡⟡

"Now!" Professor Roth demanded.

"Yes, sir," a seven-year-old Deanna said solemnly.

Staring into another room, The Professor watched as the table rose from the ground about three feet.

"Good girl. Now, gently set it down," Professor Roth instructed.

Deanna set the table down.

"Good girl. Do it again."

Deanna looked toward the other rooms where she could see the other kids doing similar experiments. Charlie was in a room by himself. He lifted a table, and set it back down. The twins, Freya and Gemma, were taking turns with their telekinesis, lifting weights of different colors and weight amounts, sorting them by color. Isabelle was glaring at the nurse in the room with her. Her test was to read the mind of the nurse as she flipped a card up from the stack. The nurse would see the card, and Isabelle was to tell her what it was, like reverse flashcards. Adam was in a room with a whiteboard. Even at seven years old, Adam did phenomenally difficult calculations. He was to predict outcomes to certain situations. He was accurate one-hundred percent of the time. He never made a mistake. It was as if his mind worked faster than time itself. Meanwhile, Eddie was in the observatory room watching all the children from above.

"Again," the male nurse with Charlie instructed. "Your daddy wants you to do it several more times to strengthen you."

"I can't. My head hurts," Charlie complained, wiping away the blood from his nose.

"Do it, or it's solitary," the nurse warned.

Charlie grunted in agony, as he grabbed his head with both hands.

"Now," the nurse commanded.

Charlie let out a yell. The table went flying across the room, slamming the nurse into the wall with the table. In that instant, Charlie's eyes rolled to the back of his head. His nose and ears bled, as he dropped to the ground in a seizure.

"Professor Roth and Medical to room C," came over the intercom. "Professor Roth and Medical to room C."

⊕⊕⊕⊕

Nine-year-old Deanna stood in a sixty-by-eighty-five-foot room made of concrete with Gemma and Freya. Adam and Isabelle were in their own trials. Unfortunately, Charlie was not there. His seizures progressively got worse each time he was pushed. A few weeks ago, he was pushed to the point that the seizure was too strong for him to recover from, and he died. This threw the kids further than the clinic could handle. They had to give the children about a week before any of them would use their gifts again. This day was the first set of trials since they lost Charlie.

Within the massive room, there was a window which ran the length of the room along the top, creating a viewing room. The glass was three-and-a-half-inch thick bulletproof glass. This allowed Professor Roth, along with several staff members to watch safely.

Eddie was in a wheelchair in the observation room as well. His normal vantage point allowed him to see all the rooms and observe all the trials. It allowed him to watch as the nurses showed the kids various tricks. It also allowed him to take mental notes on how the kids were pushed to do amazing things.

There were several items in the room with Deanna, Freya, and Gemma. There was a semi-truck and trailer, a giant log, a five-hundred-pound weight, a feather, a car, a stocked bookshelf, a barrel of water, and a kite on the table.

"Okay, Deanna, pick up the car first," Professor Roth instructed.

"When do we get to see Adam and Isabelle?" she asked. The nurses separated the kids the prior night. This was considered exam time for them. The two different groups had these once a week. They would push the kids beyond what they thought capable, to see just how strong they were. One from each group would win the trials. The winners were given the special treat of watching a movie, along with eating popcorn and drinking a root beer. The movies were all documentaries.

To the average child, this would be boring. However, to the child who does not know any better, it was fascinating to see other people and situations in the world outside of the clinic. The kids each longed to find out what life was like outside the walls of the compound.

"When you complete the trials," The Professor said to Deanna. "They're doing their trials as well."

"He said his was tomorrow, not today. I want to see Adam," she demanded. She and Adam were very close. They were not twins, but they were inseparable.

"You'll see him when you complete your trials," Professor Roth said sternly as he crossed his arms. "Now, move the car over three feet."

Deanna crossed her arms and stomped her foot in defiance.

"Do you want to quit for the day?" Professor Roth asked, raising an eyebrow. "You know what happens when you decide to quit early."

"No." Deanna shook her head as her shoulders slumped. She sighed, before focusing on the car. Reaching her hands out, she grunted and groaned for a few minutes, until the car finally rose from the ground. She moved it three feet, and then let it go.

When it slammed onto the ground, Professor Roth said, "Next time set it down gently."

Deanna narrowed her eyes at The Professor as she wiped the sweat off her face.

"Now, pick up the kite," he instructed.

Deanna scanned the items in the room. Done with this test and her dad's attitude, she glanced at the viewing area. Picking up the five-hundred-pound weight, she slammed it into the glass of the viewing room. The window cracked, so she slammed it over and over again.

Just as she was about to crack through the glass, she heard the door open behind her. Four security guards ran in and tackled her. When she hit the ground, one of them injected her with a sedative while the twins cowered in the corner, afraid they were next.

Squirming underneath the four officers, Deanna felt the familiar wave wash over her. She was in trouble again. She knew this meant she would not see Adam for several days while she sat in the dimly lit six-by-six-foot hole in the wall called isolation room four.

SEVERAL DAYS LATER, Deanna was brought back to the trial room. The same objects were in the room, along with The Professor and Adam. Adam had a bruise on his cheek, while The Professor held his arm tightly. Deanna saw the bruises forming under The Professor's grip. The other kids were all watching from the observation room.

"You want me to hurt Adam?" The Professor asked.

"N-no," Deanna stammered, seeing the tears already in Adam's eyes.

"Then, you do as you are told. Understand?"

"You hurt Adam because I didn't do what you wanted?"

"I have before. Why did you think that would change? You will do as you are told. Do you understand?" he demanded. He used the twins against each other, and before Charlie passed, Isabelle and Charlie were used against each other. When the one did not cooperate, the other would face the consequences. Since Charlie's passing, Isabelle was threatened to 'join Charlie where he was if she did not cooperate.'

"Yes, sir," Deanna said somberly.

"Now, move the car three feet," Professor instructed.

Deanna complied, this time setting the car down gently.

"Pick up the kite gently, and set it on top of the car," The Professor instructed.

Deanna did as she was told.

"Pick up the log, and set part of it on the big truck, and part on the car and kite."

The log was massive. Deanna picked it up, and carefully maneuvered it so it was positioned on top of the truck. She set it down to take a breather.

As soon as she did, The Professor slapped Adam.

Hearing Adam yelp, and then seeing him cover the spot with his hand, Deanna quickly picked up the log and positioned it correctly.

"Now, place a feather on top of the log...gently," The Professor said, with a hint of satisfaction in his voice.

Deanna looked over at him, anger churning inside her.

"Do it!"

Narrowing her eyes at him, she waved her hand through the air, and threw The Professor across the room. When he hit the wall, he groaned as he dropped to the ground. Deanna placed the feather on the log, and then ran over to Adam. "Are you okay?"

"He won't be happy," Adam warned.

"I don't care! He hurt you! Are you okay?"

Adam glanced from her, to The Professor, and back again. "We need to go!" He grabbed her hand, and together, they ran for the door. When the door opened, Deanna gasped. There were four big guys standing in front of them blocking their exit.

She waved her hands in two different directions, sending them by pairs into opposite walls. Adam stood slightly back, as Deanna snapped the neck of one of the guys. Then, she broke the leg of another. Turning toward the other two, she slammed their heads together. When one scrambled up, she threw him against the wall, cracking his head. Blood coated the wall as he slid down.

Grabbing Adam's hand again, she started to run, only to see that Professor Roth had Adam's other hand.

"Deanna?" Adam whimpered.

"Where do you think you're going?" The Professor demanded.

"I-I-I…please don't hurt him?" Deanna's bottom lip trembled, as she looked from Adam to Professor Roth. "Please don't hurt him, Daddy."

"You disobeyed me again. Hurting you does not seem to work."

"I obeyed you. The feather is on the log," she protested.

He turned to see if she was telling the truth. When he saw the feather on the log, and the shape his men were in, he knelt in front of Deanna, and said, "You have a stubborn streak in you that needs to be broken. You will listen to me. Do you understand?"

Tears crawled down her cheeks as her tiny body shook. "Wh-what are you going to do?" she asked.

"What happens when you disobey?" he asked.

"But, I didn't! I moved the feather."

"Deanna, you hurt me, and really hurt these men. At least two are dead. You killed two of my men!" Professor Roth snapped.

"But, I –"

Before she could say another word, she felt the all-to-familiar prick of the needle jam into her arm. The wave washed over her, as she dropped to her knees, and the darkness took over her body once again. She groaned, knowing she would wake in room four.

⬩⬩⬩⬩

Waking up several hours later, she was in the isolation room once again. She closed her eyes, imagining what life was like outside the walls of the clinic. Here, she was tortured and forced to do things, bad things, against her will. She heard there were two more just like her and the other kids out there. The Professor would periodically refer to them, saying that the kids at the clinic were stronger because the other two did not train. He insisted they be stronger than the other two.

"You need to be stronger!" The Professor shouted at the children. "You will be the only ones who can take them out!"

"But they're my brother and sister too," Deanna said, confused and hurt at the same time.

"You must kill them!"

"Why?"

"If you don't, they will kill you. It is either you, or them. Do you understand? It's you, or them!"

⟨⟩⟨⟩⟨⟩⟨⟩

THIRTEEN-YEAR-OLD DEANNA WAS in the trial room once again. This was Adam's trial, though. He was blindfolded as he sat at a table also in the trial room. Adam had a headset on, connected to Professor Roth, who was in the observation room. Adam's job was to tell The Professor what Deanna would pick up before she did it. Her job was to move something at random in the trial room with them. She also had on a noise-canceling headset so she could not hear Adam. The only person she could hear was The Professor. He had to flip channels, depending on who he was speaking with at the time.

Into his headset, Adam quietly said, "Barrel of water."

"Okay, Deanna, pick an item and move it," The Professor instructed into Deanna's headset.

Deanna surveyed the room. There were certain items she normally picked up. Deciding to throw The Professor's experiment off, she picked up an item that was not normally chosen.

When she moved the heavy water barrel, the scientists in the observation room cheered. Furrowing her brow, she made a conscious decision to throw the test off as much as possible.

"The semi-truck across the room," Adam said into his headset.

"Go ahead, Deanna," The Professor said.

Deanna, her stubborn streak kicking into gear, flipped the semi-truck across the room. When it hit the wall, the crash was ear-shattering, and the debris sprayed all over the room. Adam flipped the table to escape getting impaled from the debris. He knew it was coming. Deanna's temperament toward The Professor was at an all-time high. Deanna was across the room from the truck, so she ducked behind the car to escape the massive amounts of flying debris.

The door to the trial room flew open. Multiple security and scientists ran into the room, splitting between the pair to make sure they were okay.

Meanwhile, Professor Roth stayed where he stood in the observation room. "You will regret that," he warned Deanna into her headset. She was the only one to hear it.

Turning toward The Professor, she narrowed her eyes at him in defiance. He just laughed an evil laugh.

⬥⬥⬥⬥

"YOU WILL GO DOWN THERE and you will kill them!" The Professor shouted. "This is what we have worked for years to accomplish!"

"They are my brother and sister!" Sixteen-year-old Deanna shouted back.

"We don't want to kill them!" Adam insisted.

"You will!" The Professor demanded.

"Why?" Deanna challenged. "Where are the others?"

"Freya, Gemma, and Isabelle are busy," The Professor explained. "This is your assignment. If you do not kill the other two, I will send my men after you, and they will kill all four of you!"

"Won't killing us ruin all your work? You said it took you twenty years to get us!" Deanna objected.

"Ask your brother if I would kill you," Professor Roth challenged.

When Deanna turned to Adam, Adam simply nodded in response.

"But, we're your life's work," Deanna objected. "You've told us that many times."

"If you fail, there are other groups," The Professor said with a tone of satisfaction.

"There are?" Deanna said, stunned. "Where?"

"That's my secret," The Professor said. "You don't seriously think your group was the only one? There are other compounds."

"Why have we not seen them before?" Deanna asked.

Adam rested his hand on Deanna's arm and shook his head. "You need to stop," he said. "We have a job to do."

"Have you run the numbers?" Deanna asked Adam.

"Yes."

"And?"

"I'll tell you on the way. We need to go."

"Your bags are packed. You leave in an hour. Take the time to prepare," The Professor said, and left the room.

Once he was gone, Adam whispered, "The room has cameras. But, know we won't succeed. While we have strength, they have something stronger."

"What's stronger than strength?" Deanna asked, confused.

"Love."

◑◑◑◑

"Wow," Blake said, standing up as he took his hands off her head. "They had an extremely rough childhood. Next time we see them, remind me to thank Mom and Dad profusely for what they did for us by getting us out."

"What happened?" Holly asked.

"Long story. We'll talk about it in the room. In the meantime, I need to move to Adam."

"Go ahead," Wyatt said. "They're still out, and Holly won't let anything happen to you while you're in there."

Blake nodded, and then moved over to Adam's bed. Resting his hands on either side of Adam's head, Blake closed his eyes to concentrate.

⟨⟨⟨⟩⟩⟩

Six-year-old Adam sat in a room. Freya, Gemma, Eddie, Charlie, and Isabelle were coloring, but Deanna was nowhere to be found. He knew his sister had done something to anger Daddy again.

"Morning, Adam," Professor Roth said, coming into the room.

"Morning, Daddy," Adam responded. "Do I get to see Deanna today?"

"That depends on her."

"What did she do?"

"She disobeyed…again. I'll have to use a different tactic today. Come. We have some work to do."

"Yes, sir," Adam said, climbing out of bed. Leaving his stuffed bear on the bed, he followed his daddy out of the room.

When they walked into the concrete room, Deanna was already in there. She glanced from Adam to The Professor, nervous as to what this meant.

"You will obey today," The Professor insisted.

Deanna did not say a word.

Adam's stomach churned. He ran the calculations through his mind. He knew what was coming if she did not obey. There was no question in his mind as to what was about to happen to him.

"Move the weight from that side of the room to the other side," The Professor instructed.

Deanna crossed her arms as she shook her head.

"Move it!" The Professor insisted.

Deanna shook her head again.

The Professor left Deanna and Adam in the room for a moment. Adam's heart raced at what he knew was coming. He studied people and could gauge their reactions with one-hundred-percent accuracy. His brain worked quickly, almost faster than time itself. His ability was kin to precognition.

The Professor sat Adam down on a chair. He then zip-tied Adam's wrists and ankles to the chair. Adam's heart raced. He gulped as he looked wide-eyed at Deanna.

The Professor leaned on the back of the chair with his hands. "Move the weight across the room."

Deanna stood her ground. "No!"

The Professor nodded toward the guard at the door. The guard walked over to Adam and slammed his nightstick onto the top of Adam's hand. Adam let out a shrill scream, as his hand immediately pulsated in sheer pain and agony.

Deanna stood there, jaw-dropped and frozen.

"Move it, NOW!" The Professor shouted.

Deanna picked up the weight with her mind, and flew it across the room, narrowly missing the trio.

"That was uncalled for!" The Professor snapped. "You need more quiet time?"

"No, I…no!" Deanna said. "I moved it!"

"You almost hit us!"

"Deanna, please do as…." Adam sniffed. His tears continued to stream down his cheeks. "Please?"

Deanna nodded. "Don't hurt him anymore!"

"Then, do what you are told."

"Yes, sir."

◁◁◁◁

"TELL me what it says at the beginning of chapter 43?" The Professor instructed. He had *Pride and Prejudice,* a book open that ten-year-old Adam read four days ago.

"It says, '*Elizabeth, as they drove along, watched for the first appearance of Pemberley Woods with some perturbation; and when at length they turned –*'"

"That's enough," The Professor cut him off. He opened *The Great Gatsby,* a book Adam read about a year ago, and said, "Start chapter five."

"*When I came home to West Egg that night I was afraid for a moment that my house was on fire. Two o'clock and the whole corner of the peninsula was blazing with light which –*"

"Good. Very good. Now, do these math equations," The Professor said, handing him two pages of calculus equations.

Adam quickly scribbled the answers without working out the problems manually. He did them in his head in an instant. It was as if his brain worked on overdrive.

Handing the pages back, he held his breath while The Professor checked the answers with the answer key. "Excellent. Your math and retention skills are remarkable." Folding his hands in front of him, The Professor said, "I'm going to give you a challenge."

"Okay."

"Here is a stack of files from a few serial killer cases. I want you to read this stack of evidence, and tell me what you think this man looks like and acts like. And, if you know who did it, tell me. There are three stacks. You have two hours."

"Yes, sir," Adam said, and immediately went to work.

Studying serial killer after serial killer, the accuracy in which he profiled the killers was nothing short of remarkable. He was able to tell The Professor by name who did it, without initially knowing anything about the case before looking at the files.

However, reading file after file, seeing the horrific pictures, and what one human did to another was traumatic. The darkness was unmistakable, especially since he could not forget anything he read. His ten-year-old mind had difficulty processing what he had read, and why one human would do this to another.

⟨D⟨D⟨D⟨D

"WE'RE GOING to test your amazing hearing abilities today," The Professor said to twelve-year-old Adam, as they sat in a room with a table and two chairs.

"Yes, sir. May I see Deanna today?"

"That depends on Deanna," The Professor said.

"Yes, sir," Adam said. Over the years, he took a number of beatings. He knew better than to challenge Daddy at all. Deanna did it all the time, and more times than not, Adam paid the price.

"Okay, there is a man two doors down. He will say words, and I want you to tell me what he says."

"Yes, sir," Adam agreed.

The Professor had an earbud in his ear to hear the man in the other room. With each word the man spoke, Adam repeated it word-for-word.

"Okay, move him two more doors down," The Professor instructed one of the nurses. Turning to Adam, he explained, "I'm going to go to the observation room, which allows me to hear what you say. I will still be able to hear the man. I want you to tell me what the man says. This way, I can be sure you are not hearing it from the earbud."

"Yes, sir," Adam said. Adam complied with The Professor. He saw what Deanna and the others endured when they did not obey. He and Isabelle were the two peacemakers of the group. They were also the two mind readers. In addition to that gift, Adam could calculate people and equations at unprecedented and incalculable speed, predicting how someone would react. Meanwhile, Isabelle could project feelings onto others. She often used her gift to keep the kids in the room calm. After the incident regarding Eddie and Charlie, she made it a priority to keep the gifted group as peaceful as possible so no more gifts got out of hand.

Adam did as he was told. He passed the test. When he finished, The Professor gave him more cases to study and identify who the perpetrator was in the situation.

Adam sighed as he opened the file. He hoped, with every bone in his body, the people outside the walls of the clinic were not really like those within the files. The visions of mutilated bodies and dark, sinister people often gave him night terrors. He did not want to look at them anymore, but he had seen what happened to Deanna, so he complied.

◁▷◁▷

FIFTEEN-YEAR-OLD ADAM WAS LYING on his bed reading a book when Eddie wheeled up to his bed. "What's up?" Adam asked, setting the book aside.

"What would you do if you could get out of here?" Eddie asked. "If you could get out past the walls of this clinic, out into the real world, what would you do?"

"That's easy. Deanna and I are being trained to take out the other two."

"Why though?"

"Because that's what the Daddy wants."

"Why though?" Eddie challenged. "Why does he want you to kill our brother and sister? What's the logic behind it?"

"What are you thinking?" Adam asked, sitting up. "You know you're the only person in this entire place whose mind I can't read? Daddy forbids me to read his thoughts, but I sometimes try to look. I can get some things, but he is difficult to read over the anger. However, I can't read yours no matter what I try."

"I know."

"Why is that?"

"Not sure," Eddie said, sitting back in his wheelchair, resting his hands on his lap. He knew full well as to the reason why Adam could not read his mind. "But that doesn't answer my question."

"When I look into Daddy's mind, all I get is a bunch of red – anger. He's furious those two nurses took two of his prodigies away," Adam explained. "Holly's stronger than he wants to let on. So is Blake."

"What do you mean?" Eddie asked.

"Blake's brain dives deeper than even he knows. He can push thoughts into a person's mind, and not just as an influencer. When he pushes it, he can actually make someone do something against their will. He doesn't know just how strong he is. As for Holly, all she thinks she can do is telekinesis, but she's wrong. If she pushes, she can do more than that. They also can talk to each other without verbally speaking with each other."

"How do you know?"

"I study patterns. As you know, I can sort of predict the future."

"True," Eddie said, stroking his chin in thought. Leaning forward, he asked, "Knowing you the way I do, what do you think will happen if he doesn't get those two back?"

"He will kill everyone he has to in order to get them back."

"What about them? What if they choose not to come back?" Eddie asked.

"I don't think I want to know what he'll do. I don't think he'll give them a choice either."

"Think with me here. What do you think he'll do?"

"He'll go ballistic."

⬦⬦⬦⬦

"Wow," Blake said, taking a step back from Adam. He backed all the way to the couch, and sat down. Dropping his head into his hands, he took deep, cleansing breaths as the visions spun around at a dizzying pace through his mind.

"Care to share some of that?" Holly asked.

"Not here. Let's go," Blake said, getting off the couch. "In the meantime, keep them heavily sedated."

MAKE UP FOR LOST TIME

"Do what is right, not what is easy nor what is popular." Roy T. Bennett

"Y ou've been quiet since reading their minds," Holly said after Blake did not say a word for over an hour after returning to her room.

"I know. I'm sorry. It's a lot to process," Blake explained. "What those kids went through was horrific. There are more," he said, and then looked up at Wyatt and Holly for their reactions.

"What do you mean?" Holly asked.

"There's Adam, Deanna, Eddie, Freya, Gemma, and Isabelle. Charlie sustained brain damage due to an accident. Every time he used his gift, it was literally killing him. The Professor pushed him anyway. He died at age nine."

"Wow," Wyatt said, shaking his head. "And the others?"

"They sustained various levels of abuse throughout their lives. They still have hearts, and are concerned," Blake continued. "They don't want to hurt us. However, they will face severe consequences if they return without us."

"Why us, though? What's the big deal about us?" Holly asked. "We're only two. He has several."

"We're stronger than we think," Blake said. "I think we have yet to actually tap into our full potential…and Professor Roth knows it. He pushed those kids further than they ever thought possible. It wasn't always a good thing. Charlie is a perfect example of this."

"Do you know what they can all do?" Wyatt asked.

"Yes."

"What can Adam do?" Holly asked.

"He's kind of precognitive, but he does it in a unique way. He can run complex equations on sight. He studied people, and can predict how they'll behave in certain situations. He even studied serial killer files, and with each one he told The Professor who did it with one-hundred percent accuracy. He has an eidetic memory to the nth degree. He retains everything he reads and sees forever. He cannot forget, even if he tried. He has super hearing. He can hear people even through walls. While I can hear from one end of the ten acres to the other, I never tried through brick walls."

"That's a bit scary," Holly said.

"Oh! It gets better. He can read minds too."

"Does he know you were in his head?" Wyatt asked.

"I don't know."

"What can the others do?" Holly asked.

"Freya and Gemma are twins. They are strong in the gift of telekinesis. That's all they can do. Isabelle can read minds. She can also do emotions like me," Blake explained.

"What about the other one?" Wyatt asked. "You said his name was Eddie?"

"I haven't figured him out yet," Blake admitted. "He was

paralyzed in the same incident that caused Charlie's brain damage. He fell down the stairs and broke his spine."

"Oh wow," Wyatt let out a low whistle. "That's horrible!"

"As for his gifts, it's unclear," Blake explained. "There's something else," he admitted.

Wyatt's eyebrows arched. "There's more?"

"There *are* more," Blake emphasized.

"More what?" Wyatt asked, unsure if he wanted to know.

"More kids," Blake said. "I don't know how many, but there are more kids."

"Do you know where they are?"

"According to Adam's memory, they're on other compounds," Blake explained. "Wyatt, when we go up there, can we free them all?"

"I don't know if that's possible," Wyatt said. "I don't even know if or when we're going. We don't know for sure where Hope and Ben are being held."

"Yes," Holly said, "we do. We also know exactly who's holding them."

"If we're to succeed, we're going to need the other two in that room," Blake said. "We're going to need Adam and Deanna on our side."

"You cannot be serious!" Holly said, appalled. "You honestly think they'll join us in fighting against Professor Roth?"

"I don't know if they will. What I do know is we'll need more than just us to get them back," Blake explained.

"What if you try to bridge the gap?" Wyatt asked.

"What do you mean?" Blake asked.

"You can show us your memories, right?" Wyatt asked.

"Yes. You know I can. I can even show you your memories and the feelings attached to them."

"Can you show Adam and Deanna some of your memories?"

"Yes, but why would I want to?"

"Maybe if they understand your perspective, it may bridge the gap between you two and the others," Wyatt suggested.

"What do I share with them?"

The dietary person knocked on the door. "Dinner!" she called out.

"Come on in," Holly said.

"May I see your bracelet?" she asked, bringing a tray over to the bed. After Holly showed her the identification bracelet, she left the room, closing the door behind her.

"While you eat your dinner," Wyatt said, "Blake, pull a chair over here while we talk about what you saw in detail, and how we can show them that there are two sides to every story."

⬤⬤⬤⬤

"MOM, you always tell us we are a family in the heart, but not the blood," twelve-year-old Holly said to Hope, as Hope was cooking dinner. This was Ben's night off, so he chose to spend it in the workshop without interruption.

"That's correct," Hope said, cutting green peppers for a salad.

"Who are my real parents?" Holly asked.

"That's a conversation for another day."

"Are they alive?"

"Your birth father is, but your birth mother is not."

"What happened to her?"

"You really want to talk about this?" Hope asked.

"Yes, please?" Holly asked.

"She, um, died during childbirth."

"Our mom died?" Holly asked, eyes wide with sorrow.

"Yes, but God gave you a new mommy and daddy in your dad and me. He has given us the privilege of raising you, and having the both of you in our lives."

"What happens if I want to meet my father?"

"Why would you?" Hope asked, stunned.

"Wouldn't you want to know where you came from?" Holly asked.

"All he did was donate sperm," Hope explained. "He really isn't a good guy. He's actually a very bad man."

"I'm half bad?"

"No, honey. He is. He was literally just a sperm donor. That's all he did. He's not a good man. He wanted to raise you both, but he would have been mean. He would have made you do things, and possibly abused you."

"How do you know?"

"Because I knew him," Hope explained. "I used to work for him. That's the reason we have you. You do have another brother and sister, but we could only save two."

"Why did you pick us?"

"Because the other two had mothers still alive at the time we left with the two of you. We think one may have been crashing at the time, but we don't know for sure. We could only get two out, though."

"What happened to the other two?"

"Honestly, I don't think I want to know. Your birth father is a very powerful man. We wanted the two of you to be able to enjoy your childhood. We wanted you guys to live your life. We sincerely wish we could have gotten all four of you out. We barely got you two out before alarms were set off."

"Alarms?" Holly asked, wide-eyed. "Did you kidnap us?"

Hope put her knife down. She walked around the counter to the seat next to Holly's. She took both of Holly's hands into hers. "Sweetheart, I have never lied to you. I may not tell you everything, but I have never lied. I'm not going to start now."

Holly furrowed her brow. "What are you trying to tell me?"

"Yes. We took you from the clinic. When you're older, we'll tell you more. Until then, know we saved you from years of abuse," Hope explained. "I sincerely wish with all my heart we could have gotten them all."

⟨⟨⟩⟩

FOURTEEN-YEAR-OLD BLAKE and Holly were outside planting vegetable plants in the garden, while Ben was in his workshop.

"Blake, how much of our past do you know?" Holly asked.

"Quite a bit," he confessed. "I get bits and pieces when they think about it."

"What can you tell me?" she asked, planting a tomato plant.

"Well, it's like putting a puzzle together. I take the bits and pieces, and sort them out to create a picture. There are still quite a few missing pieces."

"I understand, but what portions can you tell me?"

"It's all true. What we've heard through the years is all true." Crossing his legs for a more comfortable position, Blake then worked the dirt around planting squash. "Mom and Dad were nurses in a clinic in Maine. Professor Noah Roth was doing experiments on babies in the womb. After years of it not working, he finally got it to work in the set where we were conceived. Knowing both of our moms were –"

"Wait! We're not twins?"

"No. We were born two days apart," Blake clarified.

"Are you serious?" she asked, anger flashed across her eyes. "They actually lied?"

"Relax," Blake coaxed, projecting a calmness toward Holly. "They did it to make things easier for all of us. With us supposedly being twins, it would explain why we're the same age. They were trying to blend in as easily as possible. Holly, you're my sister – twin or not. We were raised together. We literally know what each other are thinking. Just relax. If you want to know more, I'll tell you, but I won't if you don't calm down."

Holly huffed. "Fine."

"Anyway, knowing our moms were dead, they chose us. They knew for sure our moms were not going to be able to help us in any way. There was limited time, so they grabbed the two of us. They barely got away with us."

"Wow. Do we tell them we know?"

"No. Let them alone in their ignorance. They're under enough pressure. They've been hiding us for fourteen years."

"Do you really think he's still looking for us?"

"From what I saw of him, he was meaner than a baby copperhead in one-hundred-degree heat," Blake explained.

"What do you mean from what you saw of him?"

"Dad has boxes of files. He thinks about them a lot. He has them hidden in the workshop."

"What's in them?"

"The experiments through the years. There were photos of mutilated babies in the files too. That broke Dad's heart."

"I'll bet!"

"In knowing what's in the files, I can understand why they took us. We also don't know if they ran any more test groups since The Professor figured out the gene and the babies were viable."

"Ooo! That's a good point!" Holly said, thinking about it. "Do you think there are more? Do you think they know we're their brother and sister, and know we're hoping to meet them?"

"I do. I just hope if they ever find us that they realize that too."

⬤⬤⬤⬤

LIGHTLY KNOCKING on Blake's door, fifteen-year-old Holly heard Blake's voice, "Come on in, Holly."

It was around midnight when she went into his room. Sitting on the side of the bed, she said, "I had a dream."

"What happened in the dream?"

"We found the other two…or rather, they found us."

"And?"

"It started off badly. They hunted us through the country with extreme prejudice."

"Oh!" he said, sitting up. "Did your dream happen to show how to combat that scenario?"

"No. They seemed hell-bent on taking us out."

"Why?"

"Because Professor Roth told them to. He's been saying all along that we're the evil ones."

"What?" Blake's eyebrows rose in surprise. "How are we evil? Yes, we were blessed to be the ones raised outside of the clinic environment, but we're not evil. We want to get to know them. They are our brother and sister. Shoot! If we had our choice, we would have all four been raised by Mom and Dad. I would love to meet them and see what they're like. They're supposed to be a boy and girl."

"Do you really think they'll kill us?" Holly asked.

"I think they grew up with an extremely abusive father. They grew up in a lab, which pushed them past their limits. I think they were raised to think we're evil. I think they never set foot outside of the clinic's compound. I don't think they know what real love feels like. I don't think they understand the importance and value of family. I don't think they think of us as their brother and sister, because we weren't raised with the other siblings. So, yes, I think they may strongly consider killing us."

"When you put it that way…" Holly's voice faded.

"I also think we should be on our toes and alert," Blake explained. "While our wish and dream would be to reunite everyone and live happily ever after, away from the compound, their dream may not be."

"Good point," Holly said. "I only wish they would remember we're still family, and that means something."

❧❧❧❧

"How'd it go?" Wyatt asked, as Blake took a step back from Deanna in their room.

"I gave them both a little bit to chew on," Blake explained. "What they do with it, we won't know until they wake up."

"We can't do that until Holly is one-hundred percent."

"We may not have an option. There are more out there who can still come after us," Blake explained. "They're our age."

"We know what gifts they have," Wyatt said. "Use that against them."

"Wyatt, the twins, Freya and Gemma, are as strong as Deanna when they're together. Isabelle is also a mind reader, and can project feelings, too. If we're going to make it, we'll need the other two to join us. We have to wake them up."

"I wish we had more time."

"We don't."

TIME OUT

**"Nothing in life is to be feared; it is only to be understood.
Now is the time to understand more so that we may fear
less." Marie Curie**

"*Y*ou're doing what?" Shawn asked. "Is that wise?"

The group sat in various spots around Holly's hospital room or stood where there was space. Since Holly and Blake's situation was abnormal, and with the other two down the hall sedated, the hospital and police department felt better to have Holly stay until the other two were pulled out of sedation. That way if anything happened, Holly could help. Also, Holly and Blake were under police protection as long as they stayed in the room. The officers did not mind watching her room for the duration.

"Yeah. Didn't they try to kill you?" Lindsey asked.

"I mean, we just got to know you," Colby said, visibly upset. "If you wake them, one of two things will undoubtedly happen:

1) they kill you; or 2) they join you, and you take off to Maine. If number two happens, who's to say you'll return?"

"We will," Holly insisted "Our goal is for Deanna and Adam to join us. Then, we go up to Maine and free all of our brothers and sisters together. Think about it. We're all from the same father."

"They're literally our brothers and sisters," Blake said. "What would you do if your brother or sister were being held captive and tortured. The kicker is, they don't know any better. They've never known real love. They've never been outside of the walls of that compound. None of our mothers made it out alive. He got away with it!"

"I would be furious!" Tanya said, feeling the anger churn inside at the thought.

"Can you trust them if you wake them?" Megan asked. "While I understand you need them, can you trust them yet, or do you need to show them more memories?"

"She has a point," Wyatt said. "Maybe showing them what real love looks like will leave them craving what you have."

"Or it will upset them even more because they didn't have it," Mac countered.

"If we show them more, then we need to do so carefully," Holly cautioned.

"What memories do we show them?" Blake asked.

"What if you show them your memories, but exchange Adam and Deanna in your and Holly's positions for the dreams. That way they'll see and feel what it should have been like growing up in a family environment?" Megan suggested. "You've seen enough of their memories to exchange you for them. Right?"

"That's brilliant!" Wyatt said. "Can you do that?"

Blake nodded. "It's possible."

"Do you want to try it?" Wyatt asked.

"Yeah. Let's try it," Blake said. "What's the worst that can happen?"

Mac cleared his throat. When they all looked at him, he said, "They wake up and kill you."

◁▷◁▷◁▷

"OKAY, HERE'S THE GAME," Ben said to little Deanna. "You need to match these balls to the color on the basket. Now, don't use your hands. Use your mind. Make it fun. It's a game!"

"Okay, Daddy," five-year-old Deanna said with a grin. "I like this game!"

"Good. Okay, what color is this ball?" he asked, holding a ball in front of her.

"Blue."

"Which basket has the blue paper on it?"

"That one."

"Very good! Now use your gift and put it in the basket."

She took a moment before she raised the ball from out of his hand, and then levitated it over to the basket with the blue paper on it.

"Great job, honey!" Ben said, giving her a hug. "Do you want to do some more?"

Deanna grinned. "Yes! I like this!"

"Go ahead," Ben encouraged.

Every time he held up a ball, she sent it into the corresponding basket with the correct color paper. She also said each color as she put it in the basket. Each time she got it right, Ben either hugged her, gave her a word of encouragement, or gave her a high-five.

When she got it incorrect, Ben said, "That's okay. It's tricky figuring out red and orange. The colors are close. Do you know which color the ball is?" After she told him the color, he said, "Very good! Let's try it again?"

When all the balls were in the correct basket, Holly was allowed to levitate a cookie out of the cookie jar for her and her brother. She smiled as she and Adam sat on the couch eating a cookie, while Ben read Deanna and Adam a book.

◄◑◄◑◄◑

"OKAY, IT'S YOUR TURN," Ben said to six-year-old Adam. "I'll hold up a card facing me, and you tell me what it is. Let's play and see how many you can get. Don't be upset if you miss some. We'll work on sharpening your skills in time."

"Okay," Adam said, excited at the prospect of getting another cookie at the end of the game.

"Today, we're going to do something different. No cookies when you're done."

Adam frowned. "What? Why not?"

"Since there are so many, I want to do something different. This time, for every one you get correct, I'll put a piece of candy in a pile. When you get one wrong, I'll pull one out. When we're done, you and your sister can split the pile. Deal?"

Adam grinned. "Sure! That'll work too!"

Flashcard after flashcard, Adam got them right. Some were pictures of animals. Some were numbers. Others were just words.

Around card twenty, Adam got one wrong. "Dolphin," Adam said.

"Sorry, buddy. It's a shark. Good try, though," Ben encouraged.

"I'm sorry," Adam said, his bottom lip trembling as a tear dropped onto his cheek. "I wanted to get them all right."

"It's okay, bud. I know you like to get everything right, but that doesn't always happen. We all make mistakes. The key is to learn from those mistakes. Remember, I said you may not get them all correct. You have gotten nineteen correct so far. There are five left. Let's see if you can get the other five. Seriously," Ben said, resting his hand on Adam's little hand, "it's not something to beat yourself up over. You'll get better in time. I'm proud of you for getting nineteen in a row! Great job! You two are going to have a lot of candy to share!"

"Okay," Adam said, wiping the tears away.

"Ready to go again?"

"Yeah. I want to see if I can get the other five."

"Remember, if you don't, be proud of the ones you did get correct. Okay?"

"Okay," Adam said, sitting upright in order to concentrate. "Go ahead."

Ben held up the card.

"Angel."

"Awesome! Great job!" Ben said with a wide grin. "Next?"

"The word, ocean."

"Good. Next?"

"The number 650259."

"Wow! Excellent! Next?"

"Fire."

"Good job! Only one more left. The last one is…?"

"A trick," Adam said with a grin. "It's a picture of the four of us at the pumpkin patch."

"See? I knew you could do it! You have to have as much faith in yourself as I have in you. You're brilliant, son. You'll grow to be a strong man. Stay focused. You got this."

"Thanks, Daddy!" Adam said, getting up, giving Ben a hug. When Ben wrapped his arms around Adam, Adam had tears in his eyes, as he felt the love from Ben.

⬫⬫⬫⬫

"Okay, you got this!" Ben encouraged thirteen-year-old Deanna. "I know it's tough, but you can do this."

"I got this," Deanna said, looking at the mess. An F2 tornado passed near the house the previous night. While the house and buildings were fine, the acreage had a lot of downed trees and debris. Slowly and methodically, she separated the different debris into piles of like material.

"Wow! You did it!" both Adam and Ben cheered when she set the last piece of debris into the pile.

"Not done yet," Deanna said, looking at the piles with a look of sheer determination.

"You don't have to push yourself," Ben said. "Separating them the way you did is a lot."

"No. I got this," Deanna said. She took the pile of wood and separated them into two piles. The piles of smaller pieces of wood were in one stack, while the big pieces she crisscrossed into a neat pile. She did the same with the metal. She then took the trash and put them into bags. When she finished, the mountain of debris was sorted and bagged. They looked like a crew of people took all day to do what she did in a few hours.

The entire time she did the work, Ben and Adam encouraged and cheered her on. When she finished, Deanna dropped to her hands and knees. Ben rushed over and put his arms around her.

"Okay, little one. You've done enough. Time to rest. You're getting the day off tomorrow to rest as well," he said, carrying her back to the house, with Adam on his heels. "Let's not push you to the point of exhaustion again, huh?"

"Daddy?" Deanna said.

"What, sweetheart?"

A grin spread across her weary face, as she said, "I did it."

"I know you did, honey. You can do anything you set your mind to. I am so proud of the both of you," Ben said, and gave her a kiss on her head, as they continued through the woods back to the house.

Sixteen-year-old Adam said, "While you are both our parent in heart, we know we're not by birth. Care to share the real story?"

Ben topped the crockpot before slowly turning toward the pair. Leaning against the counter, he crossed his arms. "We've told you all along you're ours in our hearts. We love you as if you were ours by birth."

"That would require the pair of you to be in love," Adam said knowingly.

"Did you snoop?" Ben accused.

"Yes, but couldn't get details," Adam admitted. "That's why we're asking."

"Fine," Ben said in a sigh. Letting out a slow breath of air before he spoke, he arranged his thoughts. "You were both born in a clinic in Maine. The Doctor who runs the facility is Professor Noah Roth. He's not a good man."

"What happened to our real parents?" Deanna asked, excited be getting answers, yet nervous at the same time.

"Professor Roth used his own sperm to fertilize the eggs implanted in the mothers. Once an egg was fertilized, there were experiments done on them prior to implantation."

"What kind of experiments?" Deanna pressed.

"Genetic manipulation," Ben said to their horror. "Anyway, these experiments went on for over twenty years. Babies were born deformed, still-born, or only lived a few days…that is if they were carried to term." Seeing that the two were not phased, Ben asked, "Did you know this?"

"Parts of it," Adam acknowledged. "But please continue to fill in the details.

"Okay," Ben agreed. "Finally, about sixteen years ago, he was successful in manipulating the correct gene to produce the effect he was looking for."

"Us," Adam said in understanding.

"Yes. There were four of you at the time your mom and I

were nurses in the newborn ward. Adam, you were born two days before Deanna. Deanna, your mother died during childbirth." When he said that, Deanna's jaw dropped. "Adam, yours died the day after your birth."

Adam looked at him, momentarily wide-eyed. However, he was distracted when the kitchen table and chairs slightly lifted off the ground. Adam walked over to his sister and took her hand into his to calm her down.

"Sorry," Deanna said, realizing what she did, and gently set the table and chairs back down on the floor undamaged.

"There was a third mother who coded while we were there," Ben continued. "We knew with the mothers gone, and him being the father, Professor Roth would have free range to do what he wanted with the children. We didn't want you to grow up in a lab being pushed beyond what you should be doing, and probably tortured or abused. Unfortunately, we could only take two of the four."

"Oh!" Deanna said, wide-eyed. "So, there are two more of us out there?"

"At least. If he could figure out which DNA strand achieved the results he was looking for, there may very well be more than that out there. There were also several mothers from your test group who needed to deliver. We're not one-hundred-percent sure how many of you there are right now."

Deanna gulped. "I see."

"So," Adam spoke up, "your position in the family was to care for us, as well as homeschool us in order to stop us from potentially exposing ourselves?"

"Yes. Also, I can't use my social security number, or I'll be found. It's not that I don't have one. It's that I can't use it. If they find me, they'll arrest me…or more likely I'll die a mysterious death like those mothers."

"Then, how is Mom working?" Deanna asked.

"She's using your real birth mother's information," he said to

Deanna. "Chances are, both of your last names would have been changed to Roth, after Professor Roth."

"So, what's Mom's real name?" Deanna asked.

"Her real name is Grace Matthews. She can't use that for the same reason why I can't use my real last name," Ben explained. "My real last name is Scott. I know this may seem complicated, but –"

"No," Adam shook his head, "it makes perfect sense."

⬦⬦⬦⬦

"Okay, I need to stop," Blake said, taking a step back. "Inputting real memories into two minds is difficult enough, without having to convert the people in them and editing some of the elements." Sitting on the couch in their room, Blake explained, "I hope it was worth it."

"I'm sure it was, son," Wyatt said. "Do you want to go back to the room?"

Holly cocked her head to the side. "Wyatt?"

"What?" Wyatt asked.

"They're crying in their sleep," she pointed out, concerned. "I hope we didn't push too much information."

"We may have pushed just enough," Wyatt said, satisfied.

⬦⬦⬦⬦

Colby and Tanya came after school. They normally came a few hours before the others in order to have some time to talk to Blake and Holly on their own. While Blake and Tanya went to get food for the four of them in the cafeteria, Colby sat on the side of Holly's bed.

"How are ya doing today?" Colby asked.

"Nervous," Holly admitted. "They're weaning me off the

205

pain meds. It's only a matter of time before we have to wake them up."

"Do you think Blake did enough?"

"We'll find out."

"Are you strong enough to take them out again if you have to?" he asked.

"I would take her out first, and then him. She would probably do the same."

"Are you guys the same strength?"

"Not according to Blake. He said I'm the strongest of the telekinetics."

"The fact that you said telekinetics, meaning plural, is a bit to wrap my brain around. I was just getting used to you having that gift."

"We're just glad you guys don't think we're a couple of freaks."

"You?" Colby shook his head. "Never. You're just like us, with an extra trick or two up your sleeve."

"Good way to think about it."

"You're cute too," he added with a smile.

"Thank you!" She grinned. "You're not so bad yourself."

"Well, thank you," he said appreciatively, as his face flushed. "I was wondering something?"

"What?"

"Well, would you consider going out with me when you're out of here?"

"Are you asking me out or are you asking me to consider it?"

"I'm asking you out. Would you go on a date with me?"

"I'll tell you what. I'll be in here for a few more days. Why don't you come early like normal with Tanya tomorrow? While they go down to the cafeteria, you can bring me something to eat and we can have a date of our own here in the room."

"Really?"

Holly shrugged. "If you want to?"

"I would really like that! What if I go get our food, and I tell them to stay downstairs for a bit? That will give us some time alone."

"I think that's a great idea! That'll give them time alone as well. It doesn't take an empath to know the two of them really like each other."

"No. It doesn't. She's a tough cookie to get close to," he pointed out. "However, he seems to have cracked that tough exterior wall she puts up."

"He can get through the roughest exterior. He even got Mrs. Mueller to laugh in the store the other day!"

"Really? I didn't think she knew how to smile, let alone laugh."

"It's been his goal to get her to laugh for the longest time. He has been trying for years."

"I hope Tanya doesn't end up grumpy like her."

"She won't. You just have to learn how to take her. I like Tanya," Holly said. "She's honest and doesn't pretend. She's real."

Colby chuckled. "Yes. Yes, she is. Despite what it looks like, she does like Lindsey. She just hates it when Lindsey pretends or acts like she's not as smart as she is. Lindsey thinks that's what a guy wants. Tanya's told her numerous times not to degrade herself like that."

"Is that what you want?"

"Oh! Heavens no!"

"What do you want in a girl?" Holly asked.

"I want a girl who is honest and sincere. A girl who will stand up for herself and has a sense of pride. Dan Rather has often been quoted as saying, *Always marry a woman from Texas. No matter how tough things get, she's seen tougher.* Another good one is from John Cusak, *Texas women have an amazing sense of purpose when they lose it. They're the best girls in the world – they're loyal and fun, but when they get mad, they try to kill you,"* Colby said with a chuckle.

Holly laughed. "Those are good!"

"I know, right! Here's the thing, though, I want a woman who I know can look after herself. I want her to be my other half. What I mean by that is where I'm weak, she's strong, and vice-versa. In the Bible, women were created to be a helpmate to men. Woman was created out of man. I want that. Most importantly, I would like her to be a Christian. I want her to respect God and His word. I want her to love and honor Jesus."

"Does it bother you that I'm not a Christian?"

"Does it bother me? Yes. Only because I am concerned for your soul. Does it deter me? Nope. I like you too much for that. Can I tell you a secret?"

"Sure," she said, sitting back on the bed.

"I've seen you around town over the years, and even was able to pick you out of the crowd on Friday night football games from time to time," he admitted.

Now it was her turn to be stunned. "Really?"

"Yes, but you were untouchable. Anytime any of the youth group kids tried to talk to you two, you guys pushed us away. Now we know why."

"We couldn't let anyone get close enough to discover our secret."

"Pretty sure the whole town knows by now," Colby said in a chuckle. "Y'all can't hide it anymore. All your secrets went nuclear last week."

"True. Also, Blake read y'all's minds," Holly explained.

"Oh geez!" Colby laughed, looking at the ceiling. After he settled, he said, "I can only imagine what he read in Mac and Shawn's minds."

"I don't have to be a mind reader to read theirs. Yours, on the other hand is at times a mystery."

"Do you like a mystery?"

"I do. I imagine Blake would read your mind if I let him. Fortunately, we gave him ground rules. He's not allowed to read Tanya's either, unless she gives permission."

"Is that rule just with the two of us?" Colby asked.

"Yes, and with family. Generally, he's pretty good at sticking to that, unless he has to or has permission."

"So, when Tanya presses him, and he doesn't give her answers, it would give new meaning to the term, *I'm not a mind reader.*"

"Too true!" Holly said in a laugh.

Watching her laugh and smile, Colby soaked in the moment.

"What's wrong?" Holly asked.

"Nothing."

"No, really. What's wrong?"

"I told you I've been interested in you for years. To be not only talking to you, but also getting the opportunity to go on a date with you blows my mind!"

"That's probably the sweetest thing anyone has ever said to me," Holly said, as her face flushed in embarrassment. "Thank you!"

"Can I tell you another secret?"

She laughed. "I don't know if I can handle another one, but go ahead."

"On the Friday night games, I would look for you. If you were there, I would play my best for you, hoping you would notice me."

"Oh! I noticed you. I also saw you at the rodeos where Shawn and Mac were team roping."

"Really?"

"Sure! Since we're speaking honestly, Blake told me a long time ago that you were one of the few guys he ran across who had honorable intentions. He wouldn't dare tell me what Shawn and Mac thought."

"Yeah, don't go there. They're a different breed. There are

days I want to knock them upside the head. I don't participate in their antics anymore, but I don't preach at them or stop them either. I honestly think they drag me along for extra back-up for when they get themselves into trouble."

"Why do you hang out with them?"

"We've been friends since kindergarten. I grew up with this crew. I know they all have redeeming qualities. I also know it will take into college or after for them to sort out their issues."

"You seem to have a good head on your shoulders," Holly pointed out.

"Not necessarily."

"What do you mean?"

"Well, I used to participate in their antics," he admitted. "I don't anymore."

"What changed?"

"Honestly?"

"If you keep asking me that, I'll wonder if you're being honest all the time. Yes, please. I want complete honesty. If you don't, I'll be offended. I would rather be hurt with the truth than comforted with a lie."

"Another good saying," Colby acknowledged. "I like it. All right. Complete honesty. No asking if the other wants the truth or not."

"Agreed," Holly said, shaking his hand.

"What changed is I got a strong dose of realization. I met this one girl at a rodeo. She wanted me to kiss her and be with her. She wanted me, but not for me. She wanted me for my body. The more I thought about it, the more I felt disgusted by the thought. I felt dirty. That's when I realized that's what I was doing to a lot of the girls we ran across. I hated that for them. When the guys dragged me along again, I refused to play. When I explained why, they just said I was wuss, and let me be at the table while they hunted, as they called it. From that day forward, I was the designated driver."

"They drink?" Holly asked, appalled. "They're not old enough."

"Holly, the world in which you function is way different than mine. In mine, you can get alcohol if you want to. They do drink at parties. I did too. I'm being honest with you. I was not a good guy. I don't know how Blake read that I was honorable."

"I had him look into your mind when we were at a game," she confessed.

"Was it after my sophomore year?"

"Yes. It was this last season."

"That's because that incident happened in my sophomore year. I figured out I needed to get my head on straight that year. Not only did I change my mindset on girls, but I also figured out I didn't want to spend every weekend drunk or throwing up in a toilet bowl. I didn't want to wake up not knowing how I got somewhere anymore. I was really bad. There are times here over the last week where I couldn't figure out why we kept talking. I'm really a bad person. I don't feel like I deserve to have a friend like you, let alone be able to actually go on a date with you."

"You *were* a bad person," Holly corrected, taking his hand into hers. "You've grown up. You've matured. That's not a bad thing. You've done bad things. I'm pretty sure I'm about to do bad things. That's one of the reasons I'm resisting when it comes to Jesus. I know what He would want me to do, but I'm afraid I may not be able to control my gift when we get up to Maine. I'm afraid if I accidentally kill someone, God'll never forgive me."

"Holly," he said, keeping her hand in one of his. Resting his other hand on her cheek, making sure she looked at him, he explained, "When soldiers go into battle, they wrestle with that very thing. My dad explained it to me one time. He was military before he became a cop."

"What did he say?" Holly asked, feeling somewhat hopeful regarding her dilemma.

"He basically said when in defense of yourself or another, you do your best not to kill, but there are times where that is just not possible. Keep in mind, there were many battles in the Bible. If you're going to destroy evil, war isn't necessarily a bad thing. There is a quote by Edmund Burke, which says, *The only thing necessary for the triumph of evil is for good men to do nothing.* God forgives all sins. To Him, sin, is sin, is sin. You just have to ask with a true sense of remorse. You know you may get to Maine and do something you don't necessarily want to do. You may hurt or kill someone, but that's not a guarantee. The only person guaranteed to kill someone is a sniper."

"True, but I really don't want to kill anyone."

"God knows your heart. And you may not kill anyone. Don't think of it as going to kill someone. Think of it as you're going there to defend your family and your way of life. Things may happen. I know your heart. I know you won't do it on purpose."

"I have a temper," Holly admitted.

"You have red hair and you're a Texan. That's pretty much a given. It's the same with Megan when she gets a burr up her saddle. I would be shocked if you didn't have a temper."

"Blake is usually right there to calm me down. What do I do if he's not around?"

"You grow up and mature."

Holly pursed her lips as she nodded in understanding. "I can't continue to rely solely on him to keep me in control."

"Right. Pull up your big girl panties and get a grip."

"Wyatt said the same thing to me the other day."

"Knew he was a smart man."

"Okay. Why don't you go get our dinner, while I process what we've talked about?"

"Sounds like a plan," he said. When he stood, he leaned down and gave her a hug. "You're a good person. There is good in you. Hold onto that. Also, know Jesus wants to take that good and make it better."

"I understand," she said, and he left. Looking toward the ceiling, Holly said to God, "I really hope everything he said was true. If I accidentally kill someone, I want to know You will forgive me."

❀❀❀

AFTER COLBY GOT Holly and his dinner, Tanya and Blake stayed in the cafeteria, per Colby's request. When he left the cafeteria, Blake mentioned, "I'm glad Holly and Colby are connecting."

"He's a good guy," Tanya said. "He didn't use to be. He's made a lot of changes over the last year. I'm proud of him. Now, if we can get Shawn and Mac to do a turn-around, I would be happier."

"I can make that happen," Blake offered.

"While I appreciate it, people need to make their own choices. Some have to fall harder than others in order to see the light, but they eventually turn it around."

"Not all the time," Blake said. "Professor Roth is an evil man. The stuff I saw in Deanna's and Adam's minds were pure evil. I only relayed part of the stories. There are other parts I couldn't stomach to explain or glossed over the details."

"I'm sorry you had to see that."

"The worst was Charlie. His brain may have been damaged during the fight, but Professor Roth is the one who killed him. Can you believe he threatened one of the little girls that she would join Charlie where he was if she didn't do what he wanted her to?"

"Wow! He sounds like a piece of work!"

"You have no idea!" Blake shook his head. "He used their best friends against them. If they didn't do what he wanted them to, he would hurt their counterparts. He used Adam against Deanna. If I were them, I would be angry at us too."

"Speaking of the two sleeping beauties?" Tanya asked,

tucking a portion of her dark-brown hair behind her ear. "When are y'all fixin' to wake them up?"

"They've started to wean Holly off the pain medicine. It won't be long now. Probably just a few more days."

"What are you going to do if they wake up angry again?"

"Holly'll knock them out," Blake said with a shrug. "She's actually stronger than Deanna."

"Just how strong is she?"

"Mind-blowingly strong."

"Did you tell her yet?"

"No. I told her she was the strongest of those with the gift of telekinesis, but I won't tell her exactly how strong. If she knew the true level of her capabilities, it could prove disastrous."

"For whom?"

"Pretty much anyone within a fifty-mile radius of the compound in Maine."

"Wow!"

"Yeah."

"Do you think the kids up there will go along with you to rebel and get everyone out?" Tanya asked, picking up a french fry.

"I think we will need Deanna and Adam if we're going to succeed at all."

"What if you don't?"

"The Alamo comes to mind."

❈❈❈❈

Holly and Colby ate in silence as they weighed the upcoming events. Finally, as Holly finished her fries, she asked, "So, are you telling me if I accidentally kill someone, God will still love me?"

"The key is the word accidentally," Colby said.

"You don't understand just how angry I am at Professor

Roth. This world would be so much better without him. He is a criminal of the highest caliber. Blake showed me the memories he read off of Deanna and Adam. He put them in my mind, so I would have compassion for them when we wake them." Shaking her head, she said, "He's literally pure evil."

"He sounds it."

"He killed the mothers of those with the gene, so he wouldn't have to deal with them. If someone gets in his way, he just kills them. And the kicker? He's getting away with it! That man has left a trail of bodies a mafia boss would be proud of!"

"Do me a favor?"

"What's that?"

"Remember a few days ago when I took our picture on my phone?"

"Yes."

"I printed it. Here. When you feel yourself getting angry, pull this out and focus on my picture. Focus on the smile on your face," he said, handing her the photograph. "Remember this? It was just after I told you a funny story about me trying to help my dad birth a cow."

"Oh my gosh! That's right!" she said, laughing. "I remember you telling me about sticking your hands up the poor cow to pull it out."

"Yeah. That wasn't pleasant," he said with a smirk. "However, your face was…see?" He pointed to her in the photo. "Look at this picture, and it'll bring you back down to earth."

"I'll remember," she said, setting the picture on the table. "Thank you."

"Thank *you*! This has been the best week and a half I've had in an extremely long time."

"Me too. Knowing you're coming each day makes me happy."

"That makes me happy too." Getting a good look at her face, he asked, "What's wrong?"

"Well, besides the obvious, I've been thinking a lot about Jesus. When I heard what Pastor said, it…I can't explain how it made me feel."

"Just try. Unfortunately, I don't have Blake's gift. I can't read it on you."

"I know," she said. Looking down, she considered her words and feelings. After a few moments, she admitted, "I really hate that man. I know Jesus doesn't want us to hate or kill. The hate toward Professor Roth and all he's done is strong."

"Strength comes from the heart. We've had many deep conversations over these last several days. I know your heart. I know you don't really want to kill him. You want him to face justice. Just focus on your brothers and sisters, and your mom and dad. The situation will play itself out."

"Deanna has killed. She did it when she was younger. It was by accident, but still."

"I can't answer for Deanna. I can tell you wouldn't do it on purpose. Pretty sure it would crush you. Just do your best to use your gift as a defensive weapon and not an offensive one."

"What does that mean?"

"You're probably used to using it as an extension of you."

"It is."

"If you saw someone getting attacked, what would you do?"

"Shove the attacker away, like I did at the restaurant. I shoved the guys, and disarmed them by pushing their guns away."

"What if you saw a house on fire, and the parents were yelling their child was in the fully-engulfed house?"

"I would use Blake's mind to narrow down where they were, and then use my gift to pull the windows out of that room to get them out."

"What would you do if you saw a guy with a gun to a child's head?"

"Whip the gun out of his hand. While he was momentarily

stunned, I would pull the child toward me, and shove him back against a wall, hopefully knocking him out."

"What would you do if you were in a bank, and bank robbers came into the place with guns?"

"Throw them against the wall, and shove their guns to the other side. If they got up, I would use my gift to hold them down until someone could get to them to secure them. All of these are scenarios where I have free reign to do this. At this point, I still have to be careful where I use my gift. If the government ever found out what Blake and I can do, we would end up as lab rats for the rest of our lives."

"This is true. However, may I point out in those scenarios, you did not kill any of those perpetrators. See? Your intent is defensive. Do you understand what I'm telling you?"

"What if it was Professor Roth's life versus my mom's or dad's lives?"

"You'll have to make a decision in time. We could *what if* all day. You'll never know what you'll do until that time."

"True," she said, processing through his words.

"I have something I want to ask you."

"What is it?"

"Well, I know it's Wednesday, and per your somewhat time-line, you'll be waking the troublesome twosome here in a few days. Then your plans are to take off for Maine regardless if they are with you or not. Correct?"

"Yes."

"I have a football game on Friday night. Afterward, our youth group is doing what's called a *fifth quarter*. It's a play on words, but it's basically a little get-together. There'll be a time for fun, along with some food and soda. There'll also be a short message. Are you interested?"

"I'm on crutches," she pointed out.

"You don't have to play the games. I would just be happy you were there to see my game and know you're on a date with me. I would also love to just hang with you and enjoy some time out of the chaos that's about to happen to you. I'll be a nervous wreck the entire time you're gone, so please consider giving us this one night?"

"I would love to. However, you should talk to Wyatt first. He's our guardian until we can get our parents back. He'll also know if it's safe."

"True. I'll talk to him tonight when he comes for dinner."

"Sounds good."

⊲⊲⊲⊲

Wyatt walked into Holly's room around five-forty-five that night. The group was there talking and telling stories. "Full room," Wyatt commented. "Standing room only."

"I know. You can sit on the end of the bed if you want," Holly said, scooting to one side.

"Actually, can I talk to you in the hall for a moment? Please?" Colby asked.

"Sure," Wyatt said.

"Tanya, come on out with us," Colby said.

As the three left the room, the others looked at each other confused.

What's going on? Blake thought to Holly.

Colby wants to take me to a youth outing on Friday after the game, she thought back.

Is that safe?

Pretty sure that's why he's talking to Wyatt.

Gotcha.

Don't read their minds, Holly thought to Blake. *Let them do what they are going to do in their time.*

What does that mean?

Just —

"You two want to let us in on the conversation?" Shawn asked, cutting off their thought stream.

"Who? What?" Blake asked.

"I can tell when the two of you are talking in your minds. You have a tell," Shawn pointed out.

"They do," Lindsey agreed.

"Definitely!" Megan said.

"We'll just have to wait until they come back in," Holly said, saving Blake from any more questions.

⊕⊕⊕⊕

"WHAT'S GOING ON?" Wyatt asked, as the door closed behind them.

"Yeah. Why are we out here?" Tanya asked.

"When do you plan to wake Frick and Frack?" Colby asked.

"Friday. Why?" Wyatt asked.

"Could you postpone it one day?"

"Why?"

"Well, Blake and Tanya have gotten close. Holly and I have gotten close as well," Colby explained. "There's a home football game on Friday. Afterward, our youth group is having a fifth quarter. I would love to take Holly. And," he said, resting his hand on Tanya's shoulder, "pretty sure Tanya would love to have Blake come."

"Can he?" Tanya asked, excited.

"I don't know," Wyatt said, unsure.

"Look, they're about to run into a dangerous situation," Colby pointed out. "Wouldn't it be a good idea for them to one, have a little fun; two, get to know us all better under a safe event; and three, give them another chance to hear the gospel and maybe have the opportunity to make a decision for Jesus before they go?"

"Those are excellent points," Wyatt said, rubbing his chin in thought.

"Holly's close. She's struggling with a few issues," Colby explained. "I think it would be good for her to hear what Pastor Jay has to say."

"Blake's struggling too," Tanya added. "He can't figure out how God let this get so far."

"To be honest, I don't blame him," Wyatt said. "I can't figure it out either. However, as I said, those are good points. I'll make you a deal."

"What's that?" Colby asked.

"I'll let them go on one condition."

"What is it?" Tanya asked.

"I'll be their chaperone, kind of like a bodyguard. When they leave this hospital, I want to know they're protected. Just because Bonnie and Clyde are knocked out, doesn't mean there are not others around. I'll also have at least two other state police officers with us. We'll give them some distance, but they must be in our eyesight at all times."

Colby stuck his hand out and shook Wyatt's as he said, "Deal!"

"Agreed!" Tanya said, grinning ear-to-ear.

"Be careful, and be vigilant. If you see anything that looks even remotely suspicious, you tell me," Wyatt cautioned.

"We will," Colby said, as Tanya nodded.

"Fair enough. Go tell them."

"Can I ask Blake first?" Tanya asked. "I haven't mentioned it to him yet. Have you mentioned it to Holly?"

"Yes. She's the one who told me to talk to Wyatt."

"Okay," Tanya said, "let's go."

As the trio walked into the room, the conversation came to an abrupt halt.

Tanya thought she would try Blake and Holly's trick. *Can you hear me?* she thought to Blake.

She just about jumped out of her skin, when he responded, *Yes. I can. Can you hear me?*

"Neat trick!" Tanya grinned. "And, yes."

A smile slowly spread across Blake's face, as his heart rate picked up. Knowing he could do that with someone other than Holly was scary, yet exciting.

I want to ask you to come with me to the youth outing Friday night after the football game…as my date? she thought to him.

"No fair!" Lindsey said. "You two are talking. Aren't you?"

"Better than passing notes," Tanya said with a smile.

Yes! I would love to! And, please let me take you, and pay for you? Blake thought back to Tanya.

"Yes," Tanya said aloud.

"Yes…what?" Megan asked.

Following the cue from Tanya, Colby turned to Holly. Taking her hand into his, he asked, "Would you be my date on Friday night? Wyatt said there are stipulations. He said he has to go, and there will also be two other state police officers present at all times. Would you be willing to go with me as my date?"

"Wait! What?" Lindsey asked, stunned.

"Hold on!" Mac objected. "I didn't know that was an option! If it was, I was going to ask her."

"He's already asked me," Holly said, not taking her eyes off his. "He had to get permission from Wyatt first."

"Oh," Mac said, disappointment evident.

"And, yes," Holly said to Colby.

"Yes!" Colby said with a grin.

Linsey crossed her arms, as she narrowed her eyes at Tanya. There was obviously something she was missing. She would call Mac later and see if he knew how the two pairs got so close so fast. Until then, she would watch the two pairs very closely.

DOWN TIME

**"I have found that if you love life, life will love you
back." Arthur Rubinstein**

$\mathcal{H}$olly was released from the hospital on Friday
morning. Holly, Wyatt, and Blake would spend the
night in a hotel that night in order to not be in either home in
case they were being watched. Wyatt stopped at a clothing store
to get Blake and Holly both three sets of clothes. He did not want
to go back to their house to pick up clothing and possibly get
caught.

Once they were checked in, Holly went into the bathroom
first to clean up. She was grateful for the shower. While she had
a shower in the hospital, to her they were pathetic. In order for
her to shower, they had to wrap her leg in plastic, and tape it
closed to keep it dry.

When she finished, she got changed into jeans and a royal
blue fitted t-shirt. She would take a light jacket for the night to

stay warm in case there was a weather shift. After she did her hair and make-up, she was exhausted. Grateful to have a few hours before Wyatt took them to the football game, she rested on her bed.

With two queen beds in the room, Blake and Wyatt would share one, leaving Holly the other for the night. While Holly rested, Blake took a shower, and Wyatt went to go get dinner for the trio.

"Hungry?" Wyatt asked, walking back into the room twenty-five minutes later with dinner.

"Surprisingly, yes. Blake's still in the bathroom. He shut the shower off a few minutes ago," Holly explained.

"Great. So, according to the map I looked up, this compound is supposed to be up somewhere near Rangeley in Maine. That's about three to four day drive."

"That's what I found too," Holly said, tearing the wrapper off a ready-made sub. "Looks like a pretty area. Kind of scary to know something so dark and sinister is amongst all that beauty."

"You just focus on tonight. I want you both to have fun and be real teenagers for once."

"What does that mean?"

"You are both well-rounded young adults," Wyatt said, as Blake walked out of the bathroom fully dressed and ready to go.

"Thank you," Blake said, in jeans and a black t-shirt. His look was rugged. He had a red, white, and black plaid shirt tied around his waist by the sleeves in case it got chilly at the game.

"I'm not done yet," Wyatt pointed out. "While you are well-rounded, you have avoided being a normal teenager. You're both sixteen and just now having your first date. I promise you that if you were in public schools before now, you would have both had teens falling all over you. Having said that, the way you were raised allowed you to come through those formative years knowing exactly who you are, without the awkward mistakes most of us make in front of our classmates. So, tonight, you're both going on your first dates. I do believe the two you are going out with are both really good kids, or I would not let you go. Me, along with two other officers will be there in case some uninvited guests show up. However, I want you to ignore us. I'll let you know if something's up. If you see us running toward you, Blake, read my mind."

"Got it," Blake agreed, as he sat on the bottom portion of Holly's bed. Wyatt was on the other bed.

"I also want the pair of you to keep a close eye out. Yes, I want you to relax, but I also want you to be vigilant."

"We will," Holly agreed.

"Enjoy your dates tonight. I don't know when you'll both be back here," Wyatt said.

Blake knowingly looked at Wyatt, as he added, "Or if we'll both come back."

⊕⊕⊕⊕

THE TRIO MET the other two officers at the police station. Wyatt was not taking any chances of letting anyone know where they were staying. He checked in with cash, and left one-hundred dollars cash on the room for extra expenses so the concierge would not require a credit card. It took him showing the concierge his badge to do it, but he went around the system.

After parking the vehicles, the five went in together. Wyatt alerted the local police officers regularly at the game they were there, and why there were extra officers there, so they knew to keep an eye out.

Holly and Blake got settled on the bleachers, as Wyatt, Officer Garcia, and Officer Anderson got settled into their positions. Wyatt was five bleachers up from the pair, right in front of the announcer's box. Meanwhile Officer Garcia and Officer

Anderson each took a position at opposite ends of the stands. From those vantage points, they could see anyone walking around.

About twenty minutes later, as the bleachers filled, Tanya and Megan came up and sat with Holly and Blake. They sat Megan, Holly, Blake, and then Tanya. The guys were on the football team, and Lindsey was a cheerleader, so they were with their groups.

"Hi," Tanya said to Blake.

"Hey," Blake said. "May I?" he asked, holding his hand up.

"Of course," she said, taking his hand.

"They look sweet together," Megan said quietly to Holly.

"I agree. I've liked Tanya since we first met you guys. I'm glad she's the one he ended up with. No offense to you or Lindsey," Holly quickly added. "I just think they're a better match."

"They are. And, no offense taken. He's cute and sweet, but I have my eye on someone else," Megan explained.

"Really? Who?"

"Mac," Megan admitted, blushing.

"Megan," Holly started, feeling pressure on her to explain Mac's track record.

Megan cut her off. "I know he's not a good guy right now. He wasn't always this way. It was a slow slope. I know Colby used to be that way, too. I've seen the changes in his life over the last year. It gives me hope for Mac."

"And, I assume Lindsey likes Shawn?" Holly asked.

"She did, until Blake came into the picture. She's somewhat obsessed with Blake lately. When she found out Blake and Tanya were dating, it drove a wedge between her and Tanya even further. None of us care, though. Frankly, she should date Shawn. I think they're a better match than she and Blake. Tanya is better matched with Blake."

"And Mac?" Holly asked.

"Mac and Shawn are both involved in the rodeo circuit, and have been since they could ride. They know a lot of people, and have no problem going to parties where there's alcohol." She sighed. "I seriously miss who Mac was before he started his downward spiral."

"He'll never go back to who he was," Holly said. "We all change and evolve as we grow."

"I know. I just wish he would grow already!"

Holly chuckled.

"It's starting. There's the team," Megan pointed out. "Mac is number forty-nine. Shawn is number twenty-eight. Colby is number sixty-seven. Funny, but true story?"

"What's that?"

"Colby said he picked sixty-seven because it is a little more difficult for the referee to hold up those two numbers. I thought he was joking, but number fifty-five is Will Taylor. He's always getting called on stuff. Especially in basketball. You see, those on the football team keep the same numbers if they play basketball or baseball. It's a weird school tradition, but it works for them."

"I see. Can't buck tradition."

"Nope. Speaking of, here they come!"

The cheerleaders held up a massive paper banner, while the guys huddled under a blown-up tunnel. A few moments later, as the commentator announced the team, everyone stood, and the team crashed through the banner.

The commentor spoke about some key players, including Shawn, Mac, and Colby. Afterward, the Star-Spangled Banner was sung, and a short prayer was said.

Holly really enjoyed the games. The excitement, the athletes playing their hearts out, and of course the concession stand for snacks. It took Holly a few minutes of scanning the players before she found Colby. He turned and looked up at her and waved. When she returned the wave, he grinned, and Holly's heart skipped a beat. She liked him at that moment more than she realized. It was then a struggle ensued deep within her. She would be leaving the next day, walking into an obviously dangerous situation. She and Blake would have to give up their friends for a bit. She prayed it would not be for good.

◁◁◁▷

THE GUYS WON THEIR GAME. The cheers were deafening as the game went into overtime. When the it ended, the players left for the locker room. The cheerleaders cleaned up their area. While others dispersed for home, the officers, along with the four, remained in their seats.

"That was a great game!" Holly said. "All the guys did good!"

"Shawn did well as the substitute quarterback," Linsey said, still in her uniform, as she came up the bleachers to the group with her stuff. "The junior varsity girls have to finish cleaning up."

"Bet you love that," Megan said.

"They're the ones who left our area in a mess after the JV game." Lindsey shrugged. "They deserve to clean it up. They know better."

"They also now know not to mess with the head cheerleader," Tanya pointed out.

"Well," Lindsey smiled, "I can't help that. Those rules were there from the beginning. Being the head cheerleader is a privilege. I don't abuse it, but I won't be a push-over either."

"Don't we know it!" Tanya said, rolling her eyes.

Glancing at Blake and Tanya's hands, Linsey pointed out, "You know you can't hold hands at the youth outing. Right?"

"Why not?" Blake asked.

"Yes. We know," Tanya said to Lindsey. "However, we're not at the outing yet, mother."

"Ouch!" Lindsey cringed.

"You're not our mom, nor are you a cop, so mind your own business," Tanya snapped.

"Why can't we hold hands?" Blake asked. "It's innocent."

"Because we are not allowed to have public displays of affection at youth activities," Tanya explained. "It's nicknamed *PDA* if you hear that phrase."

"Thank you for explaining, but I don't understand why not?" Blake asked.

"Because it could make others uncomfortable," Tanya said. "We want everyone comfortable when they come to church. It's a safe place for everybody."

"Okay," Blake said with a shrug. "We'll respect that. Are there any other rules we need to know about?"

"When Pastor Jay is speaking, there's no whispering or talking," Megan said. "We're to pay attention."

"Why would you not pay attention?" Holly asked. "If his message is anything like Pastor's, then I would think you would be taking notes and looking things up. His message was fascinating!"

"Not when you've heard it a billion times," Lindsey said, rolling her eyes.

"Are you serious?" Holly asked, appalled. "This Jesus gave His life for you. He was beaten and tortured. They made Him carry the cross they were going to hang Him to die on! How can you say that the way you did and roll your eyes? That's an affront to His sacrifice!"

Lindsey looked at Holly, taken aback. "I-I'm sorry."

"Don't be sorry! Just listen to what they're trying to tell you. Stop giggling, whispering, and passing notes. I saw you guys that Sunday. You cannot tell me that's not what you were doing."

"You have to understand," Lindsey said, recovering. "I grew

up in church. I went to a Christian elementary school. I've always had Bible in my life, and heard the stories."

"Are they not real?" Holly asked.

Blake reached over and touched Holly's arm. When he touches her, it works quicker and stronger than when he projects.

"It's okay, Blake. Save your strength. I got this," Holly dismissed him.

"Okay," Blake said and stopped.

"Seriously," Holly turned back to Lindsey, "are the stories not real?"

"They are," Lindsey said.

"Then, what's your problem? Why are you so nonchalant about Jesus and the Bible? That Man prayed so hard He had blood dripping from His forehead in the Garden. He knew what they were going to do to Him, and He went willingly."

"I know that."

"Do you?" Holly challenged Lindsey. "Do you really know that, or is that what you were taught to know? Do you understand the idea of someone voluntarily giving their life for you, knowing the consequences could be deadly? Our mom and dad do. Mom willingly went with those men, so they would leave us. She knew what they were going to do to her when they got her back to Maine. Our Mom and Dad knew what they were doing when they originally took us from the lab. They changed their entire lives to save us from abuse! Jesus did more than they did. He gave His entire life just so you could enjoy a peaceful eternity with Him and God. Do you really have that Holy Spirit thing? What is It telling you right now?"

"It's telling me that I screwed up," Lindsey said. "You're right."

"Are you a Christian?" Holly asked. "It's my understanding to be a Christian, you're giving your life to the One who gave His life for you. You're giving Him control over your life."

"It is. And, yes."

"Really?" Holly asserted. "Do you think He would be proud of the way y'all act during service? The Pastor was sharing directly from the Word of God. Let that sink in – *Word of God*," Holly enunciated. "The actual and true words from the Lord God Himself. And you roll your eyes at it?"

"I'm sorry," Lindsey said.

"I'm not the one you should be apologizing to." Holly crossed her arms. Turning to Blake, she said, "I want to go wait for Colby."

"You can't," Blake said. "We have to stay here. Shawn, Mac, and Colby know to meet us here. The officers are still looking out for us."

Holly huffed, crossing her arms. "Fine."

"I'm really sorry I offended you," Lindsey apologized.

"I really think you need to have that conversation with Jesus," Holly said, not making eye contact with Lindsey.

"You're right. You're right about everything you said," Lindsey said. "And, I'll have that conversation with Him, but I also need to apologize to you."

"Thank you," Holly said.

"You're totally right."

"I already said thank you," Holly reiterated.

"I've just never heard that with such passion," Lindsey explained. "I've heard about Jesus all my life. It never occurred to me the way you said it."

"Just think about it," Holly said.

"You know, there's a big difference between your head and your heart," Megan said to Lindsey. "I know you know all of the stories in your head, but have you ever actually looked at it all with your heart?"

"Good question," Lindsey said. "Guess that's something I'll have to figure out."

⟨⟩⟨⟩

After the guys showered and changed, they all headed over to the church in separate vehicles. Wyatt's car led, with the other two vehicles with teens after his, and then the other two police vehicles. Wyatt drove, with Holly in the passenger's seat, and Colby, Blake, and Tanya in the backseat.

There was a heaviness in the vehicle after Holly and Lindsey's conversation. They did not talk the entire way to the church.

When they got there, the five stayed in the vehicle, as did the police officers. All the other teens rode in the two vans with other teens from the youth group. One was driven by Pastor Jay, and the other was by his wife, Everly.

When they arrived at Pastor Jay's house, Wyatt and the two police officers spread to various points to keep an eye on the area. Meanwhile, the other kids, along with the youth pastor and youth workers went over to the bonfire and lit the pile of wood. Afterward, they enjoyed hotdogs, hamburgers, chips, and cokes. As the fire continued to burn, Pastor Jay had everyone find a seat on logs around the fire.

At first, they sang worship songs while Pastor Jay played the guitar. Then, Pastor Jay got up to speak. "Thank you all for coming tonight to enjoy the fun. As normal, we're going to take a few minutes with Jesus. Tonight, I want to talk to you about power. The dictionary defines power as: to do or act; capability of doing or accomplishing something. Have you ever thought about power? I want you to think for a moment. Who is the most powerful human being you know?"

When he asked that question, Colby inched his fingers over and tapped Holly's hand. She smiled at him, knowing what that meant.

"Is that person big and strong, or are they small? People tend to match power with size and strength. I'm going to challenge that tonight. Let's take a look at our football team for a moment. Guys, please stand?"

As the guys each stood up, Holly noted their size, and could only imagine their power.

"Colby, you're not one of the biggest guys here, but how much can you bench press?"

"Easily one-fifty," Colby said.

"Dude! You did one-seventy the other day," Shawn objected. "He's a beast!"

"That's pretty powerful!" Pastor Jay said, surprised. "Have to say I'm impressed! What about you guys?"

"I'm at about one-twenty-five," Mac said.

"One-thirty," Shawn added his.

Several other guys said what they could bench press, before Pastor said, "These guys can all bench-press most of us sitting here. I'd say that's pretty powerful!"

Some people verbally agreed, while others nodded.

"Let me ask you a question. How many of you have been camping, or out on a trip, and an annoying mosquito got in your tent, your car, or has been in your bedroom while you're trying to sleep?"

Everyone raised their hands. Deep East Texas is known for annoying mosquitos.

"How powerful is that little mosquito?" When no one said anything, Pastor continued, "That little mosquito can annoy guys who can bench-press anywhere from one-twenty-five up to two-hundred. To me, that's pretty powerful! Have you ever had someone tell you that you can't do something because you're too young?"

Multiple people nodded, and a few raised their hands.

"They've never been locked in a room with a mosquito," Pastor Jay said with a chuckle. "Okay" he continued as people settled, "now to bring it back around. There are many stories in the Bible where normal everyday people do extraordinary things. Let's take a look at some of them…"

Pastor Jay read a few verses in the story about David and

Goliath. He told how all of the king's soldiers were afraid to fight Goliath. David decided His God was stronger, so he volunteered to fight the massive Goliath. Long story short, David killed Goliath with a tiny stone. God used that young man's bravery and faith to kill the massive giant with just a stone and a slingshot. He also shared how David started off as a shepherd boy, and ended as a king. Then he headed into Daniel versus Babylon. Despite the laws that were passed, Daniel still continued to pray and worship God. Per the King's decree, he was thrown into the lion's den for continuing to pray to God. God protected Daniel in the lion's den by shutting the mouths of the lions. The next morning, when the king found Daniel still alive, the king repented. God used Daniel in a big way. He then went on to share the story about Moses and Pharaoh. He said Moses did not feel worthy to represent the Lord. God told him differently, and proved it by using Moses to free the Lord's people.

"Philippians 4:13 says, *'I can do all things through Christ who strengthens me.'* There are many verses in the Bible where people did amazing and miraculous things with the strength that God gave them. Ephesians 6:10 tells us to, *'be strong in the Lord and in the power if His might.'* Matthew reminds us in Matthew 19:26 that, *'But Jesus looked at them and said, "With man this is impossible, but with God all things are possible."'* God created this world with just His words. He takes care of the birds of the air, and the flowers in the fields. He keeps this world spinning. He gives us what we need when we need it. He promises to help us when we need Him. It may not be what we feel we need, but He knows exactly what we need. He will always be with us. He promised in Isaiah 41:10, which says, *'Fear not, for I am with you; be not dismayed, for I am your God; I will strengthen you, I will help you, I will uphold you with my righteous right hand.'* God wants to be there for us. He even gave His Son so we could be with Him in the end. John 3:16 and 17 tells us, *'For God so loved the world, that He gave His only Son, that whoever believes in Him should not perish but have eternal life. For God did not send His Son into the world to condemn the world, but in order that the world might be saved through Him.'* He loves you, and wants to get to know you. He wants to be there for you. All you need to do is ask and He'll be there. Think about this…if God is with you, who can stand against you?"

Holly raised her hand.

"Holly?"

"I don't know if we're allowed to ask questions right now or not."

"Of course. Go ahead," he encouraged.

"Are you saying if something life-threatening happens to us, God will save us from it?"

"No. I'm telling you if something life-threatening happens, you will never be alone. Jesus will be with you wherever you go. He'll protect your heart and mind if you are one of His. I'm not going to lie. You may not make it out alive, but if you die, and you are one of His children, you'll be able to rest in His loving arms for eternity."

"Thank you," Holly said, mulling his words over in her mind. He went to continue, but Holly raised her hand again.

Pastor Jay smiled, amused. "Yes, Holly?"

"How does He protect your heart and mind if you are in the middle of terrifying, life-threatening situations?"

"Hope."

Holly raised an eyebrow. "My mom?"

"No," he said in a chuckle. "Think of it this way. If you are in a pitch-dark room what happens if you light a match?"

"There would obviously be light."

Pastor Jay pulled the box of matches he used to light the bonfire from his back pocket. Pulling one of the matches out of the box, he lit it on the side of the matchbox. Holding it in the air, he explained, "This itty-bitty flame on the tip of this tiny piece of wood can light a room enough for you to see around you, along with at least ten feet. This little light can lead you out of the darkness." Shaking the flame out, he then tossed the matchstick into the bonfire. "That itty-bitty flame represents hope. That hope will lead you out of whatever dark space you find yourself in."

"That makes sense," Holly said. "Thank you."

"Jesus came to this world, and lived like one of us, to let us know He knows how you feel. He'll walk beside you if you let Him. All you need to do is ask," Pastor Jay said. "We're going to break up and play some games. If you want to talk some more, feel free to pull me or any of the youth leaders aside. Until then, let's bow our heads in prayer."

After prayer, everyone separated into various activities.

"What did you think?" Colby asked as people dispersed.

"I think I need to talk to someone," Holly said. "I was on the fence before, but I can't continue without that hope. If I'm heading into what I know I am heading into, I'm going to need all the help I can get. If push comes to shove, and everything goes south, I want to know I'll be with God in the end."

"What if everything ends perfectly fine?" Colby asked.

"Then, I have more days where I can do what He wants me to do. There was a verse we read during our Bible time that talks about Him having a plan for me."

"That was Jeremiah 29:11, which says, *'For I know the plans I have for you," declares the Lord, "plans to prosper you and not to harm you, plans to give you hope and a future."* He does have a plan for you. You only need to ask."

"I'm asking," Holly said.

"What happens if something happens to Blake, and he hasn't made that decision?" Colby asked. "How will you feel?"

"From what I understand, that's his decision to make. I can't make it for him. I can only make it for me."

"You've learned much over the last few weeks, young one," Colby teased.

Playfully shoving him, she said, "I've had a good teacher."

"Okay, who do you want to talk to?" Colby asked, looking around.

"I don't know. Who do you think?"

"Either Pastor Jay or his wife would be good options. You really don't know any of the other youth leaders."

"True. However, I barely know any of the adults here," she said, and then it hit her, "except Wyatt."

"Oh yeah! He'd be a good one. C'mon," Colby said, giving her a hand up.

Together, they headed over to Wyatt. Once they explained why they were there, Wyatt happily prayed with Holly. After Holly asked Jesus to forgive her of her sins, and to be with her all her life, showing her what His plan is for her, Wyatt quoted a verse for her.

"In Romans 10:9, it says, *'If you declare with your mouth, "Jesus is Lord," and believe in your heart that God raised Him from the dead, you will be saved.'* You've done that tonight, Holly. You confessed with your mouth that Jesus is Lord. You asked Him to forgive you of your sins. You asked Him to take over your life. Now, you may make mistakes, but don't stress. Jesus gets it. Just do what you feel Jesus would want you to do."

"Thank you," Holly said, giving him a hug.

"Keep Him close to you as we head out in the next few days," Wyatt said. "We're all going to need Him. And, welcome to the family."

"Thank you!" Holly grinned. "I feel like a weight's been lifted off me."

"That's because it's not all up to you anymore," Wyatt explained. "You just do your best, and let God handle the rest."

"Now we need to work on Blake," Holly said.

"Agreed," Wyatt said. "It's up to him, but we all want him

and Ben to join all of us. Let God work on their hearts. We'll keep them in prayer."

For the rest of the night, Holly felt as if she were free. The idea of waking Deanna and Adam still scared her, but as long as she held onto the hope of Jesus, she knew however it turned out she would be okay.

FACE TIME

"It's better to be a lion for a day than a sheep all your life."
Elizabeth Kenny

Finally, almost two weeks after they were sedated, the trio decided it was time. Holly was on crutches, but no longer on pain medicine so her head was clear. Blake input the visions, and gave the sedated pair a few days to process. Wyatt gave Blake and Holly the night before with their friends during the fifth quarter. It was now or never.

"Are you sure you want to do this?" Colby asked, as they were outside the hospital. "You know we're not going anywhere until you guys tell us you're safe to travel with them."

"I understand," Holly said. "And, we appreciate it. We've all gotten pretty close over the last few weeks. We'll miss you, and will appreciate the prayer back-up while we're gone."

"You are coming back, right?" Lindsey asked.

"Yes," Blake said. "Whether we'll have parents or not is the question."

"You'll have me with you regardless," Wyatt explained. "I won't let anything happen to you."

"You know you can't control that," Blake pointed out. "We're not dealing with normal everyday people here. These are teens with gifts, and a lot of them. If we wake Adam and Deanna, and they choose to continue their pursuit of us, we're in trouble. We need them to do this successfully."

"Then, that's what we'll pray for," Tanya said. "That's what I've been praying for this entire time."

"Me too," Colby added.

"We all have," Mac explained. "That, and safety for Hope and Ben."

"Thank you," Holly said. "This Christianity thing is all new to us, but I understand prayer is super important."

"More than you know," Tanya said. "Speaking of which, I know we've had several conversations individually regarding Jesus. I wanted to put it out there one more time to see if you two wanted to have one last conversation regarding Him. I know I would feel better if I knew for sure you were both Christians."

"Sorry, Tanya," Blake said. "I honestly cannot think of much except getting Dad and Mom from Professor Roth. There's no telling what he's done to them over the last two weeks. The only reason we waited was to get Holly healed enough to be off pain medicine."

Taking his hand into hers, she pulled him aside as the others talked amongst themselves. "I understand what you're saying," Tanya said quietly. They spoke so she and Blake were the only two to hear the conversation.

"I know you do. We've talked enough for me to know your heart. Know I understand what you're saying as well. However, I want to make that commitment when I have a clear head. I don't want to do it just to escape going to Hell."

"And, if something happens before you get back here, that's exactly where you will be going."

"I know. I also know it's a matter of the heart. You taught me how to have time with Him each day. I'll continue to do that and pray. If I feel the Lord pressing on me, I'll do it. Until then, I want to learn more."

"What about Holly?" Tanya asked.

"Holly already prayed and asked Jesus to forgive her of her sins last night. Trust me, after the first sermon she heard, she was chomping at the bit when her head cleared. Wyatt prayed with her last night after Pastor Jay talked. She told me when we got back to the hotel."

"So, you're telling me if something happens to the pair of you, you're willing to wager your eternal security in being separated from not only Jesus, but also Holly, Hope, and Wyatt?" Tanya asked.

"And, from you as well," Blake said, resting his hand on the side of her face as he looked into her beautiful blue eyes.

"I, um, yeah," Tanya stammered, looking into his eyes as well.

"We're close," Blake said. "I don't have to be a mind reader to know we both have a strong attraction to each other. Colby and Holly are the same."

Tanya chuckled. "Mac may have something to say about that."

"No. He can't control Holly's heart any more than Lindsey can control mine. When it comes to matters of the heart and mind, trust me, there is no stopping the heart."

"Why are you running from Jesus?" Tanya asked, searching his eyes for answers.

"I'm trying to justify what all has happened in our lives up to this point, and to the lives of our brothers and sisters. You haven't seen what that man did to them over the years. I've shown you some of the visions. He is a tyrant. I can't imagine what he's doing to Mom and Dad right now. Knowing what he did to his own kids, what will he do to someone who betrayed him? He has a lot of money and power behind him."

"I've done some research on him," Tanya said, crouching on the ground. She got into her backpack and pulled out a file. Standing, she handed it to him. "You'll have a long drive to Maine. This may help you when you get there. I researched Professor Roth, as well as the clinic. There are other campuses. There isn't much, but it's a start."

"Thank you. I also have some of the files Dad stored in the shed. If Deanna and Adam agree to go with us, they're going to have some interesting things to look at along the way."

"We'll keep you in prayer," Tanya said, taking a step closer to Blake, closing the gap to less than a foot apart.

Resting his hand on the side of her face again, Blake pushed his feelings onto Tanya. "That's what I feel for you."

"You already know what I feel for you. Please be careful. This man is dangerous. People disappear without question around him."

Resting his forehead on hers, Blake said, "I'll be careful. Until then, I want to give you a memory to hold onto. May I?"

"Yes," she said.

He leaned forward and gently pressed his lips to hers in a sweet, tender kiss. It was not just a kiss. He made sure to push his feelings about her into her mind as well. "Don't let go of that memory," he whispered a moment later.

"I won't let go," Tanya promised. "Don't let me go either. Come back to me."

"I will. I promise," he said, and kissed her again.

⚛⚛⚛⚛

"OUR TURN," Colby said, resting his hand on the small of Holly's back. "Would you please come and sit with me on the bench so we can talk for a few minutes before you go?"

"Of course. Blake and Tanya are talking anyway," she said, and followed Colby over to the bench.

When they sat down, Colby took Holly's hand into his, as he said, "I'm glad you had that talk with Jesus. Now I know for sure if something happens to you, I'll see you again. I just don't want you to go too soon. Please come back to us?"

"I will. Regardless of what happens up there, I'll do my best to get back here. Willow Bend is our home." Colby cleared his throat to speak, but Holly interrupted him before he could talk, "You all have opened your hearts to us. We don't take that lightly. We don't have many friends. Actually, you're our first friends. Our brothers and sisters don't have that benefit. They've been raised in seclusion. All they know is the compound and the abuse at the hands of that man. It's our prayer to free all of them, along with Mom and Dad."

"What do you mean by all of them?"

"According to what Blake saw, there was more than just our test group. We need to find out how many groups and their locations. Those kids are all our brothers and sisters. They've been treated like lab rats their entire lives."

"I get it. I need to tell you something before you leave."

"Colby, you don't have to say anything."

"Yes. I do. I need to say it before I lose my nerve."

"Not yet," Holly said, resting her hand on the side of his face. "When I get back, we can have that conversation. I need a clear head."

"I don't want to cloud your mind."

"Not that I don't want to have this conversation," Holly added. "I just need to do it when we get back. I need to focus on rescuing everyone, and getting our brothers and sisters to safety first."

"I understand," Colby said, looking down.

Raising his chin with her fingers, Holly leaned forward and

kissed his cheek. As his face flushed, Holly explained, "I really like you, but I need to focus."

"You know I'll be terrified for all of you until you return. Are you sure you can't take a phone with you?"

"No. They can be tracked. Wyatt's even leaving his here."

"What happens if there's an accident?"

"There were accidents before cell phones were invented," Holly said with a smirk. "To ease your mind, Wyatt has a burner phone. You guys have already friended us with our new account under a fake name. We'll check that frequently. Don't use names in the messenger. Just use an initial. We will figure out who's talking."

"I know. You're under so much pressure. It's like this entire thing rests solely on your shoulders. You're strong. You're amazing. Despite all you carry, you are a light to those around you. I really wish you could see you the way I see you."

"That's Blake's gift. However, I can see the look in your eyes."

"Just be careful."

"I will," Holly promised.

"Here, I have something for you." Colby handed her a sealed plastic bead tube with a matchstick in it. When she smiled, he explained, "It's to remind you of your hope in Jesus."

"I know. I love it," she said, giving him a hug. "It's perfect. I have the picture you gave me in my wallet. This, I can keep in my pocket."

"It's waterproof too, so it won't get wet."

"True. You have no idea how much I appreciate this."

"Good. At least it makes sense. I wasn't sure."

"Of course I got it. We've connected on many levels."

"We have. Well, it looks like you need to have some face time with your siblings," Colby said, getting up. He assisted Holly off the bench, before they headed toward the group. Blake and Tanya returned about the same time.

After the teens all hugged each other, Wyatt, Holly, and Blake headed into the hospital. The rest of the teens waited outside. As the door closed behind them, Holly glanced back to see them all watching the trio go deeper into the hospital.

◆◍◆◍◆

"WHY DO I feel like we're walking into a storm?" Holly asked, as they got off the elevator for the floor, and then headed down the hall toward Adam and Deanna's room.

Seeing the four police officers still standing guard, Blake said, "Because we are."

"I have faith in you two," Wyatt encouraged.

"Glad you do. I just hope what we showed them was enough." Blake sighed, rubbing the back of his neck. "If not, we'll be waking up a tornado on the back of a hurricane. If they're still angry, this won't end well."

Standing in front of the room, Wyatt turned to the officers and instructed, "If they do not come out with us, shoot them… with extreme prejudice. If they're coming out without us, then they've killed us."

Wide-eyed, Officer Barnes said, "Are-are you serious?"

"Yes," Wyatt said sternly. "There's a reason there are four of you guarding this room since these two were brought in. You saw the Hunt home. You know about the two missing. These two are directly or indirectly responsible for all of that. We're going to wake them up. If either of these two or I don't come out first, shoot them on sight."

"Yes, sir," the officers said in unison, as they stood at attention. Each one released the holster containing their guns. Resting their hands on their weapon, the two closest to the door watched the trio go into the room, while the other two officers watched down either side of the hallway for anyone else coming.

◁◁◁◁◁

ABOUT TWO-AND-A-HALF HOURS after they stopped the sedation, Deanna and Adam started to wake.

"Morning," Wyatt said, standing between the pair as he faced them.

Holly was standing back to keep an eye on both of them, as she rested against the wall with her crutches. Meanwhile, Blake stood at the foot of Deanna's bed, pushing calmness on both of the teens.

"Wh-what happened?" Adam asked, grabbing his head. "My head feels foggy."

"You two blew into our town and turned it upside down," Wyatt explained. "Sorry, but we had to show you a few things before we woke you back up."

"How long have we been out?" Deanna asked.

"About two weeks," Wyatt said.

"Nice try, dude," Blake said, glaring at Adam. "You can't get into my head."

"Can't get into mine either," Holly added. "Blake's blocking you."

"Wyatt's too," Blake said. "It's a new trick I figured out about a week ago."

"That's not your only trick," Adam said knowingly. "Those weren't our memories. Why did you show them to us like that?"

"To show you how you should have been raised," Blake explained. "Those are our memories. I wanted to show you how we found out about you two."

"There are more," Adam said.

"I am aware we have more brothers and sisters. I am also painfully aware we lost Charlie."

"Charlie's not your brother!" Deanna snapped.

"Yes. He was," Blake said. "Just because we didn't get the opportunity to know him, doesn't make him any less our family than you two. We are brothers and sisters by blood whether you want to admit it or not. Just because we were raised in two different environments doesn't mean we aren't family."

"What do you know about family?" Deanna challenged. "We went through everything with our true brothers and sisters. You did not!"

Blake pushed a memory into both of their minds. The pair's eyes glazed as they experienced the memory…

"Blake?" sixteen-year-old Holly came into Blake's room around eleven at night on the night where the family had the conversation regarding Wyatt and Hope. Ben and Hope were already asleep.

"Did you have another nightmare again?" Blake asked, sitting up as he turned his lamp on.

Sitting on the side of his bed, Holly explained, "I feel like there are more."

"There are. There were four of us," Blake said.

"No. I feel like there are more than just the four of us. It's as if I can feel them."

"That's my gift," Blake said with a smirk.

"What if there are more than just the four of us? What if we have this huge family of brothers and sisters we know nothing about? We've missed so much of their lives. If we ever get the chance to meet them, will they consider us family too?"

"I hope so," Blake said. "I know we weren't raised together, but that doesn't make us less family. That just gives us more to catch up on."

"True. I wonder what they're like? Are they like you and me? What do they like to do? Do they like to draw like you?"

"Or write like you?" Blake asked.

"Exactly! Do they journal? Do they like sports? What's their life been like up to now?"

"Those are questions we're going to have to ask when or if we ever meet them," Blake said.

"Do you ever just sit and wonder about them?"

"I do. This is one of those situations where we're just going to have to cross that bridge when we get to it."

"What if they hate us?" Holly asked.

"Why would they hate us? They don't know us."

"What if that professor is as mean as Dad says? What if he's mean to them?"

"What if we let things level off after Mom and Wyatt get married, and then we'll see what we can find out about the clinic?"

"Can we go rescue them? I can't imagine what they went through growing up! I wish we all could have been raised together with Mom and Dad raising them all."

"Me too, sis," Blake said, tapping Holly's leg. "We'll find them."

"I don't want to let this go," Holly said. "I'm going to keep pushing."

"Oh! I know you will!" Blake said with a chuckle. "And I agree. We do need to find them. Once Mom and Wyatt get married, we'll consider it our project to find out more. When we have enough information, we'll go back to the clinic and see what we can do about helping them."

"Agreed. Thank you!" Holly said with a smile.

"Now, go to bed," Blake said, and Holly left the room.

"Nice trick," Adam said.

"You know it's the truth," Blake asserted.

"I do," Adam agreed. "You want us to trust you, but you're blocking me from seeing into your minds."

"That's offensive," Holly snapped. "Why do you need to read our minds in order to trust us?"

"Why do we need to trust you at all?" Deanna challenged.

"Because," Holly hobbled on the crutches to where Blake stood. Bracing herself on Deanna's bed, she explained, "You want our brothers and sisters released from there just as much as we do. You grew up in there. You know what you went through, and what the other test groups have gone through. Do you really want more of our brothers and sisters to face the same thing you did?"

"No," Adam admitted.

"Don't you want to rescue Eddie, Freya, Gemma, and Isabelle from there?" Blake asked.

"You know we do," Deanna said. "But, if we don't go back with the two of you, they'll hurt them."

"Don't let him pit us against each other," Holly said. "Let's work together to get everyone away from him."

"You don't want to be his toys for the rest of your life, do you?" Blake asked. "There's a saying by Elizabeth Kenny that says, *It's better to be a lion for a day, than a sheep for the rest of your life.* Do you want to continue to be under the thumb of Professor Roth?

"No," Adam said.

"You all have suffered greatly under him," Blake said. "Let's work together to get everyone away that we love."

Deanna glared at the pair. "We don't trust you."

"You don't have to trust us to work with us." Holly rolled her eyes. "Look, we'll work together to get Mom, Dad, and all our brothers and sisters out of there. We may even be able to take The Professor down. Once everyone's free, we'll figure out what to do from there."

"What do you mean?" Deanna asked.

"You guys can come down here," Wyatt suggested. "Or you can start over wherever you want."

"For the record, we would love to have you here," Holly added. "We really want to get to know our brothers and sisters. We want to show you what real love and a family look like."

"You'd do that?" Deanna asked, unsure. "There are a lot of us."

"We have ten acres," Holly explained.

"And I have twenty. We'll figure it out," Wyatt said. "Something you may not understand is just how important family is to us down here in the south."

"What do you mean?" Adam asked.

"Down here, family is everything," Wyatt explained. "We do everything we can for family. And, guess what? You two are family. So are all those other kids. You are all family, and we look out for our family."

"It doesn't matter if you trust us at this point or not," Holly said. "We are stronger together. If the four of us come together, imagine what we can do."

"That would throw him off," Adam pointed out to Deanna. "He won't be expecting that."

Deanna considered it for a few agonizing minutes, before she suggested, "What if, when we get up there, we pretend to bring you in? That way you can get inside easier."

"This will take a lot of trust on our side," Holly said, "but, I'm willing."

"Me too," Blake agreed. "We need to come together to do this. We'll play by your rules. This is your territory."

"What if they're not all on the compound?" Deanna asked. "Once you get Ben and Hope back, you won't need us."

"But you'll need us," Holly explained. "We'll all work together until we find all of them – every single one of them. If that takes months or years, then it will take months or years. We're committing to help you find all of our brothers and sisters no matter how long it takes."

"Or what it takes," Blake added. "Up to and including our lives, we'll free them all."

"Deal," Deanna said, sticking her hand out.

As Holly shook her hand, Blake went over and shook Adam's hand. When Blake and Adam shook hands, Adam said to Blake, "You know more than anyone what we went through. Can you really help us?"

"If not, then we'll die trying," Blake promised.

"I hope not. I would like to get to know you more."

"Just stay out of my head, and I'll stay out of yours."

"Agreed," Adam said with a smile.

"There are two sides to every story," Wyatt said, sitting on the corner of Deanna's bed. "You now know how you were raised, and how Blake and Holly were raised. We want to give the gift of how Blake and Holly were raised to you and your other brothers and sisters."

"We'll figure out what to do," Deanna said, "once they're all found."

BOOK 2, A RACE AGAINST TIME

*P*rofessor Noah Roth is possessive of his children – the children he created by genetic manipulation. When Ben and Hope took Holly and Blake in order to give them a better life, they knew their days were numbered. Continuously looking over their shoulders, they still missed it when the Clinic made their move by sending a group, along with two gifted after them.

Adam and Deanna Roth thought they were on the right side of things, until they ran into the other two gifted – Holly and Blake. Presented with another perspective, Deanna and Adam agree to help Holly, Blake, and Sheriff Wyatt rescue Hope and Ben, as long as they help Deanna and Adam rescue the other siblings still under the control of Professor Roth.

As the five head toward Maine, the youth group kids who became close to Blake and Holly over the last few weeks, decided to help them by doing research. Unbeknownst to them, they stumbled onto information the Clinic did not want out. After each of their homes were invaded, the kids had to make a choice – join the others in the rescue attempt, or stay home, therefore putting their families in danger. Will they make it in time to help the others, or will they be too late? It's a *Race Against Time*!

JOSHUA **1:9** – "Have I not commanded you? Be strong and courageous. Do not be frightened, and do not be dismayed, for the Lord your God is with you wherever you go."

Psalm 90:12 – "Teach us to number our days, that we may gain a heart of wisdom."

"Time slips through our hands like grains of sand never to return again. Those who use time wisely are rewarded with rich, productive and satisfying lives." Robin Sharma

BOOKS BY C.J. PETERSON

Grace Restored Series can be found: https://cjpetersonwrites.com/ series-books

Holy Flame Trilogy can be found: https://cjpetersonwrites.com/ series-books

Divine Legacy Series can be found: https://cjpetersonwrites.com/ series-books

C.J.'s Stand-Alone Books & Anthologies She Participated in can be found:

https://cjpetersonwrites.com/stand-alone-anthologies

Christmas A.N.G.E.L.s to be released OCT2021

'Tis The Season, A Holiday Anthology: 2021 Season to be released OCT2021

Sands of Time Trilogy can be found: https://cjpetersonwrites.com/series-books

Race Against Time to be released OCT2021

Out of Time to be released JAN2022

9 781952 041402